Steven Caney's
Invention Book

Steven Caney's
Invention Book

Workman Publishing, New York

Library of Congress Cataloging in Publication Data
Caney, Steven.   Steven Caney's invention book.
   Includes index.
   Summary: A project book for the would-be inventor with
activities, a list of "contraptions" in need of invention, and the
stories behind thirty-six existing inventions.
   1. Inventions—Juvenile literature.   [1. Inventions]
I. Brown, Ginger, ill.   II. Title.   III. Title: Invention book.
T48.C3 1985 608 78-73723 ISBN 0-89480-076-0 (pbk.)

Cover art © 1985 Jeff Seaver
Cover design: Tedd Arnold
Book design: Susan Aronson Stirling

Workman Publishing Company, Inc.
708 Broadway
New York, NY 10003

Manufactured in the United States of America
First printing May 1985
15 14 13 12 11 10 9 8 7 6 5

Dedicated to my creative mentors

Edward Loper
Albin Gregg
Marc Harrison

Contents

Great Invention Stories

The Inventor's Handbook

Getting Started

When people think of an "inventor" they probably conjure up the image of an absent-minded, wild-haired professor, working in a laboratory filled with bubbling test tubes and elaborate electronic machines, or at a blackboard filled with intricate mathematical calculations. To many people an inventor is a strange combination of scientist and dreamer. But in fact, there are no limitations or requirements. Anyone can be an inventor!

All inventions start as someone's idea—and nearly everyone has plenty of ideas about ways things could be improved. Some ideas are for things that do what no one has ever done before; others make old inventions better or just make jobs easier or more fun to do. Some people's ideas are futuristic and may even depend on technologies that haven't been created yet. And some, although they might seem silly to others, offer solutions that are practical answers to the inventor's needs—like eyeglasses for chickens so their eyes won't get poked, or seat belts for dogs and cats. Even though anyone can have a good idea, that does not make him an inventor.

To be an inventor you must learn to let your mind search, to think of many possible solutions to each invention problem you encounter. Even if many of your ideas seem foolish or impractical, they might lead you to a truly unique solution and a successful invention. If you can train your-

self to look at everyday things in a new and different way, as clues to new ideas, then your mind will always be inventing.

An invention doesn't have to be something radically new or profound—even the simplest ideas sometimes become clever inventions and have a tremendous impact on the market. The Hula Hoop was based on children's play hoops, which had been around for years. More than anything else, it was a new way of playing with these hoops, yet it was still considered a novelty and sold in the tens of millions. In fact, some inventions seem so obvious that after you have seen them you're apt to say, "Why didn't I think of that!" Look at the Frisbee or the Pet Rock, for example. Some people get their ideas in "brilliant flashes," whereas others create ideas by actively working on solutions to problems. An inventor considers all his ideas and then chooses the one he wants to develop.

Many great inventions have been created by novice inventors when highly competent scientists and engineers working on the same problem just couldn't see the solution. You don't have to be a mechanical engineer to invent a better mousetrap. It is true that you may need some technical help to perfect and build your idea, but your concept of how to catch the mouse is the true invention. Most inventors learn or invent their own technology as they need it.

Never Too Young

Inventors come in all ages. Age alone does not determine how creative or inventive a person is. Preschool or elementary-school-age kids can often build an invention *idea*, if not a working model or prototype of the product. The older child is more able to develop his ideas into a functioning model, but the quality of the idea itself has no age limits. Many noteworthy inventions have come from the minds and hands of young inventors. Chester Greenwood invented the earmuff when he was fifteen years old, and he then went on to invent many other successful products and ultimately became a very wealthy man.

In fact, in many ways the young inventor has a psychological advantage over the older and more experienced person. Several inventors have succeeded because they were too naive to know "it couldn't be done." Two young musicians were too scientifically unsophisticated to understand the problems Kodak was

Coat Hanger Greenhouse

1. Pull out bottom of coat hanger... until wire forms a diamond shape.

2. Bend the wire diamond across the middle to form a right angle. Straighten out the wire hook.

3. Push the wire end into the soil so the wire frame forms a canopy over the plant. Hang plastic wrap or a plastic bag on the frame.

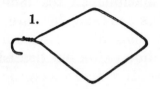
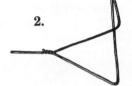

having trying to invent color picture film, and it was exactly that naiveté that allowed them to explore unconventional solutions that ultimately led to the invention of Kodachrome. The Kodak engineers were amazed.

Throughout history, inventing has been an individual art: a person recognized a need and created a product that made the job easier, faster, or more enjoyable. More recently, groups of people have been working together, with each person adding a particular expertise to what will become the complete invention. Although it seems natural that individuals invented things like water skis, Band-Aids, tea bags, Hula Hoops, and earmuffs, it is hard to imagine that just one person could create something as complex as the space shuttle. But as long as people's habits and tastes change, posing new problems and challenges, there will always be room for the individual inventor to recognize needs and find solutions. Companies with large teams of creative people backed by a lot of money and resources have no monopoly on good ideas.

Thinking Like an Inventor

Most new ideas and inventions actually grow out of old ones, and that is one of the important clues to being an inventor. You don't always have to invent from scratch. The question to ask yourself is how you can use the knowledge and materials you already have to solve a problem and create something new. How can existing materials and ideas be combined or used differently to make an invention? How can a paper cup, a roll of tape, or a hardcover book be used to invent a better fly-catcher? Or what are all the materials you can think of using to make a simple stopper or lid to keep an opened can of soda from going flat?

While the true inventor is someone who is working hard to imagine and develop new ideas or to solve old problems, some inventions are created by accident. Ivory soap was the consequence of a workman leaving the soap mixing machine on too long. Embarrassed by his mistake, he threw the "bad" batch of soap into the stream, only to see that it didn't sink but floated away. The true invention here was recognizing that the unanticipated result was a new and potentially successful product—floating soap (which ads used to show that the soap was "pure"). Often inventions are inspired by the desire to help others, but of all the reasons and inspirations, necessity is still the mother of most inventions. For example, if it had not been for Earl Dickson's wife being so accident-prone, he would never have invented the Band-Aid.

There are many different inspirations for inventions—Dr Pepper gets its distinctive name from a tale of romance. For more information, see the box on page 22.

Funnel String Dispenser

Use a funnel with a hanging hole or drill a hole near the rim. Hang the funnel on a wall and put a ball of string in it, threading the end of the string through the funnel neck.

The Long Haul

If necessity is the mother of invention, then perseverance is the father. It is often a long time from idea to patent to profit, with many successes and failures along the way. Inventors should ask themselves why they are persisting. If it is all done for the fun and adventure of inventing, then the experience can be truly rewarding.

Many inventors would like financial rewards too, and that means they will also have to consider the needs of all the people who might use their invention. Any invention that is expected to make money has to be marketable—a product that people will want to buy.

Once an inventor is convinced that his idea does have a market and could become a successful invention, he is usually stumped about what to do. The next step is to build your invention, or to create a model, and then to work out the bugs. This phase can best be characterized as build and test, build and test, and build and test some more. Each part of the development process will create its own problems and the need for more creative thinking to solve them—and that continues until the product finally "feels right."

The Art of Design

Your goal as an inventor is not only to make the idea work, but to make it work as smoothly, efficiently, and simply as possible—to use the smallest number of materials and parts to get the job done well. This means continually eliminating unnecessary parts and materials and combining functions so that one part can be made to take the place of two, three, or even more. When this is achieved, and a simple and functional construction results, it is called an "elegant" design.

Another constant concern should be the cost of producing your invention: you want to keep it as low as possible. It would be easy to design

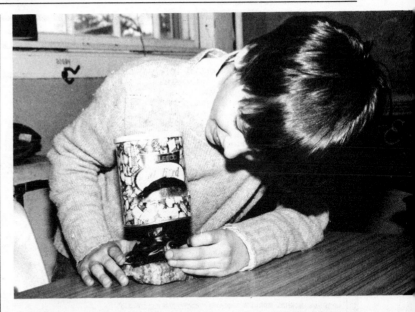

inventions if their cost were no object, but that is rarely the case. Most of the time an inventor is trying to think of alternative solutions that are less expensive than existing ones. In fact, one form of invention is simply creating ways of making things at a lower cost. However, it is not a good idea to cheapen the quality of a design just to save money, although that is always tempting. A clever and inventive design costs as little as possible while still maintaining its quality—and that should be one of your goals.

If simple, elegant invention is the result of reducing, or "subtractive" design, then "additive" design would seem to be complicated and inelegant and should certainly be avoided. A good example of additive design is the cartoon inventions of Rube Goldberg. Rube Goldberg was a popular syndicated newspaper cartoonist best remembered for his crazy and involved pseudo-scientific inventions for doing simple everyday

The Inventions of Professor Lucifer G. Butts, A.K.   By RUBE GOLDBERG

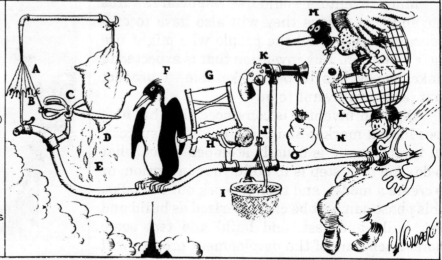

PROFESSOR BUTTS GETS HIS WHISKERS CAUGHT IN A LAUNDRY WRINGER AND AS HE COMES OUT THE OTHER END HE THINKS OF AN IDEA FOR A SIMPLE PARACHUTE. AS AVIATOR JUMPS FROM PLANE FORCE OF WIND OPENS UMBRELLA (A) WHICH PULLS CORD (B) AND CLOSES SHEARS (C), CUTTING OFF CORNER OF FEATHER PILLOW (D). AS WHITE FEATHERS (E) FLY FROM PILLOW, PENGUIN (F) MISTAKES THEM FOR SNOW FLAKES AND FLAPS HIS WINGS FOR JOY WHICH DRAWS BUCK-SAW (G) BACK AND FORTH CUTTING LOG OF WOOD (H). AS PIECE OF WOOD FALLS INTO BASKET (I) ITS WEIGHT CAUSES ROPE (J) TO PULL TRIGGER OF GUN (K) WHICH EXPLODES AND SHOOTS LOCK FROM CAGE (L) RELEASING GIANT UMPHA BIRD (M) WHICH FLIES AND KEEPS AVIATOR AFLOAT WITH ROPE (N). AVIATOR BREAKS PAPER BAG OF CORN (O) CAUSING CORN TO FALL TO GROUND. WHEN BIRD SWOOPS DOWN TO EAT CORN, FLIER, UNHOOKS APPARATUS AND WALKS HOME.
THE BIGGEST PROBLEM IS WHERE TO GET THE UMPHA BIRD. WRITE YOUR CONGRESSMAN.

One of Rube Goldberg's typical contraptions—an exercise in additive design.

tasks, like turning on the toaster or setting off a wake-up alarm. To demonstrate these absurd sequential inventions, Goldberg invented a cartoon character named Professor Lucifer Gorgonzola Butts. It was Butts' goal to make the simplest task as incredibly complicated as possible—and he always succeeded.

Professor Butts's trap of additive design is one of the dangers inventors face. Additive design typically occurs when the inventor thinks of something else—another feature or function, perhaps—*after* the basic design has been completed. Afterthoughts are fine, but rather than just tacking them onto an already completed design, you should add these new features to the original invention plan and start the development process from scratch again. Only when all features and objectives of the invention are clearly stated at the outset can an elegant design be achieved. Adding new or different functions for the invention as you go will only result in a Rube Goldberg.

There is nothing wrong with changing your mind midstream or thinking of a better way to do something after you have already done it. But don't try to modify the existing design to accommodate the new feature. Go back to the beginning and rethink the solution, using the new criteria with the old.

Unsatisfactory results should not be looked upon as failures, but rather as necessary experiments in eventually solving the invention problem. If you, the inventor, are convinced that the invention ultimately will work, that attitude will make your time worthwhile. The inventor in search of solutions knows that an elegant answer to the problem does exist somewhere, and his work is dedicated to finding it.

Anyone who wants to be helpful to an inventor at work should not criticize the immediate results but should encourage the search for the perfect solution. There should probably be a sign outside every inventor's workshop door: INVENTION IN PROGRESS—DO NOT CRITICIZE.

The true inventor is undaunted by the often-heard words "It'll never work," no matter how many discouragements or failed experiments may occur. Most inventions didn't work the first time anyway, sometimes not until the tenth, twentieth, or even hundredth time around. The invention process is one of trial and error, and each trial will usually be an improvement, or at least a learning experience, over the previous experiment. Every attempt, successful or unsuccessful, can lead to new ideas and new inventions.

How to Use This Book

The *Invention Book* explains each step of the process of being an inventor, from how to come up with good ideas and make them work to considering a patent and selling the invention for a profit. It explains the fundamentals of setting up a workshop, building models of your invention, creating a name for it, plus record keeping, planning, packaging and marketing. It also provides the inspiration to try out your own ideas and stick with them until you are satisfied with the results.

You will find stories here that tell the history of many inventions we commonly use or know about, like the ballpoint pen, drive-in movies, water skis, and color film. You can learn a great deal by seeing the many ways inventors have succeeded despite discouraging setbacks.

If you need a few ideas or inspirations to get started, look through the list of Fantasy Inventions that follows each story. Each list contains ideas for products that might be invented, to show how one invention can be the inspiration for other new ideas. Most of these fantasy inventions are only described briefly, so you can imagine, invent, and maybe even design how they might work and look. In the Fantasy Notebook one of these ideas is illustrated and labeled to show you how it might be interpreted in a preliminary sketch. But do remember, these Fantasy Inventions are only ideas, and for any one to become a true invention, the inventor must figure out how to make it work.

You don't have to read the *Invention Book* from cover to cover. Use it as a reference tool for information about some specific aspect of inventing, like the patent process, naming your invention, or marketing. Or read the invention stories just for fun. This is also a craft book. Throughout the chapters about the invention process, there are projects of things to do and simple inventions to make. Use them to give you hands-on experience in building and tinkering that will bring your invention ideas to life. You'll see for yourself how inventions go from a sketch on paper to an actual product—who knows, with a little inspiration, you may be able to adapt these sketches, ideas, suggestions and fantasies into a marketable invention that's all your own.

The Story of Dr. Pepper

Wade Morrison, a young man who worked in a drugstore in Virginia, headed west for Texas after his romance with a local girl was thwarted by the girl's father, Dr. Pepper. Morrison wound up running the Old Corner Drug Store (3.) in Waco, Texas, but he still spoke frequently of his lost romance. Charles Alderton (1.), the pharmacist at the store, would mix all kinds of flavors together in making a special drink for his patrons. The drink became named for Dr. Pepper, in hopes that it would help Morrison's romance. The drink itself was marketed by Morrison and a beverage chemist, R.S. Lazenby (2.), who developed the unusual formula further. The interesting name was matched by clever marketing methods. The bottle shown here carries the numbers "10", "2" and "4" because these were the times of day when this "friendly pepper-upper" was recommended to provide a lift of energy.

1.

2.

3.

KING OF BEVERAGES

Dr. Pepper

TRADE MARK.

VIM VIGOR & VITALITY

Dr Pepper
10 2
4
10 FL OZ

The Inventor's Workshop

An inventor's workshop is a personal space for thinking, building, experimenting, and solving problems, and as an inventor you should find a space that is inspiring for the type of work you want to do. The inspiration may come from materials for tinkering, tools, books, or even the view out the window.

A real nuts-and-bolts inventor would probably set up a workshop in the basement or garage, surrounded by scrap parts and hardware as well as mechanical things that might inspire solutions. For someone who leans more toward concoctions and kitchen chemistry, the kitchen or bathroom sink might be the best workshop. Some inventors need only a place to draw and sketch ideas; then a bedroom, desk, table, or almost anywhere might be an acceptable place. Some inventors prefer the library, getting inspiration from other people's work in books or patent drawings. The inventor who thinks of himself as an entrepreneur might feel most inspired sitting in a big chair behind a desk so he can get into a business attitude and feel like the executive he wants to be.

However, most inventors seem to take on the entire house as their workshop. In the planning or conceptual stage, you might seek a quiet space to concentrate on the design of your idea, and to solve problems by thinking and sketching. When it comes time to build a "breadboard" of the idea (the rough tryout to see if it actually works), you'll need a space that has the appropriate materials and tools to allow you to tinker. Remember that it takes time to tinker and solve invention problems, often several days or weeks, so try to find a space where your work won't be disturbed and where you are not interfering with other people's needs. If your experiments can fit into a portable carton or on a tray, you can move your "workshop" simply and quickly from one space to another.

A good workshop is well-organized and stocked with parts for tinkering. Remember to always keep a first-aid kit on hand.

For building a model or prototype of the invention you might need a workshop with tools that will allow for fine craftsmanship. You might even need help constructing some of the parts. Do you know someone who has a woodworking shop, tinkers with electronics, makes jewelry, or builds model planes? A parent? A neighbor? A teacher at school? Would they be willing to help you build a part of your invention model—or maybe show you how to do it? Remember that an inventor should be aware of all the resources available and be able to use them when needed. And for the costing and marketing phase of the invention process, you will most likely find yourself on the telephone talking to local manufacturers and suppliers. You can do that anywhere there is a quiet space with a phone and the Yellow Pages.

But of all the spaces an inventor might use during the inventing process, the most important is the space used for tinkering. Experiments have a way of spreading out, and most inventors tend to keep all of their old contraptions, so a well-lit area with a big table or desk is best. If you do not have a large work table, you can make one simply by putting an inexpensive hollow-core door or a sheet of plywood on top of two sawhorses.

Inventors are notorious for using parts and materials they have on hand. You'll find that having a good collection of invention stuff will save a lot of trips to the hardware store—and a lot of money. The type of materials needed will, of course, depend on the invention, but usually the more that are readily available the better. Inventors often find solutions to problems by just taking things apart, then putting some of the parts back together in a different way. You can find lots of useful parts in discarded items like broken toys and old appliances or leftover construction materials. As scrap parts and materials are collected, sort and organize them in bins or boxes by their type: fasteners, wire, tubes, screws, knobs,

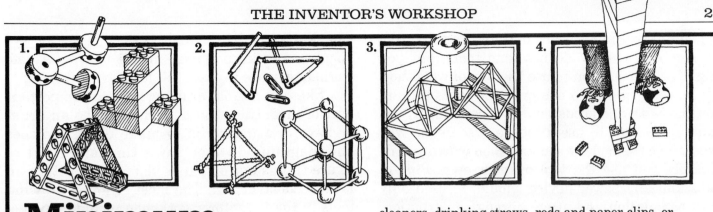

Minimum-Maximums

1. Use any toy modular building system like Lego, Tinkertoy, erector set...

2. ...or a homemade building system using pipe cleaners, drinking straws, rods and paper clips, or toothpick rods with soaked dried peas for connectors.

3. Using the fewest parts, span the distance between the arms of a chair so that the center of the span will support a roll of toilet paper.

4. Using no more than 25 building pieces construct the tallest possible freestanding structure.

switches, tape, small metal parts. Label each container clearly.

Tools of the Trade

Most jobs are easier when you have the right tools to help you, but you must also know how to use them correctly! First consider the materials and parts you will be using in your experiments and model building, then make a list of the tools you will probably need. Be sure to remember simple things like a pencil, measuring tape, and common hand tools like a hammer, screwdriver, and pliers. For tedious jobs (like cutting wood) or repetitive work (like drilling a lot of holes), you might consider using power tools like a sabre saw or an electric drill.

If you don't have all the tools you need, you might know someone who will lend them to you. Parents and grandparents are often good sources. Friends and neighbors with hobbies or home workshops might even be willing to help you do a particular job, but it is a good idea to keep the borrowing within the family. If you can afford to buy tools, *don't* buy the cheapest ones available—they frequently don't work very well (and that can be dangerous!) and don't last very long. But don't buy the most expensive industrial-quality tools either—you won't be using them every day, year after year. And absolutely do not buy or use "play tools"—they do not work at all!

Many schools have an industrial-arts workshop or an arts-and-crafts department with a variety of hand tools and maybe a few power tools. Some schools have completely outfitted workshops with specialized tools for woodworking, metalworking, jewelry making, and electronics. Schools usually do not lend tools, but you might get permission to use the school workshop.

A good rule is to use only the tools you are familiar with and accustomed to operating. If you don't know how to use a tool, ask someone who does. Have them show you and then watch you do it *before* you use the tool on your own. Plug-in tools and any power device should be used only with permission and after thorough instruction. Whenever you work with power tools and certain potentially dangerous hand tools (like a hammer, saw, knife, or drill), wear safety glasses or eye goggles, and keep a first-aid kit nearby. A safe workshop space is essential for good tinkering.

Sketching and drawing are an important part of inventing. You don't have to be an artist or have drafting skills to make quick sketches and diagrams. It often saves time and effort to figure things out on paper before committing an idea to construction. The most common drawing tools in the inventor's workshop include a pad of graph paper, a T-square, two plastic triangles (a 45° triangle and a 30°/60° triangle), a ruler,

The Story of the Jukebox

Soon after Thomas Edison invented the phonograph people started making coin-operated record players for public places, eventually named "jukeboxes" after the British slang for a place of entertainment, "juke joint." Shown here are the 1897 Edison Automatic, with stethoscope-like headphones (2.), the big 1905 multiphone (4.), the 1908 Regina Hexaphone (3.) and the flashy Wurlitzer 950 from 1942 (1.), now worth between $10,000 and $15,000.

1.

2.

3.

4.

Space, Tools and Materials

Here is a list to help you plan your workshop, including basics for your work space, useful tools for both building and tinkering, and good parts and salvaged materials for you to collect.

SPACE

workbench area
workbench light

Storage containers for parts
    cut-down milk cartons
    empty cans, jars, plastic containers
    cigar boxes
first-aid kit

TOOLS

bench vise	hand drill and bits
screwdrivers	clamps
hammer	penknife
pliers	hacksaw
tweezers	adjustable wrench
scissors	sandpaper and/or file
measuring tape/ruler	

MATERIALS

Fasteners

screws	wood scraps
rubber bands	electronic parts
tape	plastic parts
thin wire	rubber parts
glue	metal parts
brads and nails	
string and rope	

Discarded objects for taking apart
    small kitchen appliances
    radios
    tape recorders
    toys
    locks
    cameras
    lamps
    roller skates
    typewriters
    scales
    bicycles
    telephones

Common household materials and discards
    cardboard
    empty cans and containers
    electric wire
    paper tubes
    straws
    paper clips
    toothpicks
    pipe cleaners
    aluminum foil

Bookshelf Book Safe

1. Select an unwanted book large enough to hold your hideables. Mark the inside page for cutting as shown.

2. Using a scissors or sharp hobby knife, cut through several pages at a time until the entire middle section is removed.

3. Place hideables inside of the book hollow and put the book back on the shelf. Because the bookshelf book safe is homemade and not a look-alike commercial product, no one will know which book to look for.

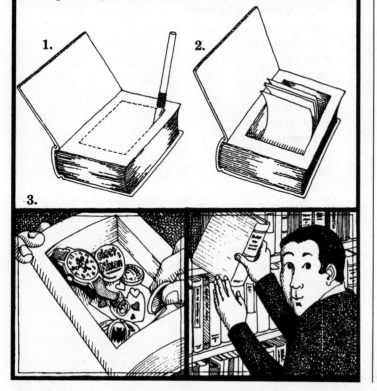

pencils, and a drawing compass or a circle template. If you have never used these tools, don't be afraid to experiment with them. They're easy to figure out, and with practice you will develop some skill.

Somewhere in or near the workshop you should keep your inventor's library of catalogs, newspaper clippings, sketch notebooks, and reference books, including books on crafts, books on building and repairing, books with diagrams that show how things work, books about inventing, manufacturers' parts catalogs, the Yellow Pages, and of course a Sears catalog. Large mail-order catalogs can help you find the kinds of tools, materials, and fasteners that are commonly available, as well as give you ideas for product design and ways to solve invention problems. If you do not have enough bookshelf space, plastic milk crates make a good portable file.

Many inventors consider their reference library indispensable while tinkering and figuring out design problems. Why invent a part if you can find an existing one that will work just as well? Also, thumbing through reference materials will sometimes give you ideas for creating your own solutions.

The Inventor's Notebooks

Once the invention process begins you may be overwhelmed by the amount of information you collect and the inspirations and ideas you have. Write the information down or sketch out the idea *immediately* in an "inventor's notebook," while the ideas are fresh and before the information is forgotten or lost.

You should carry a small pocket-size notebook or notepad with you at all times to record ideas wherever and whenever you get an inspiration. Inventors are always trying to solve problems and find better solutions, so when you see or hear something that relates to your invention—maybe a conversation, a newfound source of scrap materials, or the way someone else has solved a similar problem—it is important to have a notebook handy to write down the information. Every now and then you should transcribe the important notes and sketches from your pocket notepad to your workshop notebook so they become an official record of the process of your invention.

The workshop notebook is an ongoing record of all the events, actions, experiments and observations during the entire development of the invention. Be sure to write down everything you

do, including your new ideas for improvements—even the ones that seem harebrained. This notebook should always be kept on hand wherever you work, so you can make notes on the spot.

By reviewing your notes you can see if any solution patterns are developing. Sometimes a good idea will remain dormant until the time is right to use it. Old ideas can often yield even better solutions than new ones. In time your inventor's notebook will also become your inventor's scrapbook. Looking back at old ideas and inventions can be enlightening and amusing.

Should you decide to pursue a patent (or if you just want to play it safe), your inventor's notebook could become important evidence of the date when you first got the idea and the fact that you diligently pursued it. If this applies to you,

Flycatchers

1. Lay two pencils across a plate and put a little strip of bacon across the pencils. Then place an empty jar on top of the pencils. Flies will be attracted by the smell of the bacon and get stuck in the jar.

2. Bend a paper clip as shown to suspend a small piece of cheese underneath the top cover of your kitchen sink drain. Put the cover in place in the sink. When flies cluster around the cheese, just turn on the water.

3. Attach a small circle of mesh, or metal or plastic screen, onto a suction-cup dart gun with string or a rubber band, to make a fly swatter gun.

1.

2.

3.

Back Scratchers

Experiment with ideas by building working prototypes or a functioning model made from available materials. When the idea works, then consider how it might look and be produced as a commercial product.

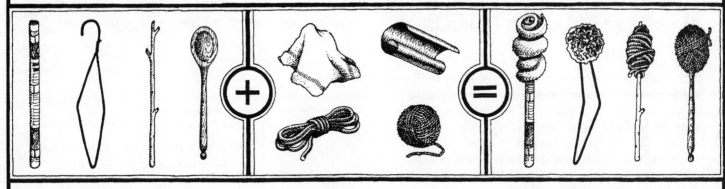

Handle
rolled newspaper
bent coat hanger
branch or stick
wooden spoon

Texture
washcloth
crumpled aluminum foil
rope
soft or rough yarn

Back scratcher
Attach a handle to a textured material to make the back scratcher of your choice

then you should keep all your notes in a bound notebook with pages that cannot be easily inserted or removed. Don't use a loose-leaf notebook or even one with a spiral binding. Number each page consecutively (skipping none), and every time you write an entry—sketches, notes of meetings, things you want to test, or anything relating to your progress and ideas—date and sign it. Don't leave a lot of blank space between paragraphs or sketches and don't leave any blank pages in the middle of your notes. During the patent process you may have to prove that you were the first to think of the idea (although this is unlikely), and blank pages or large open spaces between notes indicate to the patent examiner that you may have cheated by filling in information later.

Have a friend periodically review the most recent entries in your notebook, making sure he clearly understands what you have written and drawn; then have him sign and date a few pages as a witness. The pages don't need to be witnessed and signed on the day you write them; once every few weeks or each month should be okay. Again, the idea here is to have the proof that you were the first to think of the invention and that you worked on it diligently. A complete, signed, and witnessed inventor's notebook is the best insurance against someone's claim that they had the idea before you did.

Kitchen Ingredients Formula Guide

Common kitchen ingredients can often be combined to make new substances. A successful formula often takes much experimentation to get the proportions of the ingredients just right.

Use this formula guide as a basis for experimenting and inventing new substances—and uses. Work on a newspaper-covered table or counter, using paper cups and disposable swizzle sticks for mixing. A felt-tip pen is also handy for listing contents on the mixing cups.

Here are some sample formulas to get you started. We leave it for you to figure out the proportion of ingredients to use.

Flour + salt + water + cooking oil = paste

Water + corn starch + corn syrup + vinegar = glue

Salt + flour + water + vegetable oil + food color = play clay

Water + vegetable oil + ink + food color = liquid sandwich

Baking soda + water + lemon juice = fizz maker

Rubbing alcohol + paint thinner + food color + glass jar and lid = wave maker

Ingredient	Properties
food color	used alone or combined to give color to liquids and some solids
water	universal wetting and mixing agent
sugar	granular, sticky when wet, dries solid, can crystallize
flour	fine powder, sticky to doughy when wet, a thickener
vinegar	mild acid, strong odor, a solvent
baking soda	fine powder, absorbs odor, extinguishes flames, produces a gas when mixed with some liquids
vegetable oil	lubricant, waterproofer, burnable
gelatin	gelling agent
corn syrup	sticky and gooey
corn starch	fine powder, good thickener, separates out of mixture
soap powder	emulsifier, lubricant, good absorbing agent
alcohol	flammable, evaporates quickly
paint thinner	solvent and thinner for oil-based paints, tar, and adhesives

Planning

Once you have decided on an invention idea to build and test, and have the tools, materials, and space you will need, the practical part of the invention process can begin.

Because inventing is a process that includes many steps, you should have a plan for what you are going to do, exactly how you are going to do it, and the results you expect. However, it is usually very hard for an inventor to predict exactly how long it will take to develop and complete an invention and what problems may come up in the process. By setting several progressive goals, you will recognize more easily when one problem is solved and you are ready to go on to the next step.

For example, a first goal may be to prove that your invention idea really works. To do this, most likely you will need to build a working "breadboard" (see page 40). Once you are satisfied that that goal has been accomplished, your next goal might be to see how people will respond to your invention. Can they use it; what would they be willing to pay for it; what changes or improvements do they suggest? Or maybe your next goal is to find people with

certain technical skills who can help you solve your invention problems.

So much is learned in each part of the invention process that it is okay to wait until one goal is accomplished before setting another. But write down each goal in your inventor's notebook! By writing it out, you will have a clear sense of what

A Sample General Plan

To invent a salt shaker with a continuous adjustable control, from a light sprinkle to a fast pour.

1. Look at existing salt shakers to see what size holes they have and how much salt they hold.

2. Is there any product currently available like my idea? If so, how does it work? What about Parmesan cheese shakers or spice shakers?

3. What shapes, sizes, and styles of salt shakers work best and sell best? How much do they cost?

4. List other products that in some way control flow (water faucet, eye dropper, dump truck). How might they help you in the design? What things in nature control flow? How does the human body control flow?

5. Sketch out and draw all ideas for a flow-control salt shaker. Consider whether the same idea will work for a pepper shaker.

6. Look through reference materials (ads showing bottles with "dispensing closures," cutaway drawings that show how things work, catalogs of almost anything—hardware, laboratory equipment, kitchen appliances) for clues and inspirations to solve design problems. (Here is a good problem-solving hint: As you look through pictures for ideas, compare each product or part you see with the problem you are trying to solve. For example, "How is a kitchen sifter like a flow-control dispenser?" "How is a sponge like a flow-control dispenser?" or "How is a pair of pliers like a flow-control dispenser?")

7. Continue sketching ideas until ready to select one that is worth building and testing.

8. Draw plans as needed for building a breadboard. First design the part of the product that seems most important or most difficult—the adjustable flow mechanism.

9. List and collect tools and materials, then build the breadboard. If parts don't work together as expected, return to Step 8.

10. Test the breadboard to see how it works and determine what improvements need to be made. Return to Steps 7 and 8 as often as necessary until the breadboard works well and meets objectives.

Even though it is very important to stick with your objective no matter what, it is okay to change and update your plan as necessary. The more you experiment, the more focused your plan will become, and the closer you will be to the solution.

---

you want to accomplish. A written goal is not as easily changed as one that is only remembered.

Some inventors do not like setting goals and planning, thinking that it stifles their freedom and creativity. But quite the opposite is true. With a clear, well-defined, focused goal and a plan to reach that goal, you are much more likely to find or recognize a good solution. Sometimes an inventor arbitrarily changes his goal because he thinks he cannot solve a particular problem.

But in this case, the real problem is probably that the inventor did not clearly think out his plan. There is an inventor's adage that says "The definition is the solution." That is, the more time an inventor spends on clearly stating and defining exactly what he wants to accomplish, the easier it will be to find the solution.

For example, suppose you had an idea to make a better salt shaker so that the user could control the flow of salt, from a gentle sprinkle to a heavy flow. Your first goal is to build a working breadboard, but before you begin, you should write a plan that defines and describes what you are going to do. After a while this process will become routine. For now, *write it down!*

Time and Money

If your invention is complex or is going to require a lot of time and money to complete, then you may need a business plan to interest others in investing their own time or money in your idea. The purpose of a business plan is to establish approximately how much time and money it is going to take for each stage of the invention process, and what particular skills, people, and other resources will be required. Because a business plan is usually written before the invention

The Story of Toothpaste

Washington Wentworth Sheffield (1.) was a dentist in New London, Connecticut in the mid-1800s, who developed a tooth-cleaning powder that was quite popular with his patients. Sheffield's son Lucius (2.),

also a dentist, helped him modify the formula to make Dr. Sheffield's Creme Dentifrice, the first toothpaste. The product didn't take off until they packaged the toothpaste in tin tubes, as shown below. Lucius Sheffield became regarded as "the world's most famous dentist" and received thirty patents for inventions ranging from a way of capping teeth to an elevated tunnel railroad for cities. Tin tubes gradually became the heart of the company's business, and the Sheffield Tube Company is still in business today.

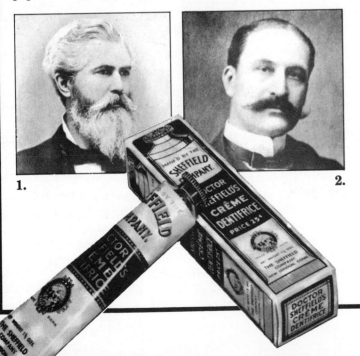

1.

2.

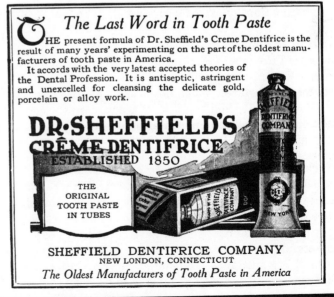

The Last Word in Tooth Paste

THE present formula of Dr. Sheffield's Creme Dentifrice is the result of many years' experimenting on the part of the oldest manufacturers of tooth paste in America.

It accords with the very latest accepted theories of the Dental Profession. It is antiseptic, astringent and unexcelled for cleansing the delicate gold, porcelain or alloy work.

DR·SHEFFIELD'S CRÊME DENTIFRICE
ESTABLISHED 1850

THE ORIGINAL TOOTH PASTE IN TUBES

SHEFFIELD DENTIFRICE COMPANY
NEW LONDON, CONNECTICUT
The Oldest Manufacturers of Tooth Paste in America

A Sample Business Plan

An adjustable bicycle kickstand for sloping, rocky, or soft ground.

Objective: To invent an adjustable kickstand that will securely keep a bicycle standing on sloping, uneven, rocky, or soft ground. I will build and improve models through to a final prototype and then try to sell the invention to a bicycle accessories manufacturer for royalty payments.

Competition: Nothing is presently available like my idea, although the manager of one bicycle shop claims some older English bikes do have a kickstand length adjustment. My idea for an adjustable kickstand is different, with a length adjustment plus an adjustable foot for greater stability on soft or rocky ground.

Product development: Most of my experiments will be modifications of existing kickstands. The length of my kickstand will be easily adjustable from long to short to accommodate uneven and sloping ground surfaces, and the foot of the kickstand will easily adjust from a single point for hard and rocky ground to a flat foot for soft surfaces. When not in use, the kickstand will conveniently fold back out of the way (in the conventional manner) and not interfere with the rider's movements.

Market research: The need for an adjustable and stable bicycle kickstand is obvious to anyone who has tried to stand a bike on sloping, rocky, or soft ground. I have talked with two local bicycle shop managers and they presently do not sell and have never heard of a kickstand like the invention I propose. Both managers think it is a good idea. The store managers also claim that most new bikes do not come with a kickstand; it is

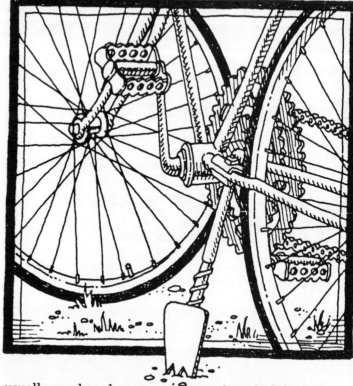

usually purchased as an accessory when the bike is new.

The first manager I spoke with claims to sell about 200 kickstands a year; the other manager estimates 250 to 300 kickstands sold per year. My kickstand will probably be more expensive than the $4 to $12 models now being sold. Both managers think that my invention could represent 10 to 20 percent of their kickstand sales if the retail price is under $20.

Marketing: When the final prototype is complete, I plan to take several photographs of the kickstand in use, to demonstrate its features and benefits. I will also write a specifications sheet listing these features and benefits along with a detailed drawing showing dimensions and other specifications.

Both bicycle store managers I spoke with have

agreed to show these materials to representatives from the bicycle accessories companies they do business with. I can also send these materials (plus a cover letter explaining that I want to sell the invention for a royalty) to bicycle accessory manufacturers. I will get these company names and addresses from the boxes of accessories I see in bicycle shops and by researching bicycle accessory manufacturers in the *Thomas Register* (a comprehensive listing of manufacturers in America) and other catalog listings at the public library.

If a manufacturer shows interest, I will try to negotiate a royalty sale agreement. My older cousin is a lawyer and he has agreed to help me negotiate for a fair royalty.

Financing: To complete a final prototype and produce marketing photographs, my only costs will be for materials. I have the tools necessary to do the experimenting and to build the prototype. Here is my estimated budget:

Buy new and used kickstands to modify, plus miscellaneous hardware:	$ 35.00
Film and processing:	9.00
	44.00
20 percent contingency for unexpected expenses, such as long-distance phone calls, postage, and bus fare.	8.80
TOTAL	$52.80

I plan to use money from my savings account and I will not need financing from someone else unless my expenses exceed $75.00. If I do need additional money I will then decide whether I should borrow it from my parents or figure out an investment plan to trade a part of the ownership in my invention for the money I need to finish development.

process is complete (sometimes even before the process has begun), most of your information will be based on past experience or educated guessing. In many ways writing a business plan is like working through the complete invention process from beginning to end without actually doing it. Of course nothing substitutes for tinkering, building, and experimenting, but a business plan will certainly help show you what to expect.

Inventing Rube Goldberg Style

Use any six action components to create an imaginative Rube Goldberg style sequential design invention for these ideas:

Automatic Fanning Machine For Hot Days

Bedroom Burglar Alarm

Remote Control TV Channel Changer

Around the Block Dog Walker

Garbage Disposal Device

Your Own Invention Idea

SUB SANDWICH   WILD CARD   FAN   FALSE TEETH   STRING   WATER CAN

A Better Mousetrap

Mouse comes out of hiding for submarine sandwich (bait) left on counter. Mouse follows line of bread crumbs. Mouse walks into path of fan and is blown across counter... into false teeth. Teeth clamp shut to hold mouse... also pulling a string... which tilts water can to drown mouse.

 CAT

 ICE CUBES

 CHAMPAGNE

 MATCHES

 CUCKOO CLOCK

 PIGEON

 CANNON

 HORN

 SPRINGBOARD

 BUCKET

 SAW

 TEA KETTLE

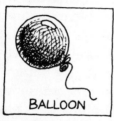 BALLOON

 WEIGHT

 CANDLE

 FROG

 MAGNET

 UMBRELLA

Record Keeping

As the process of invention goes on, you will quickly accumulate a lot of "business" papers like receipts, correspondence, and other records of money spent and money owed. Before things get out of hand, create some kind of system to organize and store these materials while also keeping them handy for easy reference. An inexpensive accordion-type manila file can easily be organized into sections for correspondence, expenses, receipts, and completed inventor's notebooks. In time, if inventing becomes a hobby, you will need a file cabinet to hold all your invention paperwork—possibly including patent papers and sale contracts!

Even if your invention expenses are minimal, it's a good idea to keep a simple financial record of all the money you spend and what you spend it on. Be sure to save all your receipts, and even keep a record of the materials you use from around the house that you do not necessarily buy. If you are ultimately successful in selling your invention for profit, you may need to have these financial records for income tax purposes. Here is a simple way to record expenses:

Invention Expenses:
Portable, Plantable Seed-Starter Box

Date	Item	Cost
8 May	Balsa wood for frames	1.75
8 May	Waterproof glue	.89
8 May	Sandpaper	.49
11 May	Corrugated cardboard	scrap
11 May	Tape	2.29
22 May	Booklet: "Planting a Home Garden"	2.98
24 May	Long-distance call to Burpee Seeds	3.20

If you need outside assistance or maybe a cash loan (usually from a parent or relative), then your business plan needs to be thorough, complete, and convincing enough for others to agree that your idea is worthy of their investment.

You can use the business plan on page 36 as a model, but do make sure that your own plan seems reasonable to you! It is very hard to follow through with a plan that you don't truly believe can work. You must have confidence in your own plan before you can convince others it will work.

Specific elements of the planning process, like royalties, marketing, and market research, are discussed in depth in later chapters.

Breadboard, Model, and Prototype

There are three physical stages an invention must go through to get from an idea to a completed product: first the *breadboard*, which proves that the invention idea works; then the *model*, which takes into consideration who is going to use the invention as well as how it will be used; and finally a *prototype* of the invention, which looks and functions exactly like the manufactured version would, except that the prototype is a one-of-a-kind, handmade sample.

Breadboard

The first step is to prove that your invention idea can work. Inventors call their first rough constructions "breadboards." A breadboard is the working proof that you have taken an idea and translated it into a physical device that can be successfully demonstrated to yourself and others. It makes little difference if the breadboard does not look good or even does not look anything like the way you imagine the finished product. The breadboard does not even have to work well; it only has to prove that your invention idea can be "reduced to practice"—that is, that your idea works.

Breadboards can be made from any materials you might have handy, including parts from other products and parts that might never be used in the final design. Often it takes several breadboards and a lot of tinkering and fine-tuning to get the idea to work right. Each breadboard should be an improvement over the previous one. For example, to build a breadboard of a newspaper roll hammock, you might begin by

Newspaper Gadgets

Roll up a section of newspaper and use it for a variety of functions. Make a bottle opener (1.), an automatic plant watering device (2.), or a newspaper duster (3.).

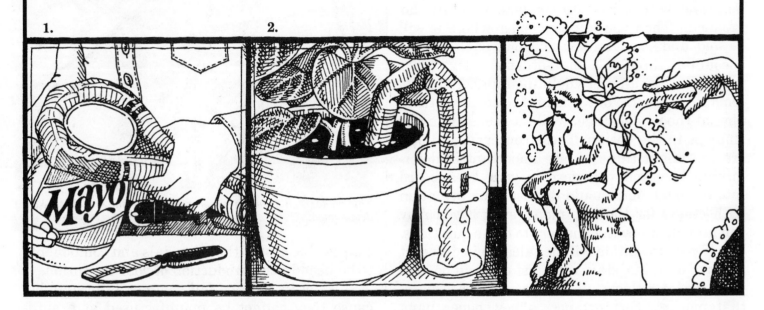

1.
2.
3.

experimenting with the ways to hold a rolled newspaper together—string, tape, glue, or wire. Next, figure out how to attach several newspaper rolls together: What type of knot holds best? How thick does the rope have to be? What is the best spacing between newspaper rolls? Then experiment with ways that the hammock can be hung. The results of each of your experiments can be considered a breadboard. You can then combine these experiments to make a complete newspaper roll hammock breadboard, either full size or smaller. But you must be satisfied that the breadboard proves that the hammock will work before you move on to the next stage, the model.

Model

An invention *model* builds on the experience acquired in making the breadboard, but it also takes into account some very important new information. For a model you must consider who is going to use the invention, who is going to buy it, what they would be willing to pay for it, and other questions whose answers will begin to dictate the function and appearance of the final design. You will also have to make your model reflect the needs of the marketplace. For every invention there are many choices to make about style, quality, size, materials, and features. And there are other factors that can influence the construction of your model. Where is the invention going to be used; are there any safety factors; what materials are available for production; how durable should the product be; how long should it last; and will it have to compete with similar products? Then you must consider where it will be sold, and how it will be sold (on a shelf, behind a counter, through a mail-order catalog). That may seem like an overwhelming number of problems to deal with, but it is best to consider them now, at the model stage, while it is easy to make changes in the design. These concerns, and others you might think of, are important in determining how you will develop your breadboard into a model. You should discuss your invention with others for their opinions, even if you may you already know the answers to these questions.

If your invention will be saleable in different types of markets, start with just one and be sure your model reflects all the special concerns of that market. For instance, a newspaper hammock that is going to be sold through a mail-order catalog should be as light as possible to keep shipping costs low, it should be easy to fold to package it for shipping, and you should be able to photograph it in an attractive way for catalogs. You should also consider who is going to use the hammock: what length and width should it be, what instructions or accessories should you include to help hang it?

While planning your model, try to design a product that meets all the concerns of the market you have selected, including the manufacturing cost and the selling price. You may need to do some research or shopping to determine the low-

This photograph shows an electronic game in the model stage of development.

est possible cost of the materials and components to be used in the production of your invention.

Many inventions fail commercially only because they cannot be manufactured at a sufficiently low cost. If a product seems too expensive, many potential users will not buy it. Thus a lot of time in the model stage is spent trying to find the right materials and components that will allow the product to be produced at a reasonable cost. As a general rule, the cost of materials and labor to manufacture an invention should be about one fifth of the product's retail store price. For example, if a product is going to sell in a store for $10 (this is the *retail* price), then you can assume that the combined cost of materials and parts plus labor to assemble the materials should be somewhere around $2.00 (1/5 x $10.00). As a rule, the higher the retail price of a product, the smaller the markup from manufactured cost to retail price. A product that retails for $50 may have a materials and labor cost of only one quarter of that price ($12.50), and a $100 retail product may have a manufactured cost of only one third or even one half of the retail price ($33.33 to $50.00). It is important for you to determine the probable retail price of your invention (often called the product's "perceived value") *first* and then calculate how much money you would be able to spend for materials and labor to build it. If you are trying to sell your invention to a manufacturer, you will need to show that your product can be produced for a cost that will allow the appropriate markups, so that the product can be sold at a price somewhere around its perceived value.

Markups are necessary in business because there are usually several people who work at producing and selling a product, and they all have expenses to pay as well as the need to make a profit on their work. The manufacturer must have a markup to pay you a royalty and to pay his salesmen, who then try to convince retail stores to buy it. The manufacturer's profit must also come out of his markup. Then the retail store owner must mark up the price to cover his own expenses for store rent, advertising, salespeople, and so on, plus his own profit. That is why it is so very important that the inventor consider the perceived value of his product and understand what that allows for materials and labor.

Now you understand why it is so important to establish the perceived value (or retail price) of your invention at the time you are planning to build the model. One way to determine perceived value is to show or describe your invention to several people and ask what they would be willing to pay for it. An even better way is to go to a retail store and look for items that are similar to yours in their market, quality, and perhaps function. See what they sell for, and ask yourself if your product is an equal value for that price. Sometimes, rather than settling on an exact retail price, it is best to determine what the lowest

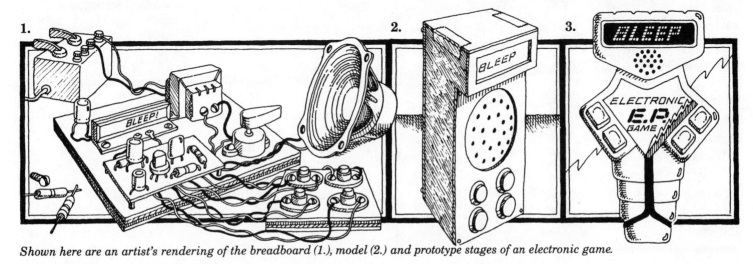

Shown here are an artist's rendering of the breadboard (1.), model (2.) and prototype stages of an electronic game.

Newspaper Hammock

1. Tightly roll about 50 pages of newspaper into a rigid tube. Roll the newspaper across the narrow end.

2. Connect several newspaper tubes using extra-strength clothesline or manila rope. When the hammock is as long as your body bring the rope ends together to form hanging loops.

3. Set up the hammock indoors or outdoors (in good weather) tying it to sturdy supports at each end.

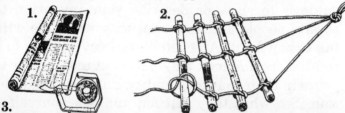

Use this example of cost calculations based on this Newspaper Hammock project to guide you in figuring out the costs and retail price of your invention.

1. Considering the market you have selected, discount department stores, what is the retail perceived value of your invention?

Because the product can wear out quickly due to abuse and weather, it has a perceived value of no more than $6.95, and it would be considered a good buy if sold for under $5.00.

2. Divide the perceived value by five (for a $10-and-under retail item) to determine how much the product should cost to manufacture.

$6.95 retail price =
  $1.39 manufactured cost
$5.00 retail price =
  $1.00 manufactured cost

3. Add up the retail costs of the materials used to build your model. If you don't know the actual cost of a part, take a guess.

2 Sunday newspapers
  (used papers free)
75 feet of heavy-duty
  clothesline $2.49
2 metal rings   .58
15 yards of waterproof
  tape   1.39
Total $4.46

4. To determine the manufacturer's probable cost for these materials, divide your total retail cost by four. That is the price the manufacturer can expect to pay for large quantities of these components when he produces the hammock.

$4.46 ÷ 4 = $1.12

5. For many products the cost of labor to assemble them is about equal to the manufacturer's cost of materials, or double the materials cost.

Cost of
   materials   = $1.12
Cost of labor   = $1.12
Materials
   and labor   = $2.24

6. Multiply the materials and labor cost by five for markup to determine the retail selling price.

$2.24 × 5 = $11.20

Compare Step 6 with Step 1. The perceived value of the newspaper hammock is $6.95 maximum, yet it would have to sell for $11.20 in order to have the proper markups and profits. What can you do? Try several things. For instance, if the newspaper hammock was sold as a craft kit, then you could eliminate the cost of labor for assembly of the finished product (although you might have to add some cost back in for packaging the kit).

$2.24   total cost of materials and labor
− 1.12   less cost of labor
  1.12   cost of materials only
× 5   markup
$5.60   retail price

Now the retail price is under the product's perceived value, but will people be willing to pay the same amount for a kit as for a finished product?

Of course, if you plan to manufacture and sell the product yourself, you might be able to reduce the markup (cut out the "middleman") and still make a good profit. Sometimes just doubling the cost of materials and labor is enough to make a profit. But do remember that it is important to make a profit while keeping the retail price of the product at or below the perceived value.

and highest perceived value of the product might be, and use that to determine the range of manufactured cost you have to work within. Much of the creativity and cleverness in the invention process goes into creating a product that can be produced at the right price.

Prototype

If you intend to sell or license your invention to a manufacturer, then often the model is all you'll need to get a company interested. But if you are thinking of producing the invention yourself, or if you want the invention to be even more impressive when trying to sell it to a manufacturer, you should then take the model to the next stage of development—the *prototype*. A prototype functions just as a model does, except that it is made *exactly* like the finished manufactured product. Even though the prototype is usually a handmade, one-of-a-kind sample, it should be exactly like the finished manufactured product right down to the very last detail, including color, graphics, and sometimes even the packaging and instructions.

In all but the simplest of inventions the prototype usually requires good model-making skills and good resources for sample component parts. If you have successfully built a model but find yourself stuck at the prototype stage, there are a few things you might try. Sometimes it is possible to "sabotage," or take apart, an existing manufactured product and adapt the parts to your own design. A lot of time and cost can be saved by starting out with already manufactured parts. However, be certain you are not merely

The Story of the Robot

Everyone agrees that the robot is still in its early stages of development. Robotics will clearly be fertile territory for inventors for years to come. This photo spread presents a survey of robots, past and present, to inspire your thoughts on robots of the future.

1.

1. This robot is a replica made in Tokyo from a design nearly two centuries old. Japan has a long tradition of trick dolls and mechanized toys. The plans of Lord Hosokawa Yorinao, who designed this robot in 1796, are still consulted by today's inventors.

2. Elektro and his robot dog Sparko were two popular creations of the Westinghouse Company, displayed at the 1939-40 New York World's Fair. The drawing above shows how Sparko works.

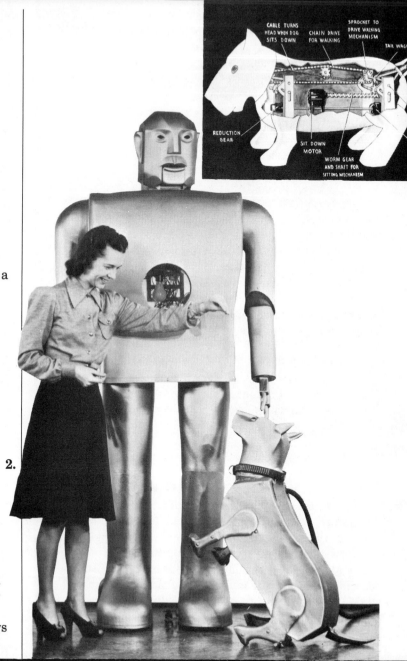

2.

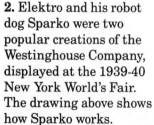

CABLE TURNS HEAD WHEN DOG SITS DOWN   CHAIN DRIVE FOR WALKING   SPROCKET TO DRIVE WALKING MECHANISM   TAIL WAGGER

REDUCTION GEAR   SIT DOWN MOTOR   WORM GEAR AND SHAFT FOR SITTING MECHANISM

3. Hero Jr. is a robot companion made by Heath Company available in kit form or fully assembled. He can sing songs, play games, tell rhymes, act as a guard and move about without bumping into things.

3.

4.

4. Scientists hope this battery-run "seeing-eye" robot, currently being developed in Japan, will lead to a workable electronic or mechanical replacement for seeing-eye dogs. Japan is one of the world's leaders in new robot technology.

5. The New York Aquarium has been testing this robot for use in its Marine Mammal Behavior demonstration.

5.

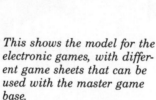

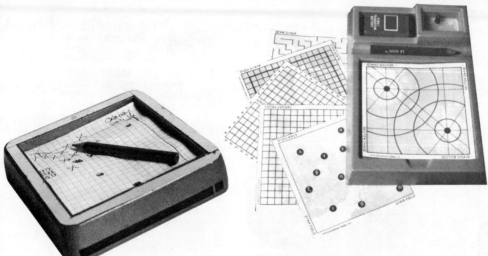

This is the breadboard for a set of electronic games invented by the author.

This shows the model for the electronic games, with different game sheets that can be used with the master game base.

The prototype looks exactly like the final product, down to the last detail. The game sheets have been further developed and refined, and the master game base is now complete.

copying someone else's design. Reshape, change, or modify the appearance of the parts so they are uniquely yours.

If that doesn't work, try talking to those manufacturers that are best suited to making the components of your product (plastic molding companies, metal stampers, woodworking plants, wire formers, printers, etc.). Check the Yellow Pages for companies that do what you need and then ask your parents if they know someone who works there. It certainly helps to get a personal introduction, but most manufacturers will be impressed (and, one hopes, convinced) when you show them your invention model and ask for assistance. Sometimes they are quite willing to build your prototype for free (in whole or maybe just certain parts of it) using the equipment and know-how they have readily available. The manufacturer's incentive is that you, or the company that buys your invention, might ultimately give him an order to build a large quantity of production parts.

Naming Your Invention

If you have created a product, then you also have the privilege of giving it a name. Naming an invention is not all that different from naming a baby or a dog or a bicycle. It is important that you like the name, but the name of an invention also has a purpose: it must help sell the invention. Sometimes the name is descriptive, so people will know what the invention is or what it does. For example, "television" describes a device that uses both "tele" (sound) and "vision" (sight). Sometimes a name is designed to have specific appeal, like Model X15 or Formula 96, or some other name that is not necessarily scientific but sounds technical. Other names may be cute, funny, alluring, or whatever seems appropriate for the product. A name, especially one that is clever and catchy, will help create enthusiasm and make it much easier for people to understand and remember your invention. A product name may even be so unusual that it makes people want to buy it. Do you remember the Pet Rock phenomenon?

Keep in mind that your invention's name will have a lot to do with the way people think about it. Some names tend to make inventions seem small, delicate, or very light, whereas other names can make an invention seem large, heavy,

1.   2.

Bubble Bath Bucket

small hole on opposite sides of the open end near the edge.

1. Using a can opener, punch several large holes around the bottom of an empty tin can. Punch a

2. Attach a loop of heavy string (or a shoelace) through the small holes so the can will hang on the tub spout. Place a bar of soap in the bubble bath bucket and turn on the water.

technical, honest, natural, or alluring. You must first decide how you want people to think about your invention, and then choose a name that is appealing and memorable. If you sell your invention to a manufacturer, the company may want to create its own name for the product. However, in the course of talking about your invention, it's good to have a name other than "the thing," or "my invention," or some merely descriptive title.

For nearly every invention with a unique beginning there is an equally unique story of how it was named. George Eastman, inventor of the Kodak camera, once said that a product name should be "short, vigorous, and incapable of be-

ing misspelled." Eastman explained his choice of the name "Kodak" by claiming that the letter "K" had always been his favorite, seeming "strong and incisive"; therefore the name of his new camera invention had to start and end with a "K." Eastman probably tried several words until he chose Kodak, which he selected, he said, because it sounded like the clicking of a camera shutter.

Sometimes a product is named after its inventor. Charles Post, an inventor of breakfast cereals, used his own name on his first cereal product, Postum, and Dr. Edward Land named his new camera the Polaroid "Land" camera. The name "Polaroid" came from his work in the polarization of light. Often a product that carries a person's name was named after someone popular or famous in hopes that the product would gain immediate acceptance. This was the case of the Baby Ruth candy bar, named for the very popular eldest daughter of President Grover Cleveland—*not* after the famous baseball player, Babe Ruth, as some people think.

Another common method for naming an invention is to use the components or ingredients of the invention. One of the most famous and valuable trademarks in the world, Coca-Cola, is a simple combination of the words "coca" (a flavorful leaf) and "cola" (sweet carbonated water), the drink's two prime ingredients. Of course it helps that the rhythm and sound of the words "Coca-Cola" is quite appealing.

Formica (the material used on many kitchen countertops) is the trademark of a plastic laminate originally developed as an imitation of a natural rock called mica. The name "formica" literally means "a substitute for mica."

Sometimes a product name refers to some special feature of the invention. The Hotpoint line of appliances began with an inventor's patented clothes iron that featured a concentration of heat at the tip, to make it easier to press around collars.

However, not all product names are the result of rational thinking. Sometimes it's inspiration that counts. Years ago, when New York City was much smaller, legend has it that while a cigar maker was developing a new line of cigars, a white owl flew in the window. Eureka! The White Owl brand of cigars shortly followed.

The Story of the Jeep

JEEP!

The jeep was created during World War II as a rugged messenger and reconnaissance vehicle. It was developed by a number of manufacturers, including the Willys-Overland Company and the Ford Motor Company. The vehicle's unusual name has two possible sources. "Jeep" was a character in the popular *Popeye* cartoon strip who was "neither fowl nor beast but knew all the answers and could do almost anything." Jeep thus became a nickname in the 1930s for any heavy-duty vehicle. The other story is that when Ford built their version of this rugged car they put the letters GP for "general purpose" on it, and people would pronounce the initials as a nickname. In either case, the name stuck, and the jeep is still used widely, by both the army and civilians, who can buy a more elaborate form of that original jeep, produced now by American Motors.

Initials and catchy acronyms (when each letter of a name stands for a word) have also been popular in naming inventions. A&P is actually a shortened form of the Great Atlantic and Pacific Tea Company. The first electronic calculator, developed in the 1940s, was called ENIAC, which stood for Electronic Numerical Integrator and Calculator. The popular ENIAC later spawned many copycats, including UNIVAC.

The Story of the Burglar Alarm

Edwin Holmes was originally a Boston notions merchant and manufacturer of ladies' hoop skirts. In 1857 he bought the rights to a burglar alarm patent from Alexander Pope and teamed up with Charles Williams, who manufactured electrical instruments. The key to building his alarm was the insulated wire to hook up the system, which Holmes concocted by taking heavy copper wire and sending it to the same manufacturer who had made his hoop skirts, to wrap the wire with cotton braiding. With his insulated wire perfected, Holmes went on to make the Holmes Protective Company a successful nationwide security firm that still thrives today.

Now even computers have gotten into the act of naming inventions. "Exxon" was selected by a computer process to ensure that the name was both reminiscent of the old company name, Esso, and unique—which explains the double x's, a combination not usually found in any language. The computer determined that both of these features meant that the new name would have high recognition.

Unless you already have a name that you're satisfied with, there are several techniques you might use to find one. If you want a descriptive title, check the invention naming menu, which lists useful prefixes and suffixes along with their meanings.

Some inventions don't sound appealing when called by their descriptive names, so you might want to think up something more melodious or intriguing. For example, let's say you have invented a "smoke-emitting pen device." That name pretty much says how the pen works, but a "sky pen" sounds like a much more attractive item to buy. You can use a "brainstorm" technique to generate a lot of names to choose from. To start the process, write a brief but very descriptive title for your product. The descriptive name should strictly say how the product works, what it does, or maybe express the feeling or attitude you wish to convey. For example, you might write "smoke-emitting pen device that writes in space," and then write down each of the words in the title that implies a major function of the device. "Smoke" might be one heading, "pen" another, and "space" yet a third. Now under each of these words write *all* the other words that you can think of that are associated in

Invention Naming Menu

Select a prefix from column A and a suffix from column B that seem most appropriate to your invention. Now put them together and say them quickly. Try reversing the order. Does the composite name both describe the product and sound good? Try several combinations and orders of words, then select the invention name that sounds best. Make sure you check your name against the dictionary, to see if you have used these terms properly.

The most popular products usually have names that begin with one of these letters: S, C, M, P, B, A, or T.

PREFIX				Technical or scientific		Consumer, fad, or image		
tele	syn	actu	vivi	tron	*intel	ine	ware	art
vege	photo	sono	para	*mobile	atric	national	etic	flex
uni	nutri	intra	cele	tech	tek	o	ical	lex
bi	contra	simpli	vari	ex	ator	trend	aid	tone
trans	deci	mic	soli	trex	*chem	old	*organo	can
centi	cyclo	socio	infra	graph	atic	apex	mite	rite
de	alti	micro	ekta	*compu	tion	um	extra	izer
poly	topo	quick	spira	*astro	mode	co	fizz	sx
metro	aqua	geri	beta	onic	gon	*mini	ary	mon
bio	ex	accu	magna	*electro	*cell	ism	work	mos
re	insti	medi	sani	meter	*disc	ix	stan	max
auto	audio	opti	thermo	osis	lab	matic	ment	vax
practi	dyna	mega	meta	*cron	*comp	trek	rep	stem
mobile	hyper	handi	vapo	*helio	*lene	trac	zine	esco
pro	exact	elec	hy	tach	nate	*oxy	dol	cor
pre	aero	inno	hydro	com	thane	tic	gram	bon
mono	homo	info	del	*milli	ene	ful	mart	lon
geo	polar	neo		ation	tro	flex	mod	*tel
di	equi	digi		ology	ite	pedic	ized	
duo	multi	omni		tric		non	mac	

*Starred words can be used as prefixes as well.

Portable Bleacher Pillow

A common plastic drawstring tote bag used to carry things to the stadium can easily be converted into a comfortable bleacher pillow. Simply stuff the tote bag with crumpled sheets of newspaper and your leftover paper trash, then pull the drawstring to form a pillow.

- Allows spectator to sit higher to view sport
- More comfortable than a hardwood or metal bleacher seat
- Nothing extra to carry
- Disposable or reusable

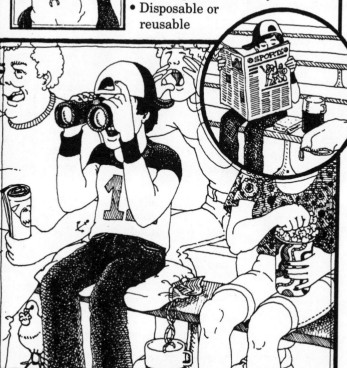

any way with that word. When brainstorming, don't worry whether a word sounds good or not; just write it down.

Smoke	Pen	Space
clouds	stylus	outer
white	point	global
fuzzy	instrument	universe
cigarette	writer	thin air
fire	marker	sky

To create a name, pick any combination of words from two or more columns, say the words together, and listen to how the name sounds. Remember that you might also combine parts of several words to make up a new word. For example, names for a smoke-emitting pen device that writes in space could be "White Writer," "Smoke Liner," or "Thin Air Marker." Here is a tip: catchy names consisting of two words frequently use the same initial for both words, like Cap'n Crunch, Kit-Kat, or Hula Hoop.

When you have finally selected a name for your invention, make sure the name is doing all it can to help explain and sell your product:

- Does the name describe the product in function or attitude?

- Will people get the impression you wish to project?

- Is the name easy to say and remember?

Patents

One of the first concerns of most inventors is "What if somebody steals my idea?" followed quickly by "Should I patent my invention?" The next question is usually "How do I get a patent?" Before you can decide whether or not to proceed with a patent application, you should have a good idea of what a patent is all about, why you might want to apply for one, and what it will cost.

Most people think of a patent as "protection" against the copying of their ideas, and many first-time inventors think that they should apply for a patent as quickly as possible, before someone else comes up with the same invention. That is not always true. The patent process can take a long time and it can cost hundreds or even thousands of dollars. Sometimes, if the inventor keeps improving on his original idea, he ends up with a patent only on the original, not on his new improved version.

A patent is a trade made between you, the inventor, and the United States government. It is actually a fancy legal document with a serial number, an official embossed seal with a ribbon, and of course the inventor's name. Through a patent, you must agree to make public all the details and technology of your invention. The *invention disclosure* should be so complete that anyone capable could build a working model of your invention solely from the information given.

After the United States Patent Office grants a patent to the inventor, it publishes the patent and makes it available to anyone who wants to see it (many large city libraries keep up-to-date files of patents issued). The idea behind this policy is that the government wants to help other inventors solve their design problems and inspire even better inventions by showing them exactly how existing inventions work. That is the government's benefit from the trade.

In return for making your invention public, the government grants you, the inventor, the exclusive right to make and sell your invention

Record Rack

1. Working on newspaper, iron across the middle of the album cover (with the record inside) using a medium to hot setting.

2. After one or two minutes of ironing the record should be soft. Bend the record and record jacket across the middle to a right angle over the sharp edge of a table or counter top. Hold the bent record in place using potholders until it has cooled to shape.

3. Use the Record Record Rack with the record either in or out of the jacket cover.

for a specific period of time. The amount of time depends on the kind of patent that is granted, usually in one of three categories—*utility patents, design patents,* and *plant patents.*

Most patents fall into the utility category and are granted for seventeen years. *Utility patents* cover all mechanical and electrical devices, including everything from a new flyswatter to outer space X-ray binoculars. Probably everything you invent will be in the utility category. When the seventeen-year period is up you cannot renew the patent and it becomes "public domain." That is, your protection has expired and anyone may copy your invention, manufacture it, and sell it without giving you credit or payment.

A *design patent* is granted for a new and original ornamental design of a product—in other words, the unique styling of a product. A design patent protects only the appearance of an item, not the way it is made or the way it works. For example, you might want to apply for a design patent if you invented a bicycle styled like the space shuttle. You did not invent the bicycle, you only changed its outer appearance. But if your "Shuttle Bike" proved successful, you would not want someone copying your idea. Depending on the fee, the Patent Office will grant a design patent for three and a half, seven, or fourteen years.

A *plant patent,* like a utility patent, is also granted for seventeen years and covers any unique new variety of plant life. People who crossbreed plants to create new ones are considered inventors. Suppose you successfully mixed a dandelion with a day lily and got a "dandy day lily" that would grow wild on people's lawns. If you wanted to protect your creation and possibly sell it to a seed company, you would probably want to apply for a plant patent.

Even if you are granted a patent, it is up to you, the inventor, to "police" your patent to make sure no one is illegally copying it during the time you have been given protection. A patent is something that you own, and once the patent is granted, the Patent Office can do no more to help you—it cannot help you license or sell it, produce it, or stop other people from making it themselves. That is all up to you and the help you might get from others.

A Patent Is Not for Every Invention

Some inventors have decided that they can get better protection by *not* patenting their inventions. One alternative to a patent is to keep the details of your invention a secret. If no one else would be able to learn how your invention works, even by taking it apart, then you might want to keep it a secret. You will have protection forever— or until another inventor figures it out.

The formulas for Coca-Cola and Silly Putty have never been patented, and the secrets are supposedly securely locked away in bank vaults

The Official Gazette *is where the US Patent and Trademark Office publishes new patents, a useful research tool for any inventor.*

and passed on only to carefully selected, trustworthy company officials and members of the inventors' families. It is true that many other companies have tried to duplicate the Coca-Cola taste, but no one has been completely successful; and several toy manufacturers have introduced products similar to Silly Putty, but no one has been able to exactly duplicate its unique stretch and bounce.

As an inventor, it is important for you to know how the patent system works, but that does not mean you should routinely apply for a patent every time you come up with a new gizmo. For almost any inventor, that would be much too costly and probably a waste of time. However, you should know enough about the system to take advantage of the invention solutions other people have created (remember, that is why the Patent Office makes patents public information).

If you are just starting out as an inventor or if you haven't yet successfully sold an invention, then it is probably wise to hold off on spending money to begin the patent process. First inventions are rarely successful (although the inventor always gains valuable experience)—in fact, fewer than one out of every hundred patents granted ever becomes an actual manufactured product. To some inventors that may be okay, especially if they don't mind spending a lot of money for a pretty patent certificate to frame and put on the wall. (And of course there is a feeling of prestige in being recognized as an inventor, with a patent as proof.) But even successful inventors know that it is most often wise to wait until you are *certain* you will be able to sell your invention before investing in a patent. If it truly deserves a patent, the company that buys your invention will nearly always be willing to pay the cost.

Suppose you have just completed a final working model or prototype of your adjustable bicycle kickstand and you're trying to decide if you should apply for a utility patent. Maybe you are concerned that someone else might copy your idea or independently come up with the same invention. You might first think of keeping it a trade secret, but then anyone who sees the kickstand will easily see how it works, so that is not a good idea.

If you have not already done so, you should

Protecting the Name

Although the copyright and trademark laws are quite separate from the patent process, many inventors nonetheless also want protection for the names they give their products and any written materials that happen to go with them. However, there is usually some confusion regarding the differences among *trademark, brand name, trade name, copyright,* and the little R in the circle (®) alongside some names, meaning "registered." *Brand name* and *trade name* are both commonly used to mean *trademark.* The trademark symbol, TM, can be used with any brand name or trade name you invent, and it serves to give notice to the public that you intend to use that name as your symbol. After the trademark has been in use for at least one year (and if no one contests it), the trademark can be registered with the Office of Patents and Trademarks, allowing the owner to use the little R in the circle, which gives notice that you own all rights to the name and that no one can copy or use it. A registered trademark must be renewed every five years, and unless it is continuously used, the owner can lose the rights to it. A trademark can have value for the life of the product, even though the product patent may run out after seventeen years. It is not uncommon that ultimately the registered trademark name becomes synonymous with the product it represents, as has happened with Xerox and Kleenex.

go to a library that keeps copies of patents and check to be sure you have not copied a kickstand that has already been patented. The librarian will help you find the proper patent area to look through. You might even get some good ideas on last-minute improvements.

Most patent lawyers and patent agents are willing to give an inventor a free consultation to determine the cost of applying for a patent. You could take advantage of that offer (call to check first) just so you know what the expense could be for your new kickstand, but remember that the patent lawyer's job is to sell his services to inventors, so don't be unduly persuaded to go ahead now. You should first try to determine if a manufacturer is willing to buy your kickstand before spending money on a patent application, or you should at least be convinced that retail bike stores think it's a great idea and could be a success.

What Is Patentable?

We all frequently have ideas about ways to improve the products we use (a ketchup bottle that pours more easily or a jacket zipper that won't snag), or we think of new things that need to be invented (a tractor-tread bicycle for riding in the snow or a tape recorder that will pick up and play back smells). These may all be good ideas but that is *only* what they are—ideas, not inventions!

All inventions begin with an idea, but in order to apply for a patent you must show how the idea actually works. In patent language, this is called *operativeness*.

Besides having to prove that your invention

A view inside the Search Room of the US Patent and Trademark Library.

works, another rule of patent is that you must show that your invention is "new and useful." In the words of the U.S. Patent Office, anyone who "invents or discovers any new or useful process, machine . . . or composition of matter, or any new and useful improvements thereof, may obtain a patent." Of course what is useful can be a matter of opinion. You might think that a smell recorder would be great to capture and play back the smells of a pepperoni pizza or a bed of blooming roses, whereas someone else may not care at all. But it is rare for the Patent Office to reject an invention because it is not useful. Only extremely frivolous inventions might be rejected, like sunglasses for hamsters or a gauge to measure how much cereal is left in the box. And even then the inventor can reapply and argue his case for usefulness. Who knows, maybe hamsters do have difficulty seeing in bright sunlight, or maybe people do want to know at a glance how much cereal is left in the box. Sometimes an inventor need only claim that the invention is useful to himself.

What is most important, however, is that you prove that your invention is "novel"—and that means that it must be truly new. You must be the first person to actually conceive of and create the invention. The Patent Office will *not* consider your invention new if something just like it is already on sale or if just one is in use anywhere in the world. Even if the invention was only described—in a magazine, newspaper, or some other publication—prior to your patent application, the Patent Office will reject it.

The Patent Office can be very strict in enforcing the rule that an invention be absolutely new. The only exception is that you, the inventor, can make your invention public before applying for a patent by putting it on display, publishing pictures or stories about it, or even selling it, *as long as you do apply for a patent within one year of your first public disclosure.* After one year neither you nor anyone else can be granted a patent, and the invention then becomes public property for anyone to make and use or sell.

Of course, in the process of developing your invention you will probably be discussing it and showing it to several people—to get their help and assistance. That is not considered a public disclosure. The one-year limit on applying for a patent begins only after you have sold one or more copies of your invention, or after the invention has been described in any publication. Be sure you remember this rule! Many inventors have lost the ability to obtain patent protection simply because they applied too late.

The Patent Office will also not consider an invention novel if you have only made a small change to an existing product—like a different size or color. And you cannot get a patent for something that is so obvious that it probably has been thought of in the course of everyday life. For example, you cannot patent a new way to tie shoelaces or a new use for pencils or paper clips, no matter how clever your idea may be. If you thought about making wooden pencils out of plastic, that may be considered new, but the idea is not unique or different enough to be considered a true invention. That does not mean that very simple inventions cannot be patented—someone always seems to be patenting a better mousetrap. The Patent Office doesn't care how simple or complex an invention might be; they only insist that it be useful, novel, and operational.

The United States Patent Office

The United States Constitution includes this clause: "Congress shall have power... to promote the progress of science and useful arts, by secur-

The Story of the Ferris Wheel

1.

2.

3.

George Washington Gale Ferris, Jr. (1.) grew up on the banks of the Carson River in Nevada, where he would watch and admire the big paddle boats that passed by. Ferris went on to become an engineer, and his initial fascination with paddle wheels inspired him to build a huge pleasure wheel to provide people with spectacular views from above. His 1893 Ferris Wheel, shown in this picture (2.), was the hit of the Columbian Exhibition in Chicago. One rider, William E. Sullivan (3.), decided to build a portable Ferris Wheel to take from town to town for amusement fairs. His company, the Eli Bridge Company, went on to build the nearly 1,500 Ferris Wheels in operation all over the United States.

Outdoor Solar Shower

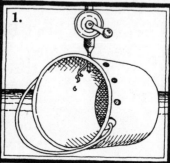

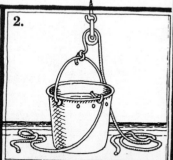

1. Drill several holes in the top side of a plastic bucket to make a sprinkler. Drill one larger hole close to the rim for attaching the pull rope.

2. Attach a strong rope to the bucket handle and run the rope through a pulley and screw hook. Attach another pull rope to the bucket rim.

3. Connect the pulley to an outdoor overhang. Fill the bucket nearly to the top with water and place it directly in the sun to warm. To shower, hoist and secure the water bucket overhead, then slowly tug the pull rope for a gentle sprinkle. For a quick rinse, give the rope a yank.

ing for limited times to...inventors the exclusive right to their...discoveries." Shortly after 1790, Congress enacted the first patent law. Since then, many patent laws have been added and revised.

At first the Patent Office was just someone's desk buried in the Department of State, but by the year 1802 the number of patent applications was rapidly growing, so the government appointed a Superintendent of Patents to be in charge of all patent business. By then the desk had turned into an entire department called the Patent and Trademark Office. Although the office still carries the same name, the official in charge is now known as the Commissioner of Patents and Trademarks, and there are several assistant commissioners plus a staff of nearly 3,000!

It is the job of the Patent Office to provide inventors (or anyone else) with information on how to apply for a patent. The Patent Office examines each patent application to determine if it should be granted or rejected. The Patent Office provides other services and offers several helpful publications for inventors (see box, page 76), but they will not help you in any way with the actual development or design of your invention. That is up to you.

The Patent Office receives about 2,000 patent applications every week, and the number keeps growing. To date, over 4 million patents have been granted. Ironically, about a hundred years ago some high government official suggested that there was probably nothing left to be invented and therefore the Patent Office should be closed. Obviously he was wrong, and fortunately the Patent Office has stayed in business to serve the more than 100,000 people who apply for patents each year.

How to Apply for a Patent

Only the inventor can apply for a patent, or if two or more persons are the inventors they can jointly file an application for patent. The process of applying for a patent can be quite complex, and it often requires a thorough knowledge of patent law. Even though you may be able to do some of the work yourself, you will almost certainly need the help of a patent attorney or a patent agent (though the Patent Office does not require you to use one).

Both a patent attorney and a patent agent are capable of helping you apply for a patent, but there is a difference between them. A patent *attorney* is a lawyer who can also help you with any legal matters in protecting your patent rights if your invention is used without permission or if another inventor claims that you have copied his idea. A patent *agent* is not a lawyer and can only help you through the actual patent process. Usually patent agents charge less for their services than patent attorneys. To find a patent attorney or agent it is best to get the recommendations of other inventors. You can also look in the Yellow Pages under "patent agents" or "patent attorneys" for someone nearby.

Before you begin working with a patent agent or attorney, get an estimate of what the entire process will cost. Even a relatively simple patent can cost $1,000 or more, and a complex, highly technical invention can cost tens of thousands of dollars to patent. Because obtaining a patent is so expensive (and nearly impossible on a kid's budget), you should certainly not rush out and hire a patent agent or attorney as soon as you think your invention works. But don't be discouraged. You can begin the patent process yourself to determine if your invention is truly unique, and then you can discuss your invention with manufacturers and store owners to see if it seems to be marketable. If you are still convinced that you should apply for a patent, then it is time to talk to your family about how to pay for it.

Once a patent application is filed, it may take several years before the process is complete. That is why you will sometimes see the words "Patent Pending" or "Patent Applied For" on products being sold. That does not mean that the patent has been granted or even that it will be granted. All it means is that the inventor has applied for a patent with the Patent Office. Once a patent is granted, the inventor *must* mark the product with the word "Patent" and the patent number that has been assigned to it. If you fail to do this, you may not be able to stop other people from copying it.

The application for a patent involves several steps that you must take to ensure that your invention is truly unique and useful and not just a copy of someone else's idea. The first step in the process is to do a preliminary "search"; that is, to look through all existing patents (and patents pending) in the same category as your invention to see if anyone else has already created your invention. The search is considered only prelimi-

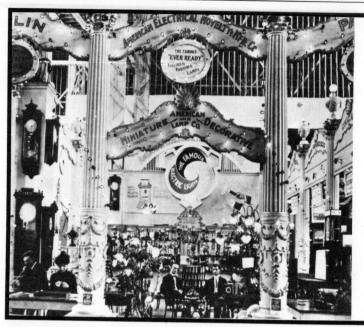

The Story of the Battery

In 1896 the National Carbon Company produced the first commercially marketed dry-cell battery, a 6-inch-high cylinder of packaged electricity. Two years later the American Electrical Novelty and Manufacturing Corporation produced novelty flashlights under the brand name "Eveready." At the first Electrical Show ever, held in 1902 in New York, American Electrical built a gaudy booth, pictured here, to show off their product. Eventually these two companies merged, giving us the well-known Eveready line of batteries and the company went on to become the Union Carbide Corporation.

nary because, after receiving a patent application, the Patent Office examiner will do an extremely thorough and official search through all the patent records that are even remotely related to your invention.

You should be able to do the preliminary search yourself at a large city library (most keep records of patents) with the help of the librarian. By reading through patents that are listed in the same product category as your invention, you will get a good idea of how an application is written and the language that is used. It might also help you improve your own invention and avoid copying the patented details of other inventions. It's best to find out at this point if some other inventor has gotten there before you, prior to spending a lot more time (and maybe a lot of money) on your invention.

In addition to looking through recent and older patents, you should also look through the patents that have just been issued. Most large libraries subscribe to the *Official Gazette of the United States Patent and Trademark Office* (you can also purchase single copies or get your own subscription from the U.S. Government Printing Office). The *Official Gazette* is published weekly and lists the patents that have been granted the previous week, along with other useful information for inventors about patent rule changes, patents available for license or sale, and indices to recent patents and inventors.

The *Official Gazette* does not publish the complete patent, only an "abstract," which includes the important highlights of the patent, to give you an idea of what the invention does and how it works. Each patent abstract contains the patent number and date of issue, the inventor's name and address, a description of the invention, one "claim" (claims will be discussed later), and the one patent drawing that most clearly shows the invention.

Each issue of the *Official Gazette* is arranged by invention subject (games, design, supports, etc.) so you don't necessarily have to look through the entire issue. Look through the abstracts that may relate to your invention to be sure your idea is original. Also, look to see how other inventors have solved invention problems by creating unique solutions. But do remember that the *Official Gazette* publishes only abstracts, and if you want to review the entire patent you will have to purchase a copy from the Patent Office. All you need is the patent number and the appropriate fee (see the publications information on page 76). Some libraries keep records of full patents and have people who are specially trained to help you search for patent information. And there you will also be able to get copies of patents just for the cost of the use of a copy machine.

Although most libraries have some information about patents, and larger libraries subscribe to the *Official Gazette* and keep files of patents issued, the following libraries keep a *complete* file (in numerical order by patent number) of all patents granted since 1836. If you live near one of these libraries, call them and ask to be put on their inventors mailing list. Many of these libraries give special talks and presentations to help people develop their inventions and apply for patents. Talks and seminars are also a good way to meet other inventors to discuss your work and learn from their experiences.

Patent Libraries

California	Los Angeles Public Library
Georgia	Georgia Tech Library (Atlanta)
Massachusetts	Boston Public Library
Michigan	Detroit Public Library
Missouri	St. Louis Public Library Linda Hall Library (Kansas City)
New Jersey	Newark Public Library
New York	Buffalo Public Library New York City Public Library University of the State of New York Library (Albany)
Ohio	Cincinnati Public Library Cleveland Public Library Ohio State University Library (Columbus) Toledo Public Library
Oklahoma	Oklahoma A&M College Library (Stillwater)
Pennsylvania	Franklin Institute (Philadelphia) Carnegie Library (Pittsburgh)
Rhode Island	Providence Public Library
Wisconsin	Milwaukee Public Library U. of Wisconsin (Madison)

There is only one place that has even more complete records of patents and more technical information about inventions: the Scientific Library of the Patent and Trademark Office in Arlington, Virginia (near Washington, D.C.). Along with thousands of scientific and technical books and magazines, the library has a Search Room open from 8:00 a.m. to 8:00 p.m., Monday through Friday, where anyone can examine any United States patent ever issued.

The Search Room is especially convenient to use because all the patents are broken down into about 300 subject classes and over 64,000 subclasses. So if you were trying to see if anyone else had previously invented and patented an adjustable kickstand just like yours, you would first look under the subject class Supports #248, and then check through the subclasses to see if one had been created for this kind of invention. There you would find all the patents that have been granted for kickstand devices, including patents presently in effect and those that have expired.

The Search Room (like the major libraries listed) also contains a complete set of patents arranged in patent number order and a complete set of the *Official Gazette* since it was first published in 1872. Elsewhere in the library there are copies of over 8 million foreign patents, and official journals (similar to the U.S. *Official Gazette*) of foreign patent offices. Only the illustrations in these journals will be of help, unless you can read the language in which the patent is written.

Anyone is entitled to use the Scientific Library and the Search Room free of charge, but it is primarily used by patent lawyers and patent agents who have been specially trained and are experienced at researching related patents that could affect a patent application. However, if you live nearby, or are visiting the Washington, D.C., area, put the Scientific Library and the Search Room on your tour list. As an inventor you might enjoy watching the search process going on and you can try searching one of your own invention ideas. Outside the Search Room is an Inventors Hall of Fame, with interesting displays of great American inventors.

Your own preliminary search of old, recent, and new patents at a local library that has patent reference information should reveal enough to determine if your idea is truly original and unique. You should be able to learn how many other inventions exist that are similar to yours, and whether there already is one that is exactly the same. If you can find nothing even remotely like your invention or idea, then proceed with developing it. If you think there is a chance that your invention may be too similar to someone's patent, then you may want to contact a patent lawyer or patent agent to discuss his fee for doing a thorough search at the Search Room, and for giving you his opinion. Most patent lawyers and agents don't actually go to the Search Room themselves, but instead hire a professional search person who lives in the Washington, D.C., area. Of course, if your preliminary search reveals that your invention has already been patented, then congratulate yourself for being so clever, and go back to the tinkering stage to see if you can invent an even better way to do it—or start work on a completely new invention.

The "Postage Stamp Patent" and the Disclosure Document Program

If, after completing your preliminary search, you are still convinced that no one else has previously patented your invention; and if, after discussing your invention with manufacturers and retail store owners, you are convinced that there is a market for your invention; and if you are concerned that someone may try to copy your invention before you have a chance to sell it, then you may want to consider applying for a patent. But don't rush into it! There are still several things you can do first to protect your idea at considerably less cost.

Many inventors cannot afford to obtain a patent until they sell their invention—and then

Patent and Trademark Office Fees

The Patent Office issues a two-page list of more than one hundred different fees for services they offer to inventors. Many of these fees are for special conditions and circumstances, like filing an appeal for a rejected application, asking for additional time to correct a problem the examiner has found, or processing an application that has been written in a foreign language. The fees listed below are the typical ones for a basic utility patent. Design and plant patent fees are somewhat less costly.

In October 1982 the Patent Office completely revised the patent fee structure, making applications much more expensive and requiring a patent holder to pay additional "maintenance" fees to keep the patent in effect for the full seventeen years. There are also two classes of fees, one for a "small entity" like an individual or small business, and a higher class of fees for large businesses (over 500 employees). The small entity fees are listed here.

To obtain and maintain a patent, these are the fees you can expect to pay to the Patent Office. Remember that these do not include the costs of a patent lawyer or patent agent.

Basic fee for filing a complete patent application including up to 20 claims. Extra fees are charged for additional claims.	$150
Patent issue fee to be paid only if the patent is granted.	$250
Patent maintenance fee to keep a patent in effect beyond 4 years. The fee is due 3½ years after the original patent grant.	$200
Patent maintenance fee to keep a patent in effect beyond 8 years. The fee is due 7½ years after the original patent grant.	$400
Patent maintenance fee to keep a patent in effect beyond 12 years to the full 17 years. The fee is due 11½ years after the original patent grant.	$600

the company that buys the invention will usually pay all patent costs if they think the protection is necessary. Many of these inventors are afraid that until they get a patent, someone else might come up with the same idea—or maybe even copy it! Sometimes an inventor just needs more time and help to work out the details before he is ready to apply for a patent, but he is afraid that by asking people to help he will be giving his great idea away.

If two or more inventors claim to have independently created the same invention, then only the inventor who can prove that he invented it first is entitled to be granted a patent. The Patent Office calls the proven date the "date of conception."

To establish a date of conception, it has been a common practice for inventors to do something called the "postage stamp patent," or the "twenty-two-cent patent" (or whatever the price of a postage stamp may be at the time).

This is how you would do it. First, write a complete description of your invention, including sketches and details if necessary to show exactly how it works; then date and sign each sheet of paper. You should also get someone else as a witness to date and sign each sheet. Put all the papers in an envelope and *seal it tight*. Now address it to yourself and send it to yourself by registered mail. When you receive the envelope, *leave it sealed*. Both the postmark date on the envelope and the dated and signed papers inside should be ample proof of your date of conception.

Although a postage stamp patent may be enough to prove when your invention was conceived, the name is misleading because it gives you absolutely no patent protection. Only with a patent will you be given the exclusive right to make and sell your invention. However, if you discover someone else with your invention, or even if another inventor applies for a patent before you, you may still be able to be the one who gets the patent if you can prove that you had the earliest date of conception.

The U.S. Patent Office now offers inventors a Disclosure Document Program to take the place of the postage stamp patent (although many inventors still use the old method). The Disclosure Document affords no patent protection and is used only as evidence to prove the invention's date of conception. The difference is that the government, in addition to you, keeps a record of your disclosure.

To obtain a Disclosure Document form, write to the U.S. Patent Office (there is no charge for the form), or call your library to see if they can supply it. The form comes with instructions.

First you must clearly and completely describe your invention and explain how it is made and how it is used. Your description can include sketches, drawings, and photographs as long as they do not exceed a size of 8½ by 13 inches. You cannot send breadboards, models, or prototypes, but the information you supply should be complete enough so that someone else could make the invention without your help.

Next you must sign a form (two copies) stating that you are the inventor. You then send to the Patent Office your invention description (with any sketches, drawings, or photographs); the two signed forms stating you are the inventor; a self-addressed, stamped envelope; and a

The Story of the All American Soap Box Derby

1.

5.

4.

3.

The Soap Box Derby, founded in 1934 by newspaper photographer Myron Scott in Dayton, Ohio, was for many years the ultimate challenge for young inventors and tinkerers. Sponsored for a long time by Chevrolet, the Derby tested the resourcefulness of hundreds of competitors every year, requiring that all cars cost no more than $75 to build. Pictured here are: (1.) Bob Gravett, the first Soap Box Derby Champion; (2.) Jeff Iula, one of the winners in 1966; (3.) Founders (l. to r.) Jim Schlemmer, Myron Scott and B.E. "Shorty" Fulton; (4.) Guest participant Ronald Reagan from 1951, and (5.) A view from the finish line, taken in 1935.

2.

$10 check or money order for the filing fee. Be sure to keep photocopies of everything you send.

When the Patent Office receives your Disclosure Documents, they will stamp them with an identification number and a date of receipt. That is the date that will be your official date of conception for the invention submitted. The Patent Office will keep one copy of your signed statement and send the other back to you in the self-addressed, stamped envelope. That is your record that your Disclosure Documents are on file.

No one at the Patent Office actually looks at the documents you submit; they are just placed in a file under the identification number assigned, in case you should need to prove your date of conception. However, if you do not apply for a patent within two years, the Disclosure Documents for that invention will be destroyed. You can, of course, resubmit the documents, but you will also get a new date of conception based on the later application.

Even though you may send yourself a postage stamp patent or submit a Disclosure Document to the Patent Office, you should still keep a detailed inventor's notebook to show that you were "diligent" in completing the invention. Sometimes, when inventors with the same idea can't prove who actually had the earliest date of conception, the Patent Office will award the patent to the inventor who can prove that he was diligent and worked the hardest on it.

Do remember that regardless of what disclosure document you send to yourself or to the Patent Office, you have only one year from the date of *public* disclosure of an invention to apply for a patent. Disclosing your invention to yourself or the Patent Office is not considered a public disclosure.

Talking to a Patent Lawyer

If after considering the alternatives you are convinced that you should apply for a patent, discuss it with your parents. They might be able to help you arrange a meeting with a patent lawyer or a patent agent. Ask if there is a charge for a brief first consultation—often it is free. If you do arrange a meeting, take along your inventor's notebook, any other notes and sketches of the invention, plus your final breadboard, model, or prototype. Here are a few of the questions you should ask:

• Is the invention patentable? Only the Patent Office, after a thorough search, can grant or deny a patent, but a patent lawyer or agent will be able to tell you if parts or all of your invention are possibly unique and useful enough to be patented.

• Is the invention ready to patent? Many inventors file for a patent too soon, before they have considered all the ways the invention can be made and all the possibilities for improving it. A patent lawyer or agent may advise you to do more work on your invention to improve your chances of getting a patent that covers all variations of your idea. It has not been uncommon for an inventor to get a patent for an invention that is an improvement on someone else's patent.

• How much will a patent cost? Ask for a break-

Computer Control

Cover the computer terminal screen with a sheet of clear plastic food wrap. Using a crayon or watercolor felt marker pen, draw a game directly on the plastic wrap, then play by the rules given, within the capabilities of your computer.

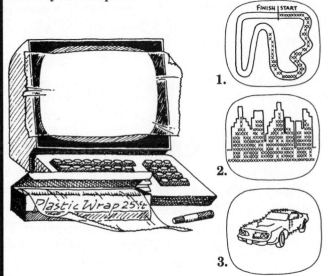

1.

2.

3.

1. Grand Prix. Draw a racetrack course with curves and straightaways about one inch wide. Using either the cursor only or a line of X's go once completely around the track from start to finish in the fastest time possible (without going off the track). **2. Skyline Art.** Draw a city skyline, then fill in the buildings by scrolling up lines of computer generated letters, numbers or symbols. **3. Picture Tracing.** Trace a magazine picture on the plastic food wrap, then put the wrap over the terminal screen. Redraw the picture using letters, numbers and symbols. Remove the plastic wrap to see the finished computer picture.

down of the Patent Office fees for filing plus the lawyer's or agent's fees for doing a search, preparing the application (including drawings), and any incidental fees that might be incurred during the patent process. Also ask when the fees must be paid. You might want to begin with only the search and then decide whether you should continue with the application.

It is important to remember that *you* are the inventor, and a patent lawyer or agent cannot necessarily judge how good or bad your invention is, or how salable it might be. One of the exciting things about inventing is that no one knows for sure if a product will be a commercial success until after it actually reaches the market.

Filing a Patent Application

Four things are required by the Patent Office when filing a patent application:

1. A clearly typed or handwritten document that fully describes the invention and states specifically which things about it you claim to be unique and useful.

2. A signed and officially witnessed oath that you are the original and first inventor.

3. Technical drawings (for most inventions) that show how the invention is made and how it works.

4. The appropriate filing fees (see page 67).

When all the filing materials are complete, they are sent (with the filing fees) to the Commissioner of Patents and Trademarks at the U.S. Patent Office. As soon as your application is received you will be issued an official patent serial number. In any correspondence with the Patent Office, always use the serial number so they can easily locate your file.

The first part of the patent application is the most important. Your invention will be judged by the Patent Office on the description you give and the claims you make for uniqueness. These claims must convince the Patent Office that your invention is truly new and different from other products. And you must also show that your claims do not conflict with claims made in existing patents. This is where the search information comes in handy. You can and should refer to existing patents of products similar to your invention to help support the fact that your idea is unique. An example of the claims that might be made for an adjustable bicycle kickstand appears on the facing page, along with other sample patent application papers and drawings.

Patent Drawings

For nearly every kind of invention, except formulas (like a recipe for a new soft drink) and processes (like a sequence of chemicals to dye cloth), the Patent Office requires that you submit explanatory drawings with your application. A simple invention may require only one drawing, but usually several drawings are needed to show different views and details so that every feature of the invention listed in the claims is clearly shown.

The Patent Office strictly requires that patent drawings be done in a particular way: it specifies the kind of paper, paper size and margins, ink, weight of lines, shading, and scale to be used. You can buy a book from the U.S. Government Printing Office that lists all the rules and specifications and shows you how to make patent drawings (see box, page 76). However, you should already be a pretty good draftsman before attempting to do your own patent drawings. If you are not, then there are draftsmen who specialize in patent drawings, and they usually work together with patent lawyers and patent agents. The Patent Office also has a staff of draftsmen who will do the patent drawings for you (for a fee of course), but they are usually very busy and you may have to wait several months for your drawings to be done.

At one time the Patent Office required inventors to send working models with their applications. That is no longer required except in rare circumstances. But the Patent Office now wants the description of your invention and drawings to be so complete and clear that anyone with the appropriate skills would be able to build it. No one at the Patent Office builds your invention and tests it, but they do have engineers and other technical people who should be able to figure out from the application whether and how the invention works.

After Your Patent Application Is Filed

When your patent application is received by the Commissioner of Patents and Trademarks, it will

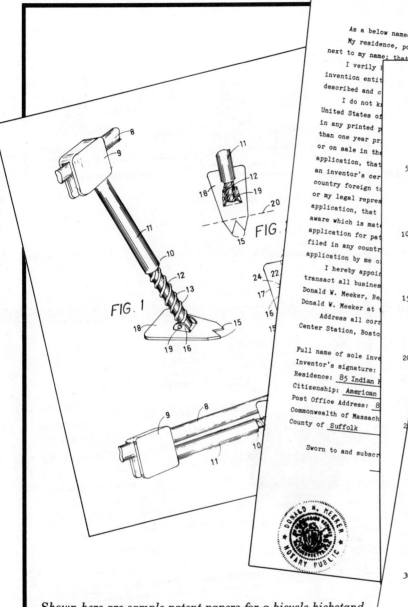

Oath

As a below named inventor, being duly sworn, I depose and say that;

My residence, post office address and citizenship
next to my name; that

I verily b
invention entit
described and c

I do not kr
United States of
in any printed p
than one year pri
or on sale in the
application, that
an inventor's cer
country foreign to
or my legal repres
application, that
aware which is mate
application for pat
filed in any countr
application by me o

I hereby appoi
transact all busines
Donald W. Meeker, Re
Donald W. Meeker at t

Address all cor
Center Station, Bosto

Full name of sole inve
Inventor's signature:
Residence: 85 Indian H
Citizenship: _American_
Post Office Address: 8
Commonwealth of Massach
County of _Suffolk_

Sworn to and subscr

Description

Adjustable Kickstand With Surface Adaptable Foot-Pad/Spike

Background of the Invention

Technical field

5   The   s props or steadying devices for two-
wheeled   for a two-wheeled
vehicl
be sta
spike

10   Back
in
whe
te
15   s
t

Claims

I claim:

1. An adaptable kickstand for supporting a two-wheeled vehicle on a
variety of different surfaces, wherein the kickstand comprises:
a rigid elongated support member rotatably secured at one end
to the two-wheeled vehicle by conventional means for pivoting the
kickstand between an elevated and a lowered position, which support
member is adjustable in length;
and pivotally secured to an opposite end of the support member
a combined foot pad and spike means for contacting the kickstand
with any of a variety of different surfaces upon which the kickstand
will rest.

2. The adaptable kickstand of claim 1 wherein the elongated support
member comprises a hollow tube rotatably secured to the vehicle,
which hollow tube is threaded interiorly along the length of the
tube and, threaded into the hollow tube, a rigid solid shaft threaded
exteriorly along the length of the shaft, which solid shaft fits
slidably within the hollow tube to adjust the length of the support
member by turning the shaft.

3. The invention of claim 2 wherein the threads of the tube and shaft
are matching fast threads for rapid adjustment.

4. The adaptable kickstand of claim 1 wherein the combined foot pad
and spike means comprises a substantially flat rigid plate with a
centrally positioned pivot means connecting the plate to the end of
the support member, and which plate is pointed at one end and broad
in width at an opposite end.

5. The invention of claim 4 wherein the pivot means comprises a hinge and
locking means to retain the plate in a stationary position with the
pointed end pivoted downwardly.

6. The invention of claim 5 wherein the hinge is formed by cutting two
opposing tabs in the center of the flat plate, bending the tabs to a
vertical position and drilling aligned holes through the two tabs to
receive a pin passed through a corresponding hole in the end of the
shaft.

Shown here are sample patent papers for a bicycle kickstand. The claims describe the novel features of the invention. The drawing shows the style to which all patent drawings must conform.

be thoroughly checked to be sure everything is complete and done by the rules. The Patent Office will overlook some irregularities that they can correct, but if there is a major defect with your application you will be notified by the Patent Office and will be given six months to correct the problem. When everything is considered complete, the Patent Office officially accepts the application by assigning a serial number to it, listing the acceptance date as the official filing date, and sending you a receipt giving you that information.

Next, your patent application file is assigned to a particular examiner who has expert knowledge in the field of your invention. The examiner reviews the patent documents and drawings and then begins a very thorough search of United States and foreign patents to determine if your invention is truly new. (If your invention is already patented in another country, you cannot receive a patent for it here.) Although the examiner will repeat much of the search work that was done to prepare the application, he will usually go much further, checking several related invention classifications.

The examiner is actually checking your patent claims against the claims already made in existing patents. Very often the examiner will accept some of the claims and disallow others. Sometimes the examiner will rewrite a claim so it is acceptable.

Only about two out of three patent applications are approved the first time they are examined. You may be asked to supply additional information or to correct a drawing before a decision is made. When the examination process is

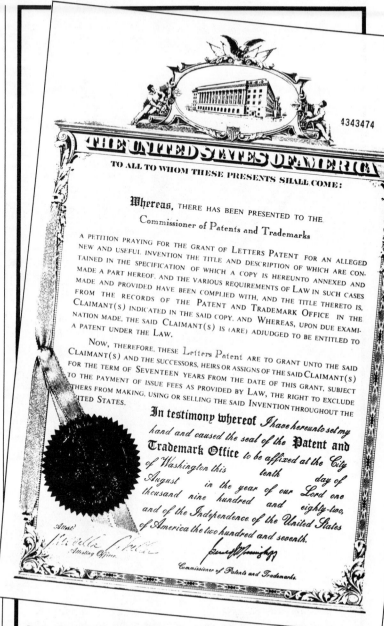

Some inventors frame their patents—others publish them. Shown here is inventor/author Steven Caney's patent for an electronic game.

finally complete, you will be notified by mail of the examiner's findings and decision.

If the examiner found your invention to be not new at all, and therefore not patentable, then probably all your claims will be refused or rejected. If the examiner does consider it new and unique, you will then be eligible for an invention patent for those claims accepted by the examiner. If you are notified that your patent application has been examined and rejected, there are several ways to appeal the decision and have your application reexamined. Unfortunately, it takes a lot of work and a lot of money to appeal for reexamination, and most inventors can't afford it unless they are being supported by a company interested in the invention.

Occasionally two or more people file patent applications claiming to have invented pretty much the same thing. Since a patent can be granted to only one of the applicants, the Patent Office determines which inventor first figured out the way to make it work (date of conception) and built a working breadboard, model, or prototype (reduction to practice).

Who gets the patent is not necessarily decided by who was first to file an application. In fact, an inventor can even file a patent application to challenge a patent that has already been issued (but only within the first year) by claiming that he thought of and built the invention earlier. The competing inventors must then present evidence and proof to determine who actually was the first inventor, and therefore who should be granted the patent.

The complete patent examination process, from first filing to final decision, can take as long as two or three years. It isn't that the process itself takes that long; the problem is the large backlog of applications at the Patent Office. Remember that your application must wait for an examiner who is a specialist in your type of invention. If there is some crucial reason why the patent process should be hurried, you can write your request to the Commissioner of Patents—but you'd better have a good reason. In the meantime, while you are waiting for a decision from the Patent Office, you could be planning what you are going to do with the invention.

If you are granted a patent, the Patent Office will send you an official document called "Letters of Patent." Your patent gives you protection only from copiers in the United States (it is also possible to apply for foreign patents). For the next seventeen years, you, the holder of the patent, control all rights to make, use, or sell the invention in America. A patent is considered to have value like any other piece of property, so you can sell your patent to anyone, license it, lease it, loan it, and even leave it to someone in your will. (Most first-time patent holders frame it!)

The same week that your patent is granted it will be published in the *Official Gazette*. But don't expect that to bring around any hot buyers. Potential manufacturers probably won't come knocking at your door. Only about one out of every hundred patents issued actually makes money for the inventor. It is even rarer that an inventor becomes a millionaire. Most inventors usually need to sell several inventions to earn a living and pay for their new experiments. And remember that no one is going to buy your invention unless you promote it.

Publications of the U.S. Patent and Trademark Office

The Patent Office offers several publications to help inventors determine the patentability of their inventions and to apply for a patent. You can also get copies of any patent granted.

Because the cost of these publications does change, you should first write and request the current price. You should also be able to find most of these publications in major city libraries.

The following publications are available from:

Superintendent of Documents
U.S. Government Printing Office
Washington, D.C. 20402

The Story of the United States Patent Office—A history of the Patent and Trademark Office and how the patent system works.

Patents and Inventions: An Information Aid for Inventors—A guide to help you decide if your invention is patentable, telling how to apply for a patent.

Patent News—The current laws that determine the operation of the Patent Office.

The Official Gazette of the United States Patent and Trademark Office—A weekly publication that lists the patents that have been granted that week, plus other information about patent suits, patents available for license or sale, and changes in patent rules. Available by yearly subscription or in single issues.

Index of Patents—An annual index to the *Official Gazette.*

Manual of Classification—Listings of all the classes and subclasses of inventions used by the Patent Office plus an explanation of the classification system.

Manual of Patent Examining Procedure—An explanation of the procedures used by the Patent Office for examining patent applications.

Guide for Patent Draftsmen—A detailed guide showing how to draft patent drawings.

Directory of Registered Patent Attorneys and Agents Arranged by States and Countries—A geographical listing of patent lawyers and patent agents.

You can get a copy of any patent issued as long as you know the patent number. Send your request with payment (currently one dollar for each copy) to:

Commissioner of Patents and Trademarks
Washington, D.C. 20231

Marketing Your Invention

The process of inventing does not end when you have completed a working model or prototype, or even after you have applied for a patent. Some of the hardest work may still be ahead. If you want to make money from your invention, you will need to get it to the people who will want to buy it—and that process is called *marketing*.

Many people confuse marketing with selling. Selling is actually only one part of marketing, which includes all the advance planning that is necessary before you are ready to sell the product. Marketing decisions concern the appearance of the product, its name, packaging, sales literature, and advertising. To successfully sell your invention, you need a marketing strategy that will catch people's interest.

When you plan to market your invention, you generally have two choices: Sell your invention to a manufacturer for either a one-time fee or a royalty, so that the manufacturer makes the product and sells it for whatever profit he can make; or, start your own business to produce and sell the invention to retail stores or directly to the customers who will be using it (see page 84).

Selling Your Invention to a Manufacturer

Most inventors try to sell their inventions to a manufacturer, who usually takes care of all the details of producing the product on a large scale

Disclosure Forms

Some inventors, especially those without patents, are afraid to show their inventions to manufacturers for fear that someone might steal or copy the idea. Although that can happen, it is very, very rare—most businessmen are honest. However, you can ask a manufacturer to sign a *disclosure form* before he sees your invention. A disclosure form states that you, the inventor, are asking the manufacturer to review your invention in confidence, and that the manufacturer promises not to reveal the nature of the invention to anyone else.

If you want a manufacturer to sign a disclosure form, send the form with a cover letter giving a brief but enticing description of the product you are offering for sale (don't discuss how it works), and request that the form be signed and returned to you so you can send the complete presentation. Some companies will gladly sign; others will not.

Some manufacturers may not be willing to consider your invention until you sign *their* disclosure form. It is not uncommon for a company to review an invention that is very similar to or even exactly the same as something they have already thought of. And so a manufacturer's disclosure form states that you cannot make any claims against them if they later produce and sell a product like your invention without paying you anything. That may sound risky, but the only way you can sell your invention is to show it!

and getting it into the marketplace. This allows the inventor to go back to work on other inventions. It may sound simple, but there is one big catch: it is not that easy to sell your invention to a manufacturer!

Each manufacturer knows the kind of customers he has and what they will and will not buy. You will have to find just the right manufacturer who knows how to market your invention, or you may have to change and modify your product to be more like those an interested manufacturer already sells. What is most important is that you find a manufacturer who is just as excited about your invention as you are.

Everyone who looks at your invention will have his own ideas of what it needs in order to sell well—including ideas about how to manufacture it, design the packaging, and ways to advertise and promote it. You don't have to agree with all the suggestions, but each time you discuss your invention with a manufacturer you will learn something new, and many of their ideas will contribute to the product's final success.

Listen especially to what they say *not* to do. Selecting a winning product is not a science, and no one knows for sure what combination of elements makes a smash hit. But most experienced sales and marketing people do know what customers will *not* buy. To successfully sell your invention to a manufacturer, you need a marketing plan that covers these three major steps:

1. Finding the most appropriate companies to approach;

2. Presenting your invention as effectively as possible; and

3. Negotiating a fair agreement.

Finding a Buyer

One way to find potential buyers is to go to a store that sells products of the same sort as your invention, or to the kind of store you think might best sell your product. Look for items that are similar to yours or that appeal to the type of customer you think would buy your invention. If your product will be made of wood, look at wood products; if your product is a board game, look at board games; if your product is a new type of table-napkin dispenser, look at products made by manufacturers of kitchen accessories, and so forth. You can copy the names and addresses of appropriate companies from the purchases. You might also look up your product category (toys, sporting goods, housewares) in the Yellow Pages in order to find local manufacturers. Or go to the library and look in the *Thomas Register* for a listing of all American manufacturers in that category, especially those located nearby.

Presenting Your Invention

Before you consider approaching out-of-town companies, try to make a personal presentation to a manufacturer in your neighborhood or town. This will give you some valuable marketing insights that you can then use in the presentation you mail to companies elsewhere. (A verbal presentation doesn't have to be as thorough as a written one, since you are right there to answer any questions.)

After speaking with one or more manufacturers, you will have an idea of what they like about the product and what they think should be

Inventor Beware

Sometimes you will see advertisements in newspapers and magazines with headlines meant to catch an inventor's attention: "Do you want to sell your invention?" "Buyers looking for new inventions," or "Inventions wanted." There are several companies that claim to offer marketing services to inventors, but very few inventors have actually sold their inventions through these services.

Invention-marketing companies often claim they will review your invention, prepare copy and presentation drawings or photographs, and then send the presentation to a list of manufacturers that they think are potential buyers. Some of these companies publish a newsletter with descriptions of new products, which they mail to manufacturers. Invention-marketing companies usually make no evaluation of your product nor can they determine how successful it may or may not be. If someone should be interested, all negotiations for sale are strictly between you (the inventor) and the manufacturer.

Getting that type of exposure for your product may seem quite appealing, but unfortunately it rarely works. These companies almost never deliver the kind of attention and effort needed to get your product sold. They will often entice you with increasingly ambitious sounding plans and services, for which they charge you additional fees, but the results are usually the same. You will do much better if you contact manufacturers and make the presentation yourself, and learn from the experience.

The Story of the Computer

T he computer is a sophisticated invention that reaches new heights every year. The personal computer revolution began in the late 1970s and 1980s, but computing machines have been in development for centuries. This essay shows a sampling of machines and inventors, past and present.

2. Joseph-Marie Jacquard invented this Jacquard loom in 1801. The loom produced intricate woven patterns based on a long series of punched cards (see center, top), the forerunners of computer punch cards.

1. The abacus, an ancient Chinese calculating device, is considered by many to be the first "computer."

4. Lady Augusta Ada Lovelace, a friend and collaborator of Babbage's, is known as the first programmer.

3. This is one portion of Charle Babbage's Difference Engine, the first true calculating machine, and precursor of the adding machine, developed by Babbage in the 1820s and 30s.

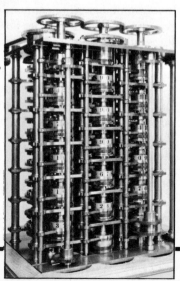

5. Dr. Herman Hollerith completed his Hollerith tabulator in 1890, the first electromechanical counting machine, which used punched cards to process data. His machines were used to calculate the US census (depicted here) and his company went on to become the computer giant IBM.

6. ENIAC, the first programmable electronic computer, was built by electrical engineer J. Presper Eckert and physicist John Mauchly during World War II at the University of Pennsylvania's Moore School of Electrical Engineering.

7. John Bardeen, Walter H. Brattain and William Shockley received the Nobel Prize in 1956 for their invention of the transistor. This technological breakthrough led to the development of the tiny microchips that power today's computers.

8. No one can predict where development of the computer will lead, the possibilities are so great. This photo shows a part of the dashboard from a Lincoln Continental 100 concept car, with a display that produces maps and directions for any area of the country.

OPERATION
FEATURES & USES
MARKETING
VIEWS

SPECS

A well-organized presentation is essential when trying to get a manufacturer to buy your invention, or when trying to get investors to help you start your own company.

changed. The chances are that other manufacturers will have some of those same concerns. If there has been a consistent objection or problem, you might have to change or correct the product before you prepare a written presentation.

A typical written presentation, which you will send to manufacturers you cannot visit in person, should include a page of information that describes what the invention does, how it works, what its features are, and how it benefits the user. If you have a good-looking model of the product, send a photograph of it (do *not* send the model). If you have a patent, include a copy of the patent abstract as it appeared in the *Official Gazette.*

To complete the presentation, write a cover letter to go with the other materials. A neatly handwritten business letter is fine, but a type-written one is better. Simply state that you are submitting your invention for their review and

consideration, and that if interested they should contact you to discuss it further. Be sure to give your mailing address, and your phone number and calling times if you want to be contacted by telephone. Address the letter and the envelope to the manufacturer, "Attention: Director of New Products" (unless you already know the name of the person you are sending it to). Be sure to keep a photocopy of everything you send for your files.

Because you are sending the presentation unsolicited (the manufacturer did not request it), it may be a few weeks, a month, or even longer, before you get a reply. You should not expect the presentation materials to be returned, so do not mail anything valuable or anything you cannot do without, and keep extra copies of all your materials. Don't be upset if most responses say something like this: "Thank you for sending us your invention. Unfortunately we cannot consider it at this time. We encourage you to continue inventing and wish you great success." Rejections are a part of inventing, and experienced inventors are not discouraged by them. Remember, you are trying to find just the right manufacturer, who will be as enthusiastic and optimistic about your invention as you are. Keep sending out presentations until you find him.

If you do get a positive response, the potential buyer will probably want to see a working model and to know all the details of the invention. Send whatever has been requested—by registered mail or express mail, so you will have proof that it was delivered and received. Enclose a letter asking that everything you are sending be returned at your request when they have finished reviewing it. Again, make a photocopy for your files.

Once a manufacturer says he is interested in buying your invention and wants to talk about a contract or agreement, you should get the help of a lawyer. This is not because there is any reason to distrust the manufacturer or imagine that he might cheat you. Most established businessmen are honest and will make a fair offer, but the terms of any legal agreement can get complicated. A lawyer will also advise you about what is fair and will help you to negotiate with the manufacturer. If the manufacturer says that he wants to negotiate with you (or your family) alone, without a lawyer, watch out! Anyone running an honest business and wanting to make a fair deal will welcome your lawyer's participation.

Negotiating an Agreement

The two most common ways to be paid for your invention are a *flat fee* and a *royalty*. In an outright flat-fee sale you receive a one-time payment for giving the manufacturer the right to produce and sell your invention. If your invention is patented, you are literally selling the ownership of your patent to the manufacturer. You will receive no additional money from the company regardless of how successful the product might become, but you also won't have to give any of the money back if it is a flop.

Because a manufacturer can only guess at how well your product might sell, flat-fee offers are usually low and based on pessimistic sales projections. That protects both of you if it doesn't sell well: the company loses just the fee, and you still get to keep the money. But what if the invention is a success? Many an inventor has cringed when a product he sold outright—for what seemed to be a reasonable fee—went on to become a big seller. If the inventor had negotiated a royalty agreement instead of a flat fee, he would have shared in the success of the product and probably would have made a lot more money.

In a typical royalty agreement, both the inventor and the manufacturer take some risk, and usually they win or lose together. For every one of your products sold, you will receive a percentage of the price the customer pays. So, the more successful the product, the more money you and the manufacturer will make. But if the product does not sell well, the manufacturer may not collect enough money to pay for his production and marketing expenses and you will probably not receive enough money to pay for the time you spent inventing it.

The royalty percentage is based on many factors agreed upon between you and the manufacturer. In general, the lower the market price of the product, the smaller the percentage, and likewise the higher the price, the higher the royalty. For items with a retail price of less than $1, the royalty might be only 1 to 2 percent. For items selling from $1 to $10, you might get a 3 or 4 percent royalty. For more expensive items, the royalty might be 5 percent or even higher. Each industry has a royalty schedule that is typical for the products they produce. After speaking with a few manufacturers, you will have a good idea of the royalties you can expect.

Because there is usually a gap of one to two years between signing an agreement and the time the product goes on the market, royalty agreements almost always include a cash advance ("up-front money") to seal the bargain and reward the inventor for his work until he begins to receive royalty payments. This payment is usually an advance against royalties, which your invention must "earn out" before you receive any more royalties. In other words, if you receive an advance of $500, you will not receive any more money until sales of your product have generated over $500 in royalties. But no matter how poorly the product sells, or even if the manufacturer never produces it (which does happen sometimes), the cash advance is yours to keep. There is no set formula for calculating advances, but an average would be about one-quarter to one-half of the anticipated first-year royalties. Usually, the advance is lower than what you could expect to be offered as a flat fee.

Some royalty agreements also contain a "minimum performance guarantee," which promises that the inventor will receive a certain minimum royalty payment each year, regardless

Starting Your Own Business

Going into business to manufacture and sell your invention is a major undertaking that involves more time, money, and energy than most people imagine. It is also very risky. Every new enterprise begins with optimism and enthusiasm, but fewer than 25 percent survive the first year, and many others go out of business soon after that. And yet, the few that do succeed and grow become an inspiration to future entrepreneurs. With dedication and diligence, it can work!

If your invention is simple and inexpensive enough for you to manufacture in some quantity, you might decide to *test-market* the product. To do this, you manufacture and package a limited amount of the product, and then on your own, or with some help, try to sell it to friends and neighbors or to a certain group of people you think would want it (such as selling the adjustable bicycle kickstand mentioned earlier at a local bike race). Perhaps a neighborhood store will agree to sell your invention for you.

Test-marketing can provide important information for you, which can help when you go into business full-scale, or which could also persuade a manufacturer to take another look at your invention. Listen carefully to the reactions of the people you try to sell it to—you want to know why they like it and, even more, why they don't. Try to make changes that take these reactions into account, and then go out and sell some of the improved version to see if people are more enthusiastic. If you have found a store owner who will help, he or she may be able to make some useful suggestions about packaging and displaying your product.

If your test-marketing still hasn't convinced a

manufacturer to buy your invention, or if you've decided you prefer to expand the business on your own, here are a few of the basics you will have to consider. Your public library is a good source for books on starting up a business. Try to do as much research as you can before you plunge in.

MARKET RESEARCH—Determine why customers would buy the product, the product style they like best, and how much they are willing to pay. Also look at the features and benefits of products you might be competing with.

PRODUCT ENGINEERING AND DESIGN—Figure out what the product will look like (based on your market research) and how to manufacture it at the lowest possible cost.

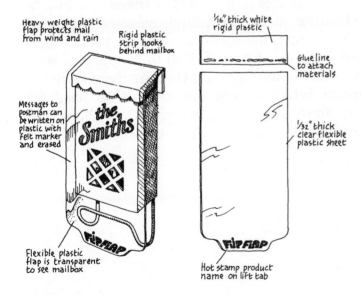

Heavy weight plastic flap protects mail from wind and rain

Rigid plastic strip hooks behind mailbox

Messages to postman can be written on plastic with felt marker and erased

the Smiths

Flexible plastic flap is transparent to see mailbox

FLIP FLAP

1/16" thick white rigid plastic

Glue line to attach materials

1/32" thick clear flexible plastic sheet

Hot stamp product name on lift tab

FLIP FLAP

MANUFACTURING—Work out a way to mass-produce the product from components you make or buy from vendors, or arrange with a manufacturer to produce the complete product for you.

SALES—Develop a plan to locate potential customers, show them the product, convince them to buy it, and take orders.

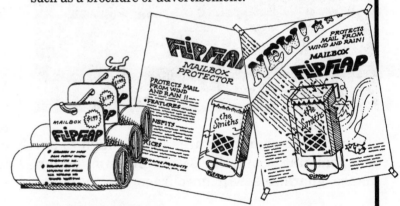

ADVERTISING AND PROMOTION—Based on your products features and benefits, and your market research, design and write copy for the package, instruction sheet (if required), and any promotional materials necessary to sell the product, such as a brochure or advertisement.

DISTRIBUTION—Determine where you will store the inventory and how you will deliver or ship it to your customers.

FINANCE AND ACCOUNTING—Do a cost projection of all anticipated expenses and sales income, and the sales it will take to make a profit. Also, keep accurate and thorough records of all money spent and received.

MANAGEMENT—Write a detailed marketing plan based on the above information, with a time schedule for getting everything done. Then take charge and see that everything does get done.

turer to get the product to market more quickly, or to promote it more effectively.

Part of the fun of being an inventor is the gamble and the excitement of waiting to see if your invention will become a big success. Most inventors are optimistic about their products and so they prefer to take a chance with a royalty agreement.

Once you have a signed contract, you can begin to dream about your product taking the market by storm and bringing you royalties for years to come. Sometimes that does happen. But selling your invention should also be an incentive for you to get right back to inventing something else. Most inventors find happiness and success not just in creating a single invention but in continuing to create unique solutions to problems. In time, nearly all inventions become outmoded and obsolete and need to be replaced with newer and better products that are more suited to current interests and life-styles. The need for inventions will always be great, so there will always be a need for creative inventors.

of whether the manufacturer sells enough to pay that amount. Sometimes a minimum performance guarantee will encourage the manufac-

Great Invention Stories

The Invention of
Earmuffs

A well-defined need often dictates the solution.

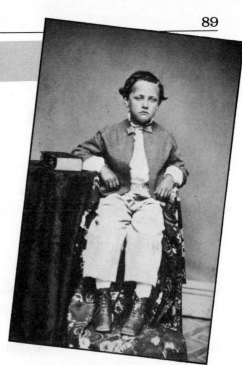

Inventor-to-be Chester Greenwood, pictured here at age seven.

Chester Greenwood suffered more than most from the problem of cold ears. He grew up in Farmington, Maine, where the winters are long and severe. Everyone's ears were cold there, but Chester's ears, which would turn from vivid red to purple to deathly white to an alarming deep blue, were the talk of the town.

In the winter of 1873, Chester Greenwood got a pair of ice skates for his fifteenth birthday. Eager to try them out, he raced down to the pond and onto the ice, but within minutes a harsh wind sent him running back home with his ears already white and red and ready to turn blue.

People wore socks, boots, gloves, hats, and all kinds of insulated clothing to keep all the parts of the body warm, but the ears, stuck there on the side of the head and exposed to the elements, were a special problem. So on the next day, Chester came up with an idea: he tied a heavy wool scarf around his head, hoping it would keep his ears warm, so he could try skating again. On his way to the pond, his ears were quite snug and warm, but the wool scarf was so itchy that again he had to turn back.

On the third day, Chester tried something different. He made oval loops out of baling wire and asked his grandmother, who lived with the

Chester Greenwood, teenaged inventor, pictured here at age 17 modeling his innovative creation—earmuffs.

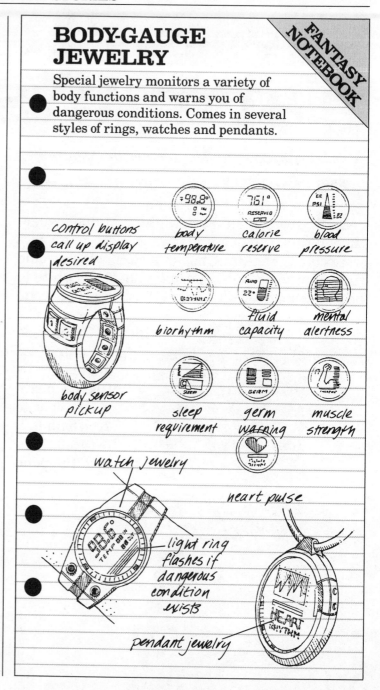

BODY-GAUGE JEWELRY

FANTASY NOTEBOOK

Special jewelry monitors a variety of body functions and warns you of dangerous conditions. Comes in several styles of rings, watches and pendants.

control buttons call up display desired

body sensor pickup

body temperature · calorie reserve · blood pressure

biorhythm · fluid capacity · mental alertness

sleep requirement · germ warning · muscle strength

heart pulse

watch jewelry

light ring flashes if dangerous condition exists

pendant jewelry

family, to sew pieces of beaver fur on one side of the loops and black velvet on the side that would fit against his ear. She then sewed a wire connecting the loops to Chester's cap.

Chester Greenwood tested his fur-covered ear flaps in the outdoor winter cold, and they worked! His ears remained a healthy shade of pink, and for the rest of the winter Chester skated in comfort. The Farmington neighbors, who had always been interested in his colorful ears, were now more interested in his new-fashioned ear flaps. They too wanted a pair of warm ear flaps, so Greenwood's mother and grandmother were soon spending all their spare time cutting, sewing, and bending wire to fill orders.

By the time Chester Greenwood was nineteen, he had improved his design with a flat steel spring to fit over the head and keep the flaps in place, and Greenwood's Ear Protectors were selling throughout New England with people commonly referring to them as "earmuffs." Although two patents had previously been issued—one to William P. Ware in 1858 for an "ear, cheek and chin muff," and one to C. Sedgewick in 1872 for another ear-protecting device—apparently neither invention caught on. Greenwood's earmuffs were much more successful, and he patented his design in 1877. Chester Greenwood is remembered to have said, "I believe perfection has been reached."

The earmuff business prospered, and Greenwood next devised a machine to manufacture his ear protectors, and he opened a factory in town. Farmington soon became the earmuff capital of the world, home of "Greenwood champion ear protectors for use in cold weather." Chester Greenwood went on to become the town's leading citizen.

As the years passed, Greenwood expanded his interests. He established a bicycle business

Fantasy Inventions

Protection from the elements was the inspiration for young Chester Greenwood, and these ideas try to accomplish that same objective.

ANTI-TICKLE BELT. Renders the wearer completely tickle-proof.

MOSQUITO-REPELLING HAT. Fabric of hat contains harmless mosquito-repelling substance that protects the entire body from bites.

ONION-CUTTING GOGGLES. Protect eyes from burning and tearing while cutting onions or hot peppers.

MOUTH MUFF. Keeps out harmful airborne particles, harmful chemicals and foods, or anything not fit for consumption. The muff will open only to allow ingestion of healthful foods and nonharmful objects.

Chester Greenwood, now a successful inventor and businessman, still sporting those distinctive ears, and the Greenwood house in Farmington, Maine.

and founded the first telephone company in Franklin County, Maine. He became a specialist in plumbing and steam and hot water heating, and manufactured the Greenwood Steam Heater and the Greenwood Pipe Vise. He is also credited with more than a hundred other inventions, some of which led to the development of modern-day airplane shock absorbers, improvements in automobile spark plugs, a new type of mechanical mousetrap, steel bows for archery, and the spring-tooth rake.

When Chester Greenwood died in 1937 at the age of seventy-nine, his earmuff factory was operating twenty-four hours a day. The Maine State Legislature eventually honored the inventor of earmuffs by officially declaring December 21 (the first day of winter) "Chester Greenwood Day." The event is celebrated in Farmington with events that include a parade and, of course, a coldest-ears contest.

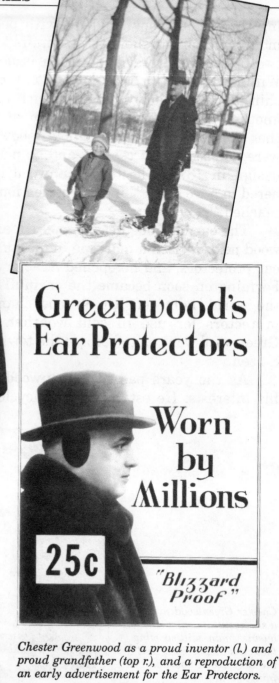

Greenwood's Ear Protectors

Worn by Millions

25c

"Blizzard Proof"

Chester Greenwood as a proud inventor (l.) and proud grandfather (top r.), and a reproduction of an early advertisement for the Ear Protectors.

The Invention of
Drive-in Movies

Create an invention that meets your own needs and others with the same needs will want it.

Maybe it was an especially hot night, or perhaps his wife couldn't stand the smell of his cigar. We really don't know why, but on an evening in the late 1920s Richard M. Hollingshead, Jr., of Camden, New Jersey, got the idea of taking his film projector outside and watching his home movies there. He placed a small screen in his driveway in front of his car, mounted the projector on the car roof, and then climbed into the front seat to watch what was, in fact, the first drive-in movie. At first Hollingshead only thought it was great fun, but soon he began to realize the commercial possibilities of an outdoor movie theater where the entire audience sat in the privacy and comfort of their own cars. He turned a lawn sprinkler on his car to see if the film could be seen through a windshield wet with rain. And he even thought about bringing food into the car to snack on while enjoying the movie.

Richard Hollingshead spent several years developing his idea and plans for an outdoor drive-in movie theater, and on May 6, 1933, he was issued a patent. For the next three weeks, a horde of architects, carpenters, and construction men worked full time to build what Hollingshead called the "Automobile Movie Theatre," located on Crescent Boulevard in Camden.

The Automobile Theatre was as big as a football field, with seven rows of inclined grades and room for 400 cars. The patented design featured a 5 percent grade from the back to the front of each row, permitting the patrons to have an uninterrupted

Opening night, June 6, 1933, at the world's first drive-in theater in Camden, New Jersey (below), and a variation of the drive-in that provided each car with its own screen, in Urbana, Missouri (r.).

view of the 30-by-40-foot screen from any spot in the parking area. Guardrails at the front of the inclined rows were low enough for the cars' bumpers to clear, but high enough to serve as a block for the tires, so cars would not fall off the front of the ramp. Each row was 50 feet deep, leaving more than 30 feet of space between the rows for cars to come and go without disturbing others watching the film.

The theater opened just a few weeks after the patent had been issued, during the height of the Great Depression. Movies were very popular at the time because they were a diversion to help people forget their problems. Camden moviegoers especially liked the idea of Hollingshead's Automobile Theatre because a carful of people could get an evening's entertainment at a cost of only $1 per car or 25¢ a person. On opening night, over 600 people came to watch a film called *Wife Beware*. After the first week, Hollingshead provided a food and drink concession so people could watch films, be outdoors, and eat at the same time—just as he had envisioned originally.

At first the sound came from individual speakers placed in the ground. Cars were supposed to park over the speakers so the sound would come up through the floorboards. It didn't work very well. What *did* work was something called controlled directional sound, a technological breakthrough introduced by the RCA company at about the same time Hollingshead re-

SATELLITE SUN SERVICE

Satellites reflect sunlight to darkened areas of Earth—just call the satellite subscription service to order. An energy-efficient light source that can also provide warmth and alter the weather.

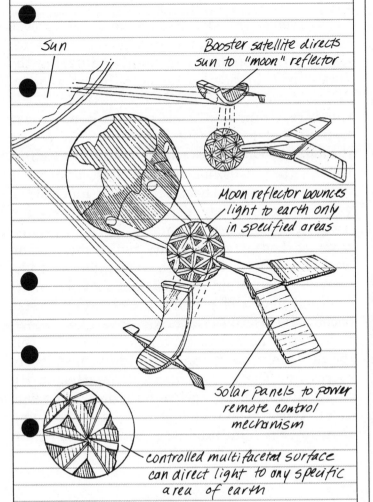

Sun

Booster satellite directs sun to "moon" reflector

Moon reflector bounces light to earth only in specified areas

Solar panels to power remote control mechanism

controlled multifaceted surface can direct light to any specific area of earth

ceived his patent. The sound came from very large speakers placed alongside the movie screen. Everyone from the first row to the last could hear the sound of the movie at the same volume, but so, too, could everyone outside the theater in the surrounding neighborhood. Eventually an individual speaker for each car was developed that could be hung inside the window.

Drive-in movies turned the ordinary car into a private theater box. Smokers, who had rarely enjoyed indoor movies because of the strictly enforced smoking prohibition, could smoke in their cars without offending or endangering others. People could talk and have their refreshments without disturbing those who preferred silence. Young children, who at the time were not welcome in movie theaters at night, could go to the drive-in in their pajamas with their parents, saving the cost of a baby-sitter, and people did not

Showing the versatility of a drive-in theatre, Mr. and Mrs. George Pannenter flew in to catch the opening of the Drive-In (Fly-In) Theatre in East Dennis, Massachusetts, on July 16, 1949.

Fantasy Inventions

The drive in movie was a clever combination of a favorite form of entertainment, the movies, and an unusual place where people spend a lot of their time—the car. Use these ideas to help you think of similar innovations for other existing forms of entertainment.

VIDEO GAME THEATERS. Each person in the audience has a game joystick to control his "player" on the screen. Audience members play video games against each other.

DIAL-A-YAWN. Check the directory and call up the bedtime story you want to hear over the phone.

READING ENVIRONMENT MOOD EFFECTS. Recorded mood sound effects complement the mood of the book being read. The reader can select mood sound themes of love and romance, mystery and adventure, humor, tragedy, intrigue.

DRIVING MOVIES. Movies and other entertainment shows are projected on the car windshield from inside the car. Special angle of projection allows all passengers to view screen except the driver, who maintains a clear view of the road. Works well in both daylight and darkness.

PUBLIC SURVEY TWO-WAY TELEVISION. Yes and No buttons on the television allow viewers to voice their approval or disapproval of the show or commercial being aired.

DRIVE-IN ESTABLISHMENTS. Drive-in or drive-through services and product sales catering to the person who doesn't want to leave the car. Drive-in psychiatrist; rock concert; college; art gallery; copy service; post office; pharmacy; museum; grocery; travel information.

have to get dressed up. Old people and the handicapped were comfortable, too. They were assured of a seat without having to stand in line and did not have to move once they arrived. And obviously there was no parking problem. Hollingshead's idea was an enormous success. By the 1950s, drive-in movies had become an American way of life, with more than 5,000 outdoor locations from coast to coast.

Clever as the idea was, it eventually proved unable to compete with a new phenomenon. With the growing popularity of television during the 1960s, drive-in movie attendance began to dwindle, and so did the number of drive-in movie theaters. Improved features such as in-car heaters and better sound systems that played through the car's radio couldn't stop the decline. During the 1970s, shopping centers and malls became popular and began to take up much of the valuable land used by drive-ins. Today there are fewer than 1,000 drive-in movies in America, and many of these do double duty as flea markets on weekends. The drive-in movie theater, an ingenious and entertaining idea that met the interests and habits of people in a certain era, has become the victim of a newer invention, television, better suited to contemporary needs. But the drive-in concept continues to be enormously successful. The simple idea that started in Richard Hollingshead's driveway soon led the way to all types of automobile drive-ins, including restaurants, laundries, banks, and even churches.

The Invention of
The Frisbee

Look at local fads and amusements for new novelty product ideas.

Sometimes an invention already exists and just needs to be discovered. There is no telling how long ago the first "flying disk" was thrown, but it was probably soon after the invention of the wheel. However, the history of the Frisbee flying saucer toy disk shows how an enthusiastic and motivated marketing man turned a local college fad into a full-fledged international sport played by millions of people.

The Frisbee story began over one hundred years ago in Bridgeport, Connecticut, where William Russell Frisbie owned and operated the Frisbie Pie Company. While his sister did the baking, William Frisbie was the "outside man," traveling the daily routes between local shops to sell his pies. Although the pies came in different flavors, one thing was common to all: the unique Frisbie pie tin, a 10-inch-wide round tin with a raised edge, wide brim, six small holes in the bottom, and the words "Frisbie's Pies" stamped across the bottom.

Shortly after 1900, William Frisbie's son, Joseph P. Frisbie, took over the family business and expanded the salesmen's routes to include several other cities—including nearby New Haven, the home of Yale University. Frisbie's pies were popular at Yale and yielded a rather large

Miss Nora Frisbie, President of the Frisbie-Frisbee Family of America, compares a Master Frisbee with the original Frisbie, held by Stancil Johnson, author of Frisbee.

number of empty pie tins. At some unrecorded moment, someone discovered that with a firm flick of the wrist, the empty tin would glide through the air in a fascinating semi-floating motion.

In a short time, a simple game of pie-tin catch became a campus fad. However, all was not perfectly safe. The metal tins were a bit heavy and could be dangerous if someone were hit. So it became the custom at Yale to yell "Frisbie!" when letting loose with the throw.

Frisbie's delivery-truck driver became aware that many pie tins were not being returned to the company, and instead were being kept for play. But rather than demand that they be returned, the route driver spread the word to other cus-

tomers that Frisbie's pie tins could be made to fly, and he would gladly demonstrate the technique.

That is the Yale version of the Frisbee story and probably the most accurate, but there is also a slightly different Harvard version. Harvard students in Cambridge, Massachusetts, were also great fans of Frisbie's products and they have insisted that it was Frisbie's round tins used to package sugar cookies—not pies—that made the best flying disks.

Whatever the origin, the pie-tin game was not recognized as a manufacturable and marketable product until the late 1940s, when plastics were just emerging as a cheap, moldable mate-

A selection of early Wham-O Frisbees, including the pro size Mystery-Y (far right), the original Mystery-Y (second from right), the pluto platter (second from left) and a rare Speedy (far left).

rial. In 1948, when Walter Frederick Morrison returned from World War II, he found America buzzing with fascination, curiosity, and rumors about UFOs, Martians, and anything that smacked of outer space. Alleged observers' sketches and bogus photographs of alien spacecraft usually showed saucer-shaped devices with a flight pattern similar to the flight of the pie and cookie tins he had thrown as a youngster. Morrison got the idea of capitalizing on people's curiosity by making a flying saucer toy.

After experimenting with various materials and disk shapes, Morrison finally began the production of his plastic flying saucer toy. He did not set up his own factory, but rather contracted with a Southern California plastics company to make the disks for him. The finished product was shaped much like today's Frisbee, and it flew very well. But there was one problem: the plastic used for production became brittle in all but very warm weather and had a tendency to break into hundreds of pieces upon impact with anything hard. To satisfy complaining customers, Morrison agreed to replace any broken disk with a new one if the owner returned every single piece!

Meanwhile, Morrison went back to the drawing board and came up with a new version, this one made from a softer and more durable plastic. The marriage of product and material was perfect: the plastic was sufficiently lightweight, durable, and flexible to withstand impact, and strong enough to hold its shape. It was also very cheap to produce. Fred Morrison contracted with the plastic molder to manufacture his new version of the flying disk, and then he rented a booth at Southern California's Pomona County Fair,

Frisbee inventor Fred Morrison gives a few friendly pointers.

where he introduced a clever scheme to sell his product—"the invisible wire pitch."

With a friend as assistant, Morrison would pretend to string an invisible wire over the heads of the onlooking crowd, drawing attention to himself by walking through the mass of people yelling, "Make way for the wire!" Morrison then would instruct the crowd to observe how the

flying disk would sail
across the invisible wire.
The onlookers would in-
variably gasp with amaze-
ment as the spinning disk
appeared to float away from
Morrison's hand across the wire
to his assistant's hand. The eager buyers were
then told that the disk was free but the "wire"
cost 1¢ a foot and came in minimum 100-foot
lengths. Morrison sold a lot of flying disks.

Fred Morrison continued to perfect the flight
characteristics of his product by altering
its shape and weight distribution. The
popularity of UFOs continued to influence his design, and the 1951 version sported
a center hump to mimic a spaceship's cabin,
complete with portholes around the perimeter.
An inscription molded into the underside of the
disk instructed the owner to "play catch, invent
games, fly-flip away." Morrison named his improved disk the "Pluto Platter" and sold it anywhere he could draw a crowd—at the beach, on
crowded city streets, and outside high schools.

In 1955, while Fred Morrison was hawking
his Pluto Platter, two other Southern Califor-
nians who had just completed college were starting a new toy manufacturing company. Richard
Knerr and A. K. "Spud" Melin were partners in
the Wham-O toy company, producers of sling-
shots. While looking for new products to beef up
their line, they noticed that Morrison's disks
were being flung up and down the beaches of
Southern California. They tracked Morrison
down to a Los Angeles street corner where he was
aggressively giving his sales pitch. Melin and
Knerr could sense the enthusiasm of the crowd
and could "smell" the signs of a potential fad.
Morrison was invited back to the Wham-O factory to discuss a marketing deal for worldwide
manufacturing and sales rights, and in January
1957 Wham-O began producing and selling its
version of the Pluto Platter.

Although Melin and Knerr were wildly optimistic, sales of the flying disk were sluggish.
Fortunately for their business, they had just introduced another new product—the Hula Hoop.

For six months the Hula Hoop sold faster than any toy in history, and the Wham-O company enjoyed great success. But the Pluto Platter was not forgotten.

On a sales trip to the East Coast, Richard Knerr heard several Harvard students tell of the long-standing undergraduate fad that involved flinging pie tins in a game of catch. Everyone on campus called the game "Frisbie-ing." With the instincts of a good marketing man, Knerr decided to drop "Pluto Platter" and use the name that had already been established. Interestingly, at the time Knerr had no idea of the historical origin of the Frisbie name, and he spelled it

Clark Edwards shows off one of the many tricks performed by experienced Frisbee players.

Fantasy Inventions

There's more you can do with a flying disk than just throw it back and forth, from different sorts of games all the way to super-sized disks for more serious uses.

FORK AND SPOON FLIPPERS. A dinner table game using ordinary table forks and spoons. Each player tries to flip and catch a fork or spoon by pounding on the end of the spoon bowl or fork prongs to make them flip. Points are awarded based on the complexity and style of the flip.

MOTORIZED FRISBEE. A self-propelled, radio-controlled, flying disk.

FRISBEE BACKBOARD. For solo play, toss the flying disk at the backboard and it will bounce back to you.

PIZZA PAN PONG. Players using pizza pan paddles must keep round dough balls bouncing in the air, without allowing them to go flat.

FRISBEE TRANSPORT VEHICLE. Large cargo-carrying Frisbee transport vehicles. Flying disks are launched from Frisbee ports by powerful tossing machines.

ALL-MEDIUM SCREW TRANSPORTER. Vehicle in the shape of a large boring screw that can work its way through any medium including earth, water, rock, sand, surface structures, and foliage.

Frisbee—which is the trademarked spelling used today.

The Hula Hoop craze died as quickly as it had started, and Wham-O focused its energy on making the Frisbee its next big success. Sales did improve, but it was not until the 1960s that Frisbees really began to soar. This was partly the result of the efforts of the vice president and

FANTASY NOTEBOOK

FREESTANDING SPINNING UMBRELLA

A heavy-duty umbrella that deflects rain away from you and has a base for stability.

"folds for storage" as an ordinary compact umbrella

opens like a regular umbrella

tilt adjust for driving rain

handle telescopes to become free-standing

pumping causes umbrella top to spin and deflect rain

gripper leg tips won't slip on any surface

steady tripod base folds into handle

A selection of the various flying disks that have been patterned after the original Frisbee.

general manager of Wham-O, Ed Headrick, who decided to promote Frisbee not as a toy but as a sport. Headrick tinkered with the Morrison design and produced a longer, more stable flight pattern by introducing thin raised edges called "flight rings." In 1964 Wham-O produced the first Frisbee Professional Model and sponsored Frisbee tournaments through another of Headrick's creations—the International Frisbee Association. The idea of turning an idle game into a full-fledged sport worked, and Wham-O was selling Frisbees by the millions.

Today the Frisbee is no longer just a fad, but a popular toy and sport played almost everywhere. Various manufacturers have devised flying disks that glow in the dark, battery-operated, blinking-light disks, specially designed disks for stunt acrobatics, cloth pocketable disks, and foam disks that can be used indoors. The Frisbee is here to stay.

The Invention of

The Band-Aid

Most inventions are inspired by a personal need.

In the early 1900s, the newly married Mrs. Earl Dickson was a fairly inexperienced cook, and she often cut or burned herself in the kitchen. Earl Dickson worked for the Johnson & Johnson Company, which at the time made most of the surgical tape in America. Dickson was getting so much practice bandaging his wife's hands with gauze pads and tape that he was becoming an expert. He realized that if he could prepare bandages that his wife could apply herself, he wouldn't have to worry that she might cut herself when no one was around to help. So Dickson began experimenting. He reasoned that if the gauze pad and tape were combined, his wife would be able to put the bandage on with one hand. So he took a strip of Johnson & Johnson surgical tape and laid it out on a table, sticky side up. Next he took a strip of gauze, folded it into a pad, and put it in the middle of the tape. But there was a problem. Preparing the bandage in advance meant that the adhesive tape had to be unrolled, exposing the sticky surface, which would dry up if it was left out too long. Dickson tried different kinds of cloth to cover the sticky tape, hoping to find one that wasn't too hard to remove when the bandage was needed. Crinoline, a fabric similar to satin, did the job very well. The next time the accident-prone Mrs. Dickson cut herself, she simply peeled off the crinoline and bandaged her cut with her clever husband's invention.

RING BAND
WOUND PROTECTOR

FANTASY NOTEBOOK

A one-size-fits-all bandage that stays in place without adhesives. Comes pre-medicated, with a place to add your own medication.

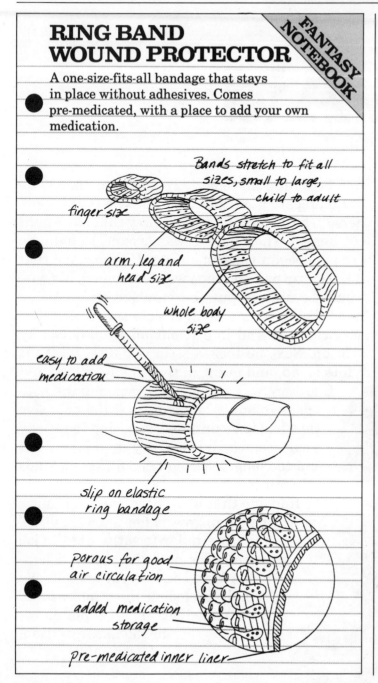

Bands stretch to fit all sizes, small to large, child to adult

finger size

arm, leg and head size

whole body size

easy to add medication

slip on elastic ring bandage

porous for good air circulation

added medication storage

pre-medicated inner liner

Earl Dickson (second from left), his wife (far left), and the actor and actress who portrayed the couple in a play.

Dickson's ready-made bandage was the beginning of his rising career with Johnson & Johnson. When company executives saw his new idea, they liked it enough to introduce the ready-made adhesive bandages as a new Johnson & Johnson product. The bandages were sold without a brand name until 1920, when W. Johnson Kenyon, the mill superintendent, suggested the name "bandaid"—"band" for the tape strip, and "aid" for first-aid. Eventually the Band-Aid

Fantasy Inventions

Most inventions, like Earl Dickson's Band-Aid, are inspired by a personal need. These fantasies expand on the basic bandage and may inspire you regarding your own safety or protection needs.

SAFETY CLOTHES. Lightweight air-bubble fabric clothing that protects the wearer from body scrapes, bruises, and other injuries while insulating from heat and cold.

CLEAR CUT GLUE. A clear paste wound protection that holds the cut together and lets you see the progress of healing. Glue peels off when cut is healed.

BARE TOE PROTECTORS. Hard-tipped toe socks keep toes from being stubbed.

LOOSE TOOTH PULLER. An adjustable loop cord fits around the loose tooth. When the handle of the cord is yanked the loop tightens and pulls out the tooth.

SUPER-STRETCH ADHESIVE STRIP AIDS. For temporarily repairing broken windows, bike tires, stuffed animals, injured animals, injured trees and plants, or anything that has come apart.

SECOND-SKIN CREAM. A body cream—applied to elbows, knees, and any body area—that protects the skin from scrapes, bruises, cuts, dirt, and germs. The cream forms an impenetrable but flexible and clear skin covering that washes off.

TATTOO BANDAGE PATCHES. Clear bandages with printed tattoos disguise wound while it is healing. Tattoo bandages can also be used at the beach to make suntan tattoos.

name was given to all sorts of first-aid and surgical tape products manufactured by Johnson & Johnson, and the Band-Aid name became synonymous with the bandage. Earl Dickson was rewarded for his efforts with several promotions; at the time of his retirement in 1957, he was a vice president of the Johnson & Johnson Company and probably could afford to take his wife *out* to dinner!

A selection of Band-Aid packages from over the years.

The Invention of
Chocolate Chip Cookies

The unexpected result of an experiment can become the invention, but only if you recognize its value.

The words "Toll House" have come to be synonymous with the best in chocolate chip cookies. Here's the story behind this delicious concoction and its intriguing name.

In 1709 New Bedford, Massachusetts, was one of the world's largest whaling ports. Halfway along the heavily traveled route between Boston and New Bedford was a stretch of private road with an inn. While the stagecoach driver was paying the toll and changing horses, his passengers would stop off at the "Toll House" for some-

thing to eat. The inn survived the days of stage-coaches, and it still carried the same name, the Toll House Inn, when Ruth and Kenneth Wakefield purchased it in August 1930.

At this point the inn was somewhat dilapidated, but the Wakefields wanted to restore the place to its original appearance and purpose—a charming New England roadside stopover and restaurant. Unfortunately, America was in an economic depression, and starting a new restaurant was a very risky business. Determined to succeed, however, Ken Wakefield supervised the restoration while Ruth Wakefield began developing a menu for the restaurant.

Mrs. Wakefield wanted to make all the New England favorites. Of course there would be traditional desserts, including apple pie, squash pie, and Indian pudding. But she also had an imaginative touch, and she decided to make a special kind of cookie. She started with a favorite American recipe for Butter Drop-Do's and added a new ingredient: bits of Nestlé semi-sweet chocolate. She took the chocolate candy bar and broke it into small pieces, adding them to the batter. Mrs.

Wakefield had expected the chocolate chips to melt and marble into the cookie, but to her great surprise and delight, that wonderful first bite revealed that the chocolate chunks were just a little softened but still deliciously intact. A new cookie had been created, and when the restaurant started serving her "chocolate crispies," the customers' response was overwhelming. The cookie quickly became a Toll House favorite.

The Wakefields had a good friend, Marjorie Mills, who happened to be the food editor of a Boston newspaper. She gave out Ruth Wakefield's new cookie recipe on a Boston radio show, and the word spread quickly. Everyone passed the recipe on to a friend.

Fantasy Inventions

New cookies are invented in people's kitchens almost every day. Try taking one element from each of these columns to create a new cookie of your own. You might want to use the basic recipe for chocolate chip cookies, as described on the wrapper on page 109, to get you started.

INVENT-A-COOKIE RECIPE BOOK.

vanilla	chip	sandwich
chocolate	crunch	bar
almond	nugget	cookie
coconut	flake	spreads
strawberry	squeeze	slices
licorice	dip	rods
coffee	chunk	puffs
pecan	slice	circles
pepperoni	crush	snacks
grape	paste	wafers
clam	flavored	biscuit

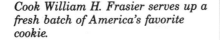

Cook William H. Frasier serves up a fresh batch of America's favorite cookie.

In the meantime, Nestlé had been thinking about discontinuing its semi-sweet chocolate bar because of poor sales—poor everywhere, that is, except around Boston. So the company sent one of its executives to Boston to see why so many semi-sweet bars were being sold in the area. They were very excited to learn about the new cookie and wanted to let as many people as possible know about the recipe and its use of their chocolate bars. Nestlé decided to keep making the bars, and they even began to put score lines on them so they would break more evenly and easily.

They also invented and sold a special chopper to break the chocolate into little cookie-size pieces. As the fame of the cookie spread farther, the name "Toll House" became so popular that the Nestlé company bought the name from the Wakefields in 1940 and put it on the back of the wrapper of every semisweet chocolate bar. Shortly thereafter, they began making chocolate chips in the now familiar form of small morsels—ready to pour out of the package and into the cookie dough. To this day, Nestlé's chocolate chip package still carries Ruth Wakefield's inventive recipe. The Toll House Inn was struck by a tragic fire in early 1985, but the Wakefield's cookie factory still stands on the original site.

Year after year, more chocolate chip cookies are sold in America than any other type. Recently the chocolate chip cookie has been the center of large-scale commercial competition. Many varieties have sprung up as bakers all over

The original Toll House in Whitman, Massachusetts.

the country claim that their recipe makes "the best" chocolate chip cookie; some have added walnuts or pecans, others feature slightly different flavorings, shapes and sizes, and baking methods vary. Whole books have been written on chocolate chip baking, but the original Toll House recipe is still America's hand-to-mouth favorite.

Smooth Rich Delicious

NESTLÉ'S SEMI-SWEET SWISS PROCESS CHOCOLATE

The wrapper from the Nestle's chocolate bar that inspired the chocolate chip.

PORTABLE SMELL RECORDER

Record and play back favorite smells, both of specific objects and general environments. Controls allow you to change smells and create new ones.

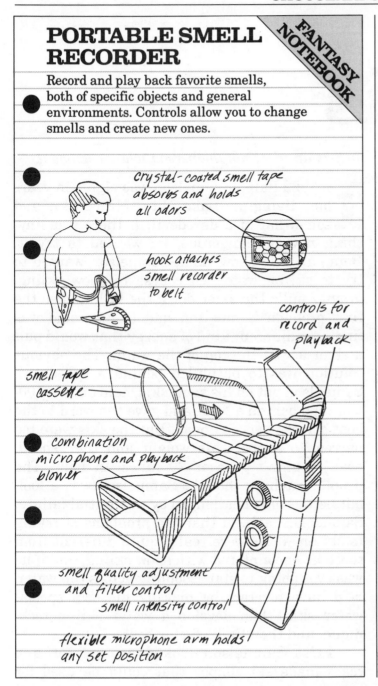

crystal-coated smell tape absorbs and holds all odors

hook attaches smell recorder to belt

controls for record and playback

smell tape cassette

combination microphone and playback blower

smell quality adjustment and filter control

smell intensity control

flexible microphone arm holds any set position

Mr. and Mrs. Wakefield pictured with fellow baking businessman Duncan Hines (center). The modern trademarked logo used by Nestlé's for their chocolate chips, and the famous original recipe, still found on the back of the wrapper (below).

TOLL HOUSE™

ORIGINAL NESTLE TOLL HOUSE® COOKIES

2¼ cup-all-purpose flour
1 measuring teaspoon baking soda
1 measuring teaspoon salt
1 cup butter, softened
¾ cup sugar

¾ cup firmly packed brown sugar
1 measuring teaspoon vanilla extract
2 eggs
One 12-oz. pkg. (2 cups) Nestlé Semi-Sweet Real Chocolate Morsels
1 cup chopped nuts (optional)

Preheat oven to 375°F. In small bowl, combine flour, baking soda and salt: set aside. In large bowl, combine butter, sugar, brown sugar and vanilla extract; beat until creamy. Beat in eggs. Gradually add flour mixture; mix well. Stir in Nestlé Semi-Sweet Real Chocolate Morsels and nuts. Drop by rounded measuring teaspoonfuls onto ungreased cookie sheets.
BAKE: at 375°F.   TIME: 8–10 minutes

Makes: 100—2" cookies

The Invention of
Water Skis

The profit often goes to the person who successfully markets an idea, not the person who develops it.

In 1922 Ralph Samuelson was eighteen years old, living in Lake City, Minnesota, and somewhat of a daredevil. If there was anything new or dangerous, he wanted to try it. Being an avid snow skier, Samuelson wanted to try to ski on water. Of course in snow skiing, gravity pulls the skier down the hill, and so the first problem Samuelson had to overcome was finding a different kind of energy that would pull a skier across the top of the water. The obvious solution was to be pulled behind a speedboat. Samuelson put on his snow skis, held on to a 100-foot rope behind a boat, and gave the word to the boat driver to speed ahead. But the skis were too narrow to support his weight and the "speedboat" couldn't go over 20 miles an hour. The people watching thought Samuelson was a fool, but he was only challenged by this initial failure. Samuelson realized that the problems of trying to ski on water were really quite different from those he encountered with snow skiing, and if he was ever going to start zooming across the water, he'd have to start by making his own special water skis, then develop a water skiing technique, and then find a faster boat.

First Samuelson looked around for any ready-made ski shapes that could be used for

Ralph Samuelson, shown with an airplane he used to pull himself across the water faster than just a boat, and an early shot of Samuelson in action.

skiing on water. He selected two barrel staves (slats from an oak-wood barrel) and strapped them to his feet. The front tips of the staves weren't curved up enough, though, and when he tried them he kept "tripping" into the lake.

Next Samuelson went to a lumber yard and bought two 9-inch-wide pine boards. Knowing something about woodworking, he curved up the ends of the boards by first boiling them in water and then clamping the softened wood to curved molds. When the boards dried, the new shape was permanent. The finished skis measured 8 feet long and each had a single leather footstrap in the middle.

Samuelson used his pine board skis for the very first successful water ski demonstration at the Lake City lake, where the Mississippi River widens into Lake Pepin. A crowd of nonbelievers gathered along the shore expecting Ralph Samuelson to once again make a fool of himself. But when he was finally pulled up and actually skiing on top of the water, everyone cheered wildly. Because the motorboat still could go only about 20 miles per hour, Samuelson had to zig-zag back and forth to keep himself going fast enough to stay up. The first set of pine board skis soon broke, and Samuelson built a second, improved pair. These were nearly 9 feet long and 1 foot wide, with rubber floor treading under the straps to keep his feet firmly in place. He also used a steel strap to help support the curved tip of the ski. By now the skis weighed nearly 15 pounds each.

The young thrill-seeker continued to experiment with improved equipment and skiing techniques. He developed the right type and length of pull rope, a metal ring wrapped with rubber for a good handgrip, and even the first water ski jump.

SNOW BIKE

FANTASY NOTEBOOK

A pedal-powered snow bike with ski front and tractor-tread back for both transportation and sports.

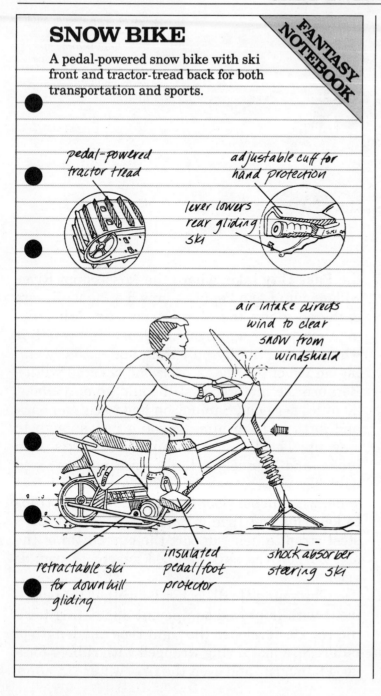

pedal-powered tractor tread

adjustable cuff for hand protection

lever lowers rear gliding ski

air intake directs wind to clear snow from windshield

retractable ski for downhill gliding

insulated pedal/foot protector

shock absorber steering ski

Soon Samuelson was putting on regular water ski shows for the crowds that vacationed on the lake, and he became something of a local celebrity. But for Ralph Samuelson, the boats available on the lake were not fast enough for the kind of thrills he wanted for himself and the spectators. So he began using a 220-horsepower, 35-mile-per-hour boat that could pull him over his newly invented wooden ski jump (greased with pork fat). Samuelson amazed the people who came to see him by sailing 50 to 60 feet in the air before coming down in a perfect landing on the lake.

Then he found an even faster boat outfitted with a World War I airplane propeller, which could pull him at nearly 50 miles per hour. And in the summer of 1925, Samuelson was skiing behind a 200-foot rope attached to a Curtis World War I flying boat that pulled him at over 80 miles per hour. At that speed, the boat became more of an airplane and would frequently begin to take off with Samuelson flying behind—sometimes 20 feet in the air! Once, when Samuelson was skiing behind the flying boat, his skis flew off and he skied on his bare feet nearly 100 yards across the water. Incredibly, he was not injured. (In fact, he was never injured in any of his daredevil water ski stunts.)

The reputation of Ralph Samuelson's feats spread, and crowds of thousands would come to watch his Sunday afternoon water ski shows. But Samuelson did not get rich as an entertainer—in fact, he refused any pay except for donations to pay for the expenses of the boats used to pull him. Samuelson was already well-to-do from his business running turkey farms, and he could afford to travel to Palm Beach, Florida, each winter, where he would also stage his one-man water ski shows. It was in Florida that wealthy people would watch Samuelson's exhibitions, and many of them would take the idea back to their hometowns where other people would attempt to do the same thing. Ralph Samuelson never taught anyone else how to water ski, and yet it was his idea that led Fred Walker of Huntington, New York, to reinvent the concept and patent his "akwa-skees" in 1925.

For over fifteen years, Samuelson was content to water ski to the cheers of onlookers. But because of several bone fractures he sustained while on land, he had to quit. The energy Ralph Samuelson put into thrill-seeking was eventually turned into a concern for the well-being and happiness of his family and community. After retiring from his turkey farm business, Sam-

An early shot of Ralph Samuelson's water ski jump in use.

uelson devoted his time to gardening, fishing, public speaking, and the practice of religion. Interestingly enough, his favorite and best-liked speech probably came from his water skiing experience and was called "How to Overcome Fear and Worry." And the pastime he invented has established itself as a favorite summer sport.

Fantasy Inventions

Ralph Samuelson was clever enough to take an existing sport, skiing, and move it to a different environment—water. These fantasies offer other skiing innovations and suggest just a few other changes in existing sports, to inspire your own new combinations.

GRASS SKIS. A gel ski base applied to regular snow skis for skiing the slopes in summer. Other gels are available for skiing on sand, mud, hay, ice, and roads.

WALL AND CEILING SUCTION SHOES. For walking or working on sloping or inverted surfaces. Can also be used for sport skyscraper climbing.

FOOT JET FLIPPERS. Swimming flippers with controllable jet propulsion.

REPLACE-A-SPORT. Any sport moved to an unusual place for playing: Grass billiards; Table golf; Rock running with rock hurdles; Mud diving; Sand surfing and sailing; Pool soccer; Sidewalk grand prix; Hill diving; Bicycle sailing; Table tag; Wall Frisbee; Carpet skiing; Fog tennis; Maze bowling; Sail walking.

WATER SKI TRACK. The waterskier's tow rope is attached to an underwater remote control pull that follows an underwater track. The skier can control speed and change ski course tracks.

SPRING-POWERED BICYCLE ASSIST. A bicycle spring motor that winds while coasting downhill and helps pedal on flat land and up hills.

The Invention of
Levi's

If you listen well the marketplace will tell you what products it needs and wants.

Levi Strauss was only seventeen years old when he left Bavaria and came to America in 1847. He could barely understand or speak English, but he went to work for his two older brothers, peddling household trinkets and cloth in the towns and villages near Louisville, Kentucky.

Making a living as a peddler was tough, and in 1849, when Levi heard of the California Gold Rush and the great fortunes that could be made, he decided to pack up his merchandise and head for San Francisco. Levi boarded a clipper ship in New York and settled in for the long journey around Cape Horn and up to California. To make money for a "grubstake" to buy land and the supplies needed to mine a piece of property, the young Strauss sold his wares and cloth to his fellow passengers, and by the time the boat docked in San Francisco, all Levi hadn't sold were a few rolls of canvas. He thought they would be easy to sell for tent material or wagon covers, but his prospecting customers had another request: "You should have brought pants....Pants don't wear worth a hoot up in the diggin's."

The businessman in Levi Strauss realized that there probably was a good market for durable canvas pants for prospectors, so he hired a

Blue jeans inventor Levi Strauss. An early advertisement for Levi's jeans, and a pair of the original trousers, now in the collection of the Smithsonian Institution.

local tailor to cut and sew his canvas into "waist-high overalls." The pants sold as quickly as they were made, and his customers were very impressed with the quality. Soon every prospector and railroad worker in the area wanted Levi's canvas pants. Levi wrote to his brothers telling them to send more canvas—and keep sending it!

Soon the young Strauss, abandoning his prospecting plans, opened a small pants manufacturing shop in San Francisco and dedicated himself to continually improving the quality of his product. Levi knew of an even stronger, more durable cloth that was produced mainly in the town of Nimes (pronounced *neem*), France. The French called the material *serge de Nimes*—meaning cloth from Nimes—but by the time it reached America, people just called it "denim." When Levi Strauss decided to switch from canvas to denim, he also decided to dye the material a dark indigo blue. It seemed that indigo blue gave the most consistent dye color, so the various

COOL SAIL CLOTHES

FANTASY NOTEBOOK

Clothing with lots of extra flaps that catch breezes as you move, to keep cool on hot days.

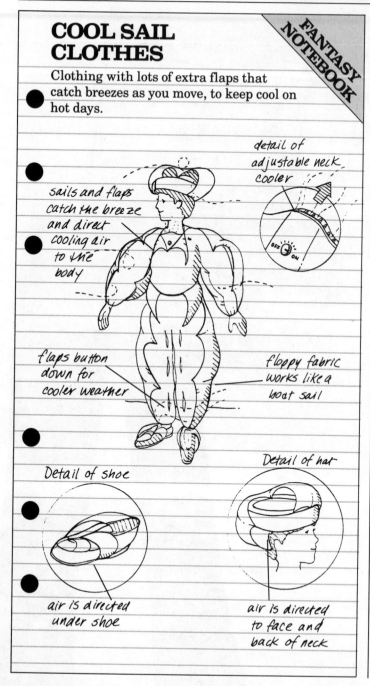

detail of adjustable neck cooler

sails and flaps catch the breeze and direct cooling air to the body

flaps button down for cooler weather

floppy fabric works like a boat sail

Detail of shoe

air is directed under shoe

Detail of hat

air is directed to face and back of neck

pieces of cloth would match when sewn together. When Levi's new improved product began to sell (at $13.50 per dozen), people still called the pants Levi's but often added "blue denims" or "blue jeans." "Jeans" was an Americanization of Genoa, a town in Italy that also produced this rugged cotton twill material.

The next big improvement in Levi's pants came in the 1860s, but he wasn't its inventor. A gold miner named Alkali Ike had the habit of stuffing the Levis pants pockets with ore samples—so much so that the pockets would frequently rip open. Ike was constantly taking his Levis to his tailor, Jake Davis, to have them resewn. After several resewings, Davis, in frustration (or maybe as a joke), took Ike's torn pants to the local blacksmith and had him put rivets at the pocket corners. It worked! Ike's pockets stopped tearing and Davis quickly had many customers wanting the same thing done to their Levis.

Jake Davis took his idea to Levi Strauss and they decided to become partners in a patent for Levi's pants with riveted pockets. Levis used the copper-riveted pocket design until 1937, when the rivets on the back pockets were replaced with heavy stitching because teachers complained that the rivets scratched school furniture.

The company's success continued to grow and so did the product line. Although Strauss intended his durable pants to be work clothes, they soon became popular for all-round use, and that popularity has helped make Levi Strauss & Company the largest clothing manufacturer in the world today.

Jeans are known around the world as the

An ad for Levi's jeans from the early 1920s, and a picture of the miners who first made the market for these rugged pants.

classic American pants. They have found a place in all segments of today's fashion, from the uniform of the young and cool to the standard rugged work outfit to the leisure wear of choice, all the way to high-priced designer versions.

Fantasy Inventions

By drawing on practicality, Levi's have become a solid staple in the ever-changing world of fashion. These fantasy ideas may inspire you on new changes in style and material for clothing.

EXPANDABLE CLOTHES. The clothing material can stretch (or shrink) to fit the changing size of a growing person. Clothes come in child and adult sizes. Also economical for a person on a diet.

WATERPROOF CLOTHES POCKETS. Keep pocket contents dry and protected regardless of the weather or work/play activity.

ORGANIC SELF-REPAIRING CLOTH. An organic fabric cloth that repairs its own rips, tears, and holes by growing new fabric to replace and connect the broken threads.

STICK-ON POCKETS. Removable pockets in a variety of sizes can be attached anywhere on clothing or skin to carry nearly anything. Available in fashion designs.

SPRAY-ON WEAR EXTENDER. A spray-on fabric coating for heavy-wear areas (such as knees and elbows) that provides extra durability and extends the life of clothing.

MEMORY CLOTH. A fabric that can be cut and molded to a permanent shape to make perfect-fit clothing.

PERSONAL MODEL ROBOT SHOPPER. Robot inflates to exact size and dimensions of the owner for clothes shopping and fitting.

STYLABLE CAR BODY. A moldable plastic car body that can be styled and restyled by simply hand-contouring the body panels. The owner can style the car himself or take it to a car styling salon.

The Invention of

Basketball

An invention can always be improved by trying new ideas.

The game of basketball is the only major sport that is completely an American invention. As is true of many inventions, it was created to fill a need—for a physically active game a class of high-school or college students could play indoors during the cold winter months.

Credit for inventing the game goes to James Naismith, who became hooked on sports during the 1880s. After graduating from college, Naismith decided to devote his life to teaching athletics, and he took a job at Springfield College in Massachusetts. Students from all over America came to Springfield College to learn to become physical-training instructors for the YMCAs back in their hometowns.

In his first few months, Naismith taught his students football and would frequently join in their game. But during the winter, when the New England weather became bitter cold and the playing fields were snowed over, Naismith was forced to bring his students indoors to the school's small gymnasium, and to switch to a less exciting program of body-training exercises.

The students were bored and they protested, but there were no sports with the intensity of football that could be played in a small gym without people getting bruised and bumped against the floor and walls and each other. In an effort to solve the problem, Naismith was given permission by the college to experiment for two weeks to see if he could come up with an active and exciting indoor sport.

Dr. James Naismith, the father of basketball, shown here in 1891.

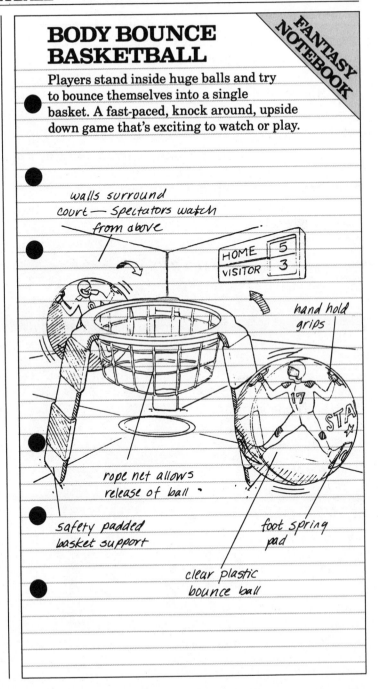

After several unsuccessful attempts to adapt football, soccer, and lacrosse for indoor play, Naismith tried to invent a totally new game instead. He decided that his new indoor sport would use some type of ball and that the rules would be simple. To minimize roughness Naismith decided that the players could not run holding the ball and could touch it only with their hands. A bat or stick was too dangerous in a crowded gym, so Naismith decided that the players would just pass or throw the ball to each other. But how was a team to score points?

Naismith first thought of using an open box on the floor at either end of the gym and having players try to toss the ball in the box to score. But it would be possible for the defenders to mass in front of the box and block all shots. Then he had a bright idea. Why not hang boxes for goals above the heads of the players so they wouldn't be able to block the shots with their bodies?

Naismith set up the game for a class tryout the next morning. He chose a soccer ball for play and went to see the school janitor to get boxes for goals. The janitor didn't have two boxes the same size, but he did come up with two wooden peach baskets. Around the school gym there was a balcony that happened to be exactly 10 feet above the floor. That seemed like a good height, so Naismith fastened the baskets to the balcony, one at either end of the playing floor.

The class was divided into two teams of nine each, and Naismith explained the rules of play:

Senda Berenson, in the long dress, with Smith College students in Northampton, Massachusetts, where women played the first public basketball game on March 22, 1893.

- The ball may be thrown or batted in any direction using one or both hands, but not a fist.

- A player cannot run with the ball and must throw it from where he catches it.

- A player cannot hold, push, trip, shoulder, or strike an opponent.

- The time of the game shall be two fifteen-minute halves with a five-minute rest in between.

- The team that tosses in the most goals in that time wins.

To start the game Naismith threw the ball up between the two team captains—thus inventing the center jump ball. As the game was being played for the first time, Naismith established rules for fouls, out-of-bound balls, and scoring. Each goal scored one point, and after each goal, play was restarted with a jump ball.

The students found this new game exciting—and much harder than they had imagined. For thirty minutes the class ran up and down the gym, passing the ball, taking shots at the peach baskets, blocking shots, and yelling instructions and cheers to each other. When a goal was scored the game had to be temporarily stopped while someone climbed a ladder to retrieve the ball from inside the basket. However, that wasn't much of a problem in the first game of "basketball"—the final score was only 1–0.

The popularity of basketball swept through Springfield College, and soon nearby schools that had heard about the new gym game were organiz-

The first basketball team, with nine men, from December 1891, at the YMCA Training School in Springfield, Massachusetts, including inventor James Naismith (center row, right).

ing their own basketball teams. It still wasn't easy to shoot a soccer ball into a peach basket, and a team rarely scored more than four or five points in a game.

In less than a year, YMCAs all across America were nailing peach baskets to the gym walls; in warm weather, baskets could even be seen on the trunks of trees and the sides of houses in nearly every neighborhood. America was quickly becoming basketball crazy.

Because the game was so new, many teams experimented with their own rules. Some schools played with as many as fifty players on a side and even tried using two balls in play at the same time. Students at Yale University began to experiment with a bounce pass and ended up inventing the dribble.

Naismith himself also continued to experiment and refine the rules of the game until ultimately he decided on five players to a side,

Fantasy Inventions

The nature and scale of competitive sports has changed somewhat since the time of James Naismith, but people are always looking for new games to play, and new ways to play existing games.

ALL-SEASON SNOWBALL MAKER. Attachment to home freezer makes and stores ready-for-play snowballs.

ROBOT REFEREE. Programmed computer referee impartially makes sports game judgments and calls. Only the master supreme computer referee can resolve player/robot referee disputes.

VIEWER PARTICIPATION TV SPORTS. During the game viewers are allowed to determine a play, move, or strategy for their home team by calling in suggestions. Viewer majority dictates the play of the game.

COMPUTER SPORTS TV. Traditional popular sports translated in detail to realistic computer games played by intellectual athletes as TV entertainment.

ROUND ROBIN RULES. The visiting team can elect to add an additional game rule for the first half of play, then the home team can add an additional game rule for the second half. Both teams must abide by the added rule.

An outdoor basketball action shot from 1892.

But the game still needed improvement. A soccer ball was difficult to bounce and too heavy for shooting long shots; the gym shoes worn by the players tended to slip on smooth wood floors; and someone still had to retrieve the ball from the basket after each goal.

Recognizing the epidemic-like popularity of the new sport, the Spalding Sporting Goods Company designed and produced a special basketball that was larger and lighter than a soccer ball and had more bounce for dribbling. The company also invented the first basketball shoe, with "suction cup soles" that were guaranteed not to slip on smooth gym floors.

Someone came up with the simple idea of drilling a small hole in the bottom of the peach basket so a stick could be poked up to push the ball out, and some other inventive player created a trap door basket that released the ball with the pull of a rope. In 1897 peach baskets were replaced with hoops and nets that caught the ball—but after each score the ball still had to be pushed out. It wasn't until twelve years after Naismith had invented the game that someone finally designed a basketball hoop with an open-bottom net that allowed the ball to drop through.

Basketball had become a full-fledged sport, and its popularity continued to grow. Today Naismith's invention is one of the most played and watched games in the country. To honor James Naismith, the Basketball Hall of Fame was named after him and located in Springfield, Massachusetts, where it all began.

The Invention of
The Trampoline

A new and novel idea must be demonstrated to gain exposure, enthusiasm and sales.

The trampoline was invented by a gifted young gymnast named George Nissen, who came from Cedar Rapids, Iowa. As a child, Nissen had fun jumping up and down on the big bed in his family's guest room. Growing up during the 1920s, young George would go to the circus and watch with amazement and fear as the high-wire performers ended their daring acts by diving into the barely visible safety net far below. George was especially excited when the bouncing performers, instead of clumsily trying to stop bouncing, did special tricks in the air between landings on the net. They would twist around in midair, do a somersault, or even bounce up and off the net to a standing position on the floor.

Safety nets and "bouncing tables" had existed for centuries in many parts of the world. Even the Eskimos had a version: they would stretch walrus skins across stakes driven deep into the ground and bounce up and down on the taut skin just for the fun of it. More recently, and closer to home, fairs, circuses, and vaudeville performers sometimes used spring-and-board bouncing tables, nets, or even mattresses as a part of the act. One famous vaudeville comedian, Joe E. Brown, used a spring bouncing table in two different ways. For one trick he would jump onto the springy table and leap up onto the shoulders of his partner. Later, Brown surprised his audience by "falling" off the stage into the orchestra pit, only to bounce off the rebound table set up in the pit and land back on stage, usually feet first.

But all these bouncing nets and bouncing tables were awkward to use, and each one had to be constructed from scratch. George Nissen thought it was about time to create a standard design for a jumping table so, while still in high school, he began his tinkering.

The inventor's first move was to remove his father's car from the garage and take over the space as his workshop. Of course, the neighbors thought he was a bit strange to be so devoted to a project that, to them, seemed to have no practical value. But he had caught the invention bug and he was determined!

Nissen spent practically no money on his early experiments. He would pick over the town dump for essential materials like springs, old rubber inner tubes, and scraps of iron. He also acquired an old heavy-duty sewing machine and rebuilt it to suit his needs. For Nissen, clever thinking and scrounged parts replaced those materials and tools he couldn't afford.

Nissen analyzed all the bouncing nets and tables then available, considering bouncing from the tumbler's point of view plus function and durability from an engineer's viewpoint. He then developed a list of criteria that he wanted his design to fulfill. He wanted it to be large enough to be safe but not so large that it would take up a lot of space. He wanted his design to be strong enough to withstand all kinds of jumping, and high enough so the bouncing surface would not hit the floor. He also wanted the jumping table to be easy to store, transport, and set up.

George Nissen's first successful model had a canvas jumping surface that was attached to a metal frame made from the rails of his own bed. Nissen used rope and strips of inner tube to connect the canvas to the frame and give bounce to the contraption.

An early trampoline demonstration, showing that a man can jump as high as a kangaroo, with a little help of course.

Fantasy Inventions

George Nissen was able to combine fun and exercise in one product—many of these fantasy inventions draw on that same clever mix.

MASSAGE HOOPS. Various size Hula Hoops with weights and textures that massage the body, arms, legs, and head as they are spun for fun.

ROCKET SNOW SKIS. Miniature rocket-propulsion engines attach to skis and replace lifts for getting uphill.

TRAMPOLINE SIDEWALKS. Light bouncy sidewalk pads are placed over concrete sidewalks to comfort shoppers' and walkers' feet.

BACKYARD MUD TUB. A backyard pool-size tub filled with silicone plastic "mud" that won't dirty or stick to clothes or skin. Great for summer sloshing.

HANGING BOUNCER. An upside-down trampoline with the jumper hanging suspended from an elastic bungie cord.

BARREL ROLL RACING. A large rolling-barrel downhill racer with a banked barrel shape that allows the driver inside to change speed and control direction through body action.

WATER JET TRAMPOLINE. The player tries to stay balanced on top of a vertical jet of water while performing various gymnastic feats.

ZERO GRAVITY BOUNCING ROOM. A recreational amusement room for floating and bouncing off of trampoline walls, ceiling, and floor.

A group rehearsal for a trampoline exhibition in San Mateo, California.

Nissen put his invention to the test at a local YMCA camp, and the kids immediately flocked to the exciting new activity. All day long, the fascinated campers lined up for turns on Nissen's bouncing table, to the exclusion of all other camp sports.

It was not until he had graduated from college in 1938 that George Nissen began to devote his full time to further developing and promoting his new jumping invention. And when all the bugs had been worked out, he patented the design and trademarked the name "trampoline"—a takeoff on the Spanish word *trampolin*, which means "diving board." Next, Nissen designed and built the machines he needed to mass-produce the invention. But the trampoline was not selling as well as he had hoped. It seemed that sporting goods dealers were not promoting the trampoline because they considered it a novelty item and a gimmick suitable only for the circus or professional performers. But George Nissen reasoned that the only reason people would not want a trampoline was because they didn't know what a trampoline was. So to educate and convince the public, he took off in his car with a trampoline strapped on top and began giving demonstrations and exhibitions anywhere there was a crowd: sports shows, schools, fairs, and playgrounds. He would also take orders for trampolines right on the spot. Any money he made selling the device he spent placing ads in sports magazines. Sales began to pick up.

When World War II began, Nissen enlisted in the Navy and left his factory in the hands of three employees. Still an ardent believer in his invention, Nissen convinced the Army and Navy to use the trampoline as part of their pilot training program. Nissen became a lieutenant and a pre-flight training instructor, and he was put in charge of using the trampoline to help with training and conditioning of pilots. Fortunately for the trampoline business, his Navy job brought him into contact with many physical education instructors who were also working on new methods of conditioning. When they returned to their jobs after the war, nearly all ordered Nissen's trampolines for their gyms and his company started to make money.

Nissen resumed his promotional touring and gave trampoline exhibitions all over Europe. Trampolining was rapidly becoming an accepted sport, and in 1948 both major intercollegiate sports organizations, the NCAA and the AAU, included trampolining as an event in the national gymnastics competitions. Even astronauts

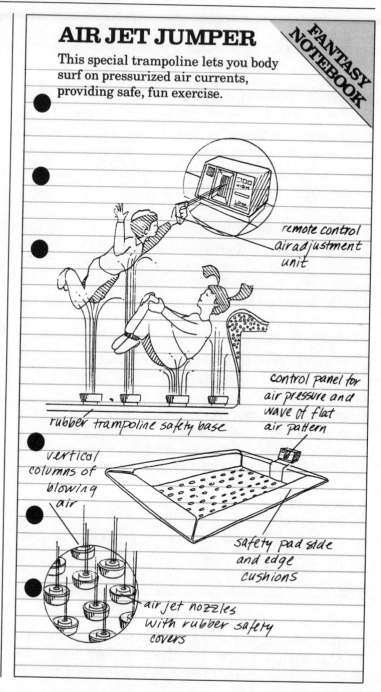

AIR JET JUMPER

FANTASY NOTEBOOK

This special trampoline lets you body surf on pressurized air currents, providing safe, fun exercise.

remote control air adjustment unit

control panel for air pressure and wave of flat air pattern

rubber trampoline safety base

vertical columns of blowing air

safety pad side and edge cushions

air jet nozzles with rubber safety covers

used the trampoline to get used to the feeling of weightlessness—a feeling that occurs for a brief moment at the very top of the bounce. By the late 1950s, the general public had finally caught on to the fun of bouncing on a trampoline, and it became a genuine fad. Trampoline centers were set up all over America, and for a few years they were very popular.

By this time, there were many other companies manufacturing trampolines, but since George Nissen had invented the name, only he could use the word "trampoline"—it had become his company's trademark. Nissen tried to get the sport renamed "rebound tumbling," so other manufacturers would not use "trampoline," but the name had become too popular. Ultimately he decided to give it up and let anyone use the name "trampoline" as long as it was spelled with a small "t."

Now that the trampoline was an accepted success, Nissen put his talents into inventing other kinds of trampoline products and games. The most successful of these was a complicated game called "Spaceball" (a combination of volleyball and basketball, all on top of a trampoline) and of course to promote it, George toured the country demonstrating how much fun it was. By 1964 the new game had become so popular that a world championship Spaceball competition was held. In Florida and California, several Spaceball parks were built, and there are even courts at the astronaut training center in Houston, Texas.

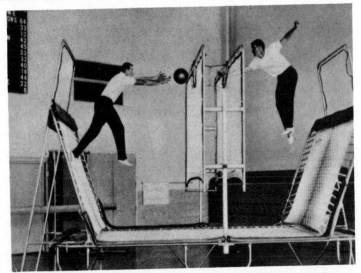

A demonstration of the trampoline game Spaceball, a novelty sport in the mid-1960s that was used at the astronaut training center in Houston, Texas.

George Nissen had showed himself to be not only a good inventor but, out of necessity, also a good promoter of his products. He never missed an opportunity to show off his trampoline. He was known for doing things like teaching a kangaroo to trampoline and even going to Egypt to bounce around on the top of one of the pyramids. As the trampoline business grew, Nissen's company began manufacturing other top-quality sports equipment of all kinds, including Ping-Pong tables, basketball equipment, scoreboards, and almost every type of gymnastic apparatus. Look in any gymnasium today and you're sure to see the Nissen brand name.

The Invention of
Kleenex

Let the consumer tell you the best use for your product.

The invention of Kleenex facial tissue followed a path characteristic to the invention process in general: it was originally made for one purpose but ultimately used for another.

The Kimberly-Clark Company had been in business since 1872 making various types of paper products. When a cotton shortage developed in 1914, just before World War I, Kimberly-Clark invented a substitute material they called Cellucotton—an absorbent wadding made primarily from wood pulp cellulose and a small amount of cotton. Cellucotton proved to be a versatile and useful material during the war. It was used in hospitals and first-aid stations in the United States and Europe to replace scarce cotton bandages, and it was also excellent as a filter in gas masks.

Hollywood stars were shown in early Kleenex advertisements to go along with the product's image of luxury. Shown here is Irene Rich, a Warner Brothers actress.

When the war ended, so did the cotton shortage, and Kimberly-Clark began looking for new ways to sell Cellucotton. Because the material felt soft against the skin, they decided to introduce Cellucotton as a disposable cloth for removing cold cream and facial makeup. In 1924 the new product, one hundred soft Cellucotton sheets to the box, was introduced to the public. However, each box of "cold cream remover" sheets cost 65¢, so the paper tissues were considered a luxury.

Knowing their product was too expensive for the average wage earner, the Kimberly-Clark advertising people tried to capitalize on the association with wealth and glamour. First the company sold the tissues directly to Hollywood makeup artists, and then they used that fact in their advertising, claiming that the best Hollywood makeup men used the new "scientific way to remove cold cream." The next generation of ads showed the popular movie stars of the day endorsing the use of disposable facial cleansing tissues. However, despite the expensive hype, the new cloth substitute sold only moderately well.

Meanwhile the creative engineers and marketing people at Kimberly-Clark were still looking for a way to make their disposable tissues more useful and appealing to the general public. In 1929 they invented and patented the "pop-up" box so that each time a tissue was pulled from the box the next one would be partially pulled out for use; that same year the tissues were also offered in a variety of colors. What would eventually prove most important was the new name of the tissues—Kleenex—to suggest the function of the product.

Two early Kleenex packages, showing the initial emphasis on the product as a cold cream remover.

WRISTBAND NOSE WIPER

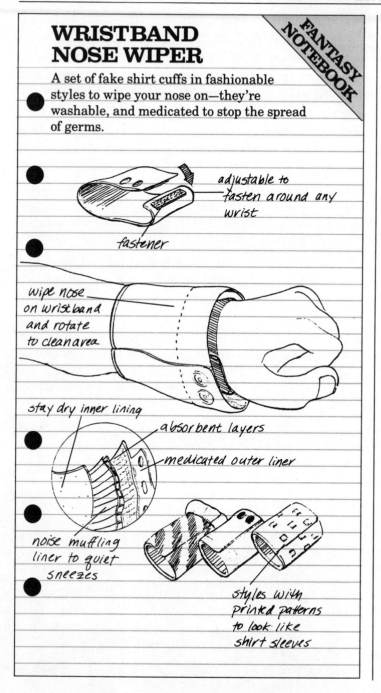

FANTASY NOTEBOOK

A set of fake shirt cuffs in fashionable styles to wipe your nose on—they're washable, and medicated to stop the spread of germs.

adjustable to fasten around any wrist

fastener

wipe nose on wristband and rotate to clean area

stay dry inner lining

absorbent layers

medicated outer liner

noise muffling liner to quiet sneezes

styles with printed patterns to look like shirt sleeves

Still, sales remained slow, and the people at Kimberly-Clark were baffled by the sluggish performance of their repackaged, brightly colored tissues. So in 1930 the marketing department tried an experiment. They went to Peoria, Illinois, with a questionnaire to learn how well people liked Kleenex, how they were using the tissues, and if they might suggest any new ideas or hints. The response was as overwhelming as it was surprising. Over half the people in Peoria who bought Kleenex used them not for removing cold cream but as disposable handkerchiefs.

Although Kleenex seems to have been the first commercial facial tissue manufactured in America, such a use of paper was not without historical precedent. There is, for instance, some evidence that the Japanese used "sneezing paper" as long ago as the seventeenth century. In 1637 an Englishman who had been in Japan wrote, "They blow their noses with a certain soft and tough kind of paper which they carry about them in small pieces, which having been used, they fling away as a filthy thing." The Japanese called this "nose paper" *hanagami*, but rather than buy it, it seems they took small scraps of paper and crumpled them to make them soft.

At any rate, all Kleenex advertising was immediately changed to emphasize this new use, and a new slogan was coined that got spectacular results: "Don't put a cold in your pocket."

Kleenex sales quickly doubled. Many people tossed their cotton hankies into the laundry for the last time and began grabbing for a Kleenex in the pop-up box whenever they felt a sneeze coming on. Within two years, sales increased 400 percent—and that was during the worst year of

Fantasy Inventions

Kleenex became successful because of their wide variety of uses—here are some ideas that take the themes of health products and clever products one step further.

DIRT-REPELLING SKIN LOTION. Spreads on the skin to create a coating that repels dirt. Keeps kids clean and protects the skin from germs.

CITY PAPER. Liquid paper pulp is piped directly into homes and businesses. A converter machine turns the pulp into any type of paper needed.

ANY PAPER PAD. A solid paper pad made up of very thin paper sheets statically stuck together. Peeling off one layer = tissue, two layers = tracing paper, three layers = writing paper, four layers = wrapping paper, and five layers or more = cardboard.

ADVERTISING TOILET TISSUE. Advertisements printed on toilet tissue for bathroom reading. Advertisements on facial tissue promote cold and fever remedies.

REUSABLE PAPER PLATES. A peel-off plastic plate surface leaves the plate clean and ready to use again. The peeled-off plastic becomes an individual garbage bag for plate scraps.

HOUSEHOLD PAPER REPROCESSOR. Accepts all used paper (including junk mail) and converts it to clean recycled paper ready to use again. Selector allows a choice of tissue, writing, wrapping, or other paper types.

SOUND-MUFFLING TISSUE. Quiets the sound of a sneeze.

SUNBURN ALARM TABS. Small transparent warning tabs placed on the body turn bright red from too much sun before the skin does.

the Depression. Today the Kleenex brand is the most identifiable and best-selling facial tissue in the world. The Kleenex brand name was so catchy that it rapidly became a commonly used word for all brands of disposable tissues. A consumer product that was first intended as a cold cream remover was reinvented by its users as a cold-germ catcher, and the handkerchief business has never been the same.

A Kleenex ad from the 1940s shows the many early uses of the tissues, along with the successful "Don't put a cold in your pocket!" slogan.

The Invention of
Dixie Cups

The benefit of new ideas must be understood to be accepted.

In 1908 a young entrepreneur, Hugh Moore, invented a vending machine that dispensed a drink of water for 1¢. Moore named his business the American Water Supply Company of New England and set up his white porcelain vending machines outside stores and at trolley stops, but sales were slow because it was difficult for him to convince people to buy what they could already get for free. At popular gathering places in most towns, there were public drinking troughs with tin dippers for scooping out a drink.

At about the same time that Moore invented his water dispenser, a young health officer, Dr. Samuel Crumbine from Dodge City, Kansas, began a national crusade against the health hazards of the communal tin dipper. When Hugh Moore read about Dr. Crumbine's campaign, he realized that he was selling the wrong product. He should sell his sanitary paper cup, not the water that went in it!

Hugh Moore and his business associate, Lawrence Luellen, went to New York City with this new idea to get the financial backing they needed to buy machinery for production. Day after day, they took their ideas and their hand-made paper cup samples to bankers, businessmen, and would-be investors. Most people just laughed. "The old tin dipper was good enough for pa and it's good enough for me!"

However, just when they were about to give up and go home, they happened to speak to one over-imaginative banker who was horrified by the prospect of people dying from diseases carried

One of the first sanitary water dispensers, from 1912.

paper cups—and cup dispensers to go with them. He also looked for new markets for his cups. Soda fountains, Moore thought, could serve drinks in his disposable cups—but he continued to encounter resistance. Most people still didn't believe that paper cups were healthier than the usual containers, and they thought it was a lot cheaper

When states started passing bills outlawing the tin dippers and public drinking troughs, like the Massachusetts legislature bill from 1910 shown here, Hugh Moore's cup business took off.

MASSACHUSETTS ABOLISHES PUBLIC C

LAW TO ENABLE THE STATE BOARD OF HE
TO PROHIBIT THE USE OF PUBLIC DRINKING CU
THE STATE. SIGNED BY THE GOVERNOR, APRIL 22,
THE BOARD WILL ENFORCE THE LAW AFTER OCT.

HOUSE . . . . No. 153

House No. 1475 as passed to be engrossed.

The Commonwealth of Massachusetts.

In the Year One Thousand Nine Hundred and Ten.

AN ACT

To restrict the Use of Common Drinking Cups.

Be it enacted by the Senate and House of Representatives in General Court assembled, and by the authority of the same, as follows:

SECTION 1. In order to prevent the spread of communicable diseases, the state board of health is hereby authorized to prohibit in such public places, vehicles or buildings as it may designate the providing of a common drinking cup, and the board may establish rules and regulations for this purpose.

SECTION 2. Whoever violates the provisions of this act, or any rule or regulation of the state board of health made under authority hereof, shall be deemed guilty of a misdemeanor and be liable to a fine not exceeding twenty-five dollars for each offence.

SECTION 3. All acts and parts of acts inconsistent herewith are hereby repealed.

SECTION 4. This act shall take effect on the first day of October, nineteen hundred and ten.

HOUSE OF REPRESENTATIVES, April 7, 1910.
Passed to be engrossed.
Sent up for concurrence.
JAMES W. KI

in germ-ridden dippers. The bank invested $200,000 in the speculative venture, and in 1909 Moore incorporated the new business as the Public Cup Vendor Company.

That same year, Dr. Crumbine was successful in convincing the Kansas state legislature to pass a law abolishing the tin dipper, and other states were considering similar action. Thinking that the publicity in favor of an "individual drinking cup" could only help his business, Moore again changed the company name to the Individual Drink Cup Company. And then in 1912 he changed the name once more, this time to Health Kups.

As more and more states passed laws barring the tin water dipper, Moore sold more and more

PORTABLE WATER FAUCET

FANTASY NOTEBOOK

Make water right from the air. Can be taken and used anywhere. Commercial and industrial models available for larger volume.

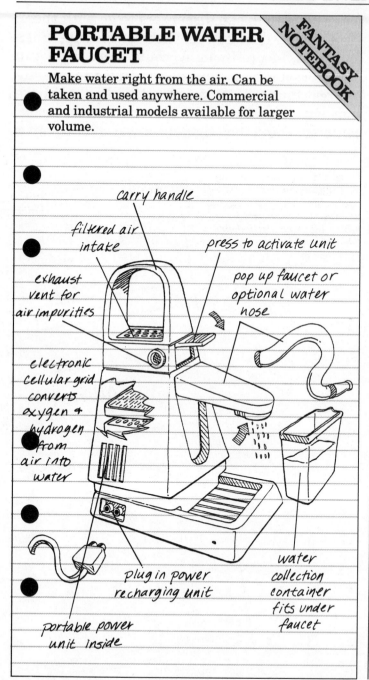

- carry handle
- filtered air intake
- press to activate unit
- pop up faucet or optional water hose
- exhaust vent for air impurities
- electronic cellular grid converts oxygen & hydrogen from air into water
- plug in power recharging unit
- portable power unit inside
- water collection container fits under faucet

An advertisement from the early 1930s shows the Dixie Cup in its new role as a sanitary ice cream container.

to hire a dishwasher than to buy throwaway cups. Moore persisted, and in time more and more soda fountains found that the convenience of a disposable paper cup outweighed the small added expense.

The final turning point in the success of Hugh Moore's company was his next and last name change. In 1919 Moore decided that the Health Kup name was too clinical and scientific to be appealing. He began to think of possible new names. It seems that a Dixie Doll Company was located next door to the Health Kup Company in New York City, and Moore and the doll manufacturer were good friends. Moore admired the name Dixie; it was catchy, short, easy to say, and nice-looking. He asked if he could borrow the name for his company and the doll maker didn't mind. The Dixie brand name worked.

Next Moore took his individual paper cups to the ice cream industry. In 1923 ice cream was sold only in bulk packages, although many other competitive products, like candy and soda, came in small individual-serving containers. After two years of research, the Dixie Company developed a 2½-ounce paper cup of ice cream that sold for 5¢, and the name Dixie Cup took on a whole new meaning for kids all over America. Hugh Moore's invention had now come almost full circle, from selling a cup of water, to selling just the cup, to selling a cup of ice cream. From a simple idea and invention, he developed a large, diverse, and imaginative business.

These etchings clearly show why public drinking troughs were considered unsanitary and eventually outlawed.

FOUNTAIN ERECTED IN UNION SQUARE.—Sketched by Stanley Fox.—[See Page 473.]

Fantasy Inventions

The concern for health that turned Hugh Moore's water dispenser into a booming cup (and then ice cream) business has grown even greater, showing a continuing need for healthier products.

GERM DETECTORS. Small tape tabs that change color to warn that harmful germs are present. Can be placed on kitchen shelves and in bathroom cabinets.

GERM ERASER. A specially treated dusting cloth that also eliminates germs.

GERM FOOD. An air-spray substance that germs ingest; it causes them to enlarge to thousands of times their normal size so they can be seen and destroyed.

GERM-FREE CUP AND TOOTHBRUSH HOLDER. An enclosed holder for bathroom cups and toothbrushes that sterilizes them for the next use.

GERM-EATING INSECTS. A specially-bred insect that is nearly invisible to humans and feeds on harmful germs.

The Invention of
Kellogg's Corn Flakes

Inventing requires both recognizing a good idea and developing it.

During the mid-1800s, a religious group called the Seventh-Day Adventists settled in Battle Creek, Michigan, bringing with them a strict dietary code that forbade the use of tobacco, liquor, tea, coffee, or patent medicines. The Adventists were also vegetarians, eating meals that consisted primarily of vegetables and grains. Their "biological living" diet and exercise methods served to promote good health, and the reputation of Battle Creek as a health center spread. People with health problems ranging from nervousness to indigestion traveled to Battle Creek, seeking a cure with the Adventists' diet. By 1866 the Adventist community had established the Western Health Reform Institute, where many of these visitors were treated.

One of the Adventist families living in Battle Creek was named Kellogg, and of the fourteen Kellogg children, two brothers were soon to make the family name a household word. John Harvey Kellogg was an especially bright student, and after completing his training as a doctor, he returned to Battle Creek to practice medicine.

John did not forget his Adventist training and he diligently combined his dietary beliefs with conventional medical practices. Using himself as a test case, Dr. Kellogg would mix up concoctions of natural grains and fruits and assess their effect on his ability to "feel healthy and think clearly."

Sometime between 1876 and 1878, Dr. Kellogg was named director of the Western Health Reform Institute, and he immediately began using some of his new dietary formulas on his patients. John Kellogg also changed the name of the institute to the Battle Creek Sanitarium, and he hired his younger brother, Will Keith Kellogg, as an administrative assistant. Although John was the more dynamic personality, devoting much of his time to surgery, lectures, research, and travel, Will Kellogg was the better businessman.

Visitors to the Battle Creek "San" were taught Dr. Kellogg's rules of good diet, but the monotonous and bland vegetarian meals often caused the patients to leave after only a short stay (or to sneak off down the block to the Red Onion Cafe for meals of steaks and chops).

Aware that his non-Adventist patients were not accustomed to such a limited diet, Dr. Kellogg, assisted by his brother, set up a food laboratory in the sanitarium kitchen and went about trying to create new and more flavorful processes for preparing wheat, corn, oats, rice, and other healthful grains. At night, the Kellogg brothers would meet in the laboratory to boil, bake, steam, and press various grains, trying to create a better flavor or a different texture. Before long, the vegetarian menu at the San included substitutes for beef, veal, pork, chicken, and coffee, all made from grains and vegetables.

Their next attempt was to invent a low-starch, whole-grain bread by first boiling the wheat. One evening, in the middle of a wheat-cooking experiment, both Kelloggs were unexpectedly called away on an important business matter. It was nearly two days before they returned to the experiment and found a pot of soggy boiled wheat that had been cooked much too

Inventor Dr. John Harvey Kellogg (l.) and his brother W. K. Kellogg.

long. However, they just picked up where they had left off and processed the wheat-mush through flattening rollers. They were astonished at the results. Instead of the sticky flat sheets they had been getting for weeks, each individual wheat berry had formed into a small flake. When the flakes were toasted, to dry them out, the result was not a new bread at all but a new, prepared, ready-to-eat cereal. The toasted wheat flakes became yet another innovative food at the San, soon to be followed by rice flakes and the patients' favorite, corn flakes. Dr. Kellogg had discovered and perfected the procedure of "tempering" grain, and in 1894 he received a patent for his process.

Dr. Kellogg had no intention of selling his

new food invention, but patients leaving the San to return home frequently requested supplies to take with them. And when those portions were consumed, they sent orders requesting more. To accommodate his patients, Dr. Kellogg and his brother Will set up a small company to manufacture their health food products and fill requests by mail order. Under the able management of Will Keith Kellogg, the Sanitas Food Company made enough money to support John Kellogg's experiments and even turn a small profit.

In 1891, thirty-seven-year-old Charles W. Post came to the Battle Creek Sanitarium to recover from a stretch of poor health. C. W. Post was an inventor who already had several patents to his credit, but he was still not a very successful man. Post could recognize a marketable product and knew the vast potential of advertising. When he saw the Kellogg brothers' food manufacturing operation and mail-order business, he immedi-

C.W. Post's original factory, from 1895, shown in front of a more modern General Foods plant, and an early advertisement for the Postum cereal beverage.

ately wanted to strike up a deal. The product that impressed Post the most was Dr. Kellogg's cereal substitute for coffee beans. But Kellogg shunned the idea of a commercial food venture. He thought that the good name of the sanitarium should not be exploited and confused with any other business, and certainly not used in advertising.

C. W. Post was convinced that if he could not use the sanitarium name, then at least the name of Battle Creek and its association with health foods would be a great boon in marketing a line of healthful food products. Post left the San to start his own retreat for the "treatment of persons afflicted with nervous prostration and over-

The Kellogg's main competitor, C.W. Post.

work"; and in 1894, with less than $70, he set up a factory in another section of Battle Creek and began producing his own cereal formula for a coffee substitute he called Postum. C. W. Post took nearly every dollar of profits and put it back into advertising his product: "Do you suffer from coffee headaches? Take Postum." Post's strongest slogan was "Postum makes red blood."

In the winter, Post's business was strong, but in the heat of summer, people preferred cool drinks and the Postum business fell off sharply. Post therefore decided to introduce a second product, a breakfast cereal, which would not be as seasonal as a hot drink. In 1897 Post introduced

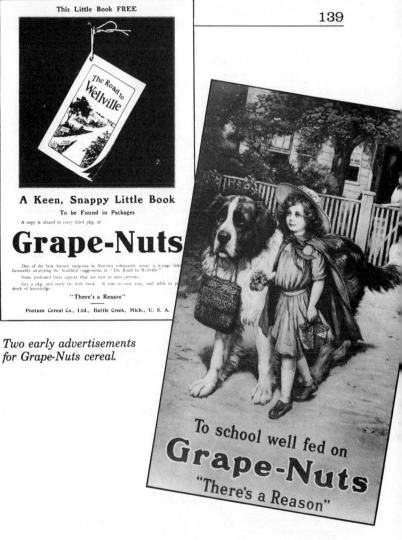

Two early advertisements for Grape-Nuts cereal.

An inside view of the Grape-Nuts production line.

Grape-Nuts, a crunchy nugget cereal made from processed wheat and barley and baked in the form of bread sticks. Although the cereal contained neither grapes nor nuts, the "Grape Nuts" name came from Post's belief that "grape sugar" was formed during the baking process, and the fact that the cereal had a nutty crunch. Post's advertising claimed that Grape-Nuts "helped the appendix, malaria, loose teeth, and

CEREAL SELECTOR

Invent your own favorite cereals from thousands of possible combinations. Have freshly made cereal every day.

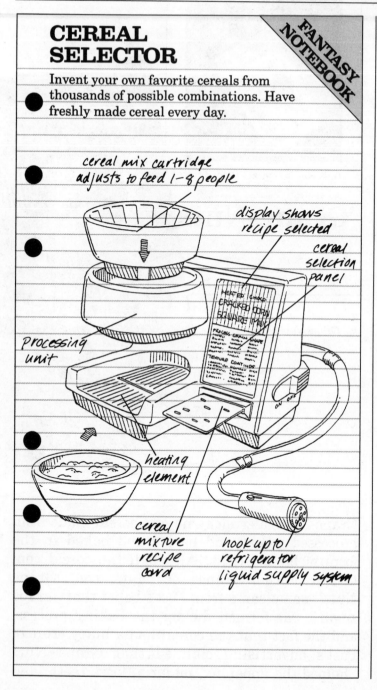

cereal mix cartridge adjusts to feed 1-8 people

display shows recipe selected

cereal selection panel

processing unit

heating element

cereal mixture recipe cord

hook up to refrigerator

liquid supply system

the brain." Every box of Grape-Nuts cereal contained a pamphlet entitled "The Road to Wellville." In less than seven years, Post's cereals made him a millionaire.

By now, many other cereal companies were being started in Battle Creek, also trying to take advantage of the town's ever-growing reputation as a health-food center. New breakfast cereals with such strange names as "Tryachewa," "Tryabita," "Nutrita," "Maple Flakes," "Cero-Fruito," and "My Food" were being produced by forty-two independent food companies. Although the Kellogg brothers were also producing breakfast cereals, they continued to shy away from commercial sales to anyone but their former patients. But Will Kellogg had watched Post's business grow and he was becoming eager to compete. So in 1906 W. K. Kellogg set up a separate business called the "Battle Creek Toasted Corn Flake Company." His brother John objected, and even though they had been partners in several food inventions, the two men decided to go their own ways. Will paid John for his share of the corn flake invention and, with other money he had raised, started an aggressive advertising program: "Kellogg's Toasted Corn Flakes, the Sweetheart of the Corn."

The corn flake business grew rapidly as Will continued to improve his product and expand his advertising. He assumed that, since there were more healthy people than ill ones, he should advertise corn flakes as good to eat and not just as a health food. To back his claims, Kellogg added salt and sugar to his boxed cereals so his customers could taste the difference between corn flakes and bland, unsweetened "health" cereals. And to make sure that he was associated with the new product, Kellogg had his name printed in big red letters on the front of every cereal box with this slogan: "The Original Bears This Signature, W. K. Kellogg."

As another promotional gimmick, Will Kellogg decided to market the cereal products to children by tempting them with contests, cutouts, package inserts, prizes, and giveaways on the panels of the cereal box. He also tempted parents by advertising new recipes using corn

Two Kellogg's Corn Flakes ads, bearing the familiar authenticating signature of W. K. Kellogg.

Fantasy Inventions

Food is something so basic to everyday life that we often take it for granted, but, like Will Kellogg, the inventor who can produce or package differently new kinds of food is bound to tap a market as big as the world itself.

VITAMIN CHEWING GUM. Enjoy the flavor and the fun of chewing while getting the daily vitamins and minerals you need.

LEFTOVER FOODS REPROCESSOR. Converts leftover table and cooking scraps into healthful foods—such as roasted beef puffs or crispy shredded liver.

DINNER TABLE CONDIMENT BAR. Handily dispenses ketchup, mustard, steak sauce, salad dressing, honey, duck sauce, and other condiments through a controlled-flow tube nozzle.

QUICK SLEEP BODY RECHARGER. A specially formulated before-bed cereal that allows the body to get a complete night's sleep in half the time.

flakes and offering premiums for collected cereal boxtops.

The corn flake business grew rapidly, soon making W. K. Kellogg and his investors very wealthy. As Kellogg invented and introduced new cereal products, he continued to follow the guidelines that had given him his initial success: produce a high-quality product, have an easily recognized trademark, and advertise aggressively. Today, of the twenty or so cereals produced by the Kellogg company, the original favorite, corn flakes, is still the most popular. The San was taken over by the federal government during World War II, and still serves as a hospital.

The Invention of
Howard Johnson's Restaurants

Inventors who anticipate future needs will be first to fulfill them.

In 1925 Howard Johnson was deeply in debt, but his positive attitude toward business and a persistent belief in his own ideas would enable him to become the founder of one of the world's largest restaurant chains.

Howard Johnson's father left a business debt of nearly $20,000 when he died, and the proud young Johnson was determined to pay it off completely and clear his father's name. At age twenty-seven, hoping to improve his income, Howard Johnson went even further into debt and borrowed $500 to take over a small drugstore in Wollaston, Massachusetts, that included a soda fountain and newspaper stand. At first the store lost money and things got even worse, but Johnson had big ideas and a little bit of money left to try some of them out.

When he had taken over the store, the soda fountain offered only three flavors of ice cream—the standard vanilla, chocolate, and strawberry—and it wasn't even very good. Johnson wanted to expand the selections, but he didn't want to serve inferior commercial ice cream. Using an old-fashioned hand-cranked ice cream freezer in the

Simple Simon and the Pieman, the famous logo associated for years with Howard Johnson's roadside restaurants.

basement of his shop, Johnson began developing his own formulas for quality ice cream. After cranking out dozens of batches of interesting flavors and textures, he settled on a recipe calling for twice as much rich butterfat as the commercial mix, and he used only natural ingredients and flavors. As the reputation of Howard Johnson's ice cream spread through the community, customers stood in line to try each new specialty. The little drugstore had turned into an ice cream parlor.

The demand for Howard Johnson's ice cream led to expansion, and within a year Johnson was selling ice cream at small stands at nearby beaches. In three years, the ice cream business had done so well that Johnson had completely paid off his father's debt as well as his own small loan. By now, the ice cream parlor had become a full-fledged restaurant, serving hot dogs, hamburgers, and other easily prepared foods. With his profits, Johnson decided to open a second restaurant in nearby Quincy, Massachusetts.

It was at this point that Howard Johnson's dream—to own a large chain of restaurants— began to take shape. But the year was 1929. The Great Depression had begun, and his restaurants were losing money. Yet even then, Johnson could see that the country was headed for a new era of better roads and better cars, with more people on the highways looking for comfortable and friendly places to stop, rest, and eat. He also saw that, rather than taking a chance at any old "greasy spoon," the traveler would want to eat at a place with predictably "good food at sensible prices."

Using his own two restaurants as learning and testing laboratories, Howard Johnson developed his own techniques and formulas for processing food so he'd be ready to start up his

The original Howard Johnson's drugstore in Wollaston, Massachusetts.

restaurant chain when the economy improved. Johnson was confident that he had created a formula for success that could be applied to any restaurant business, but when he was ready, he didn't have the money to make his dream come true. Not letting this stand in his way, he came up with another new idea—franchising.

His brilliant concept was to sell his techniques to other restaurants. The restaurant owner would use Howard Johnson's name in exchange for a fee and would buy the special-formula Howard Johnson foods to serve.

The first person to franchise was a restaurant owner on Cape Cod. The idea worked well for both businessmen, and in a short time Johnson was making similar agreements with other restaurant owners. The Howard Johnson reputation began to grow, supplying an image of "instant good repute" for every new franchise that opened.

Howard Johnson's dream of a chain of roadside restaurants was beginning to come true. In an attempt to catch the eye of passing motorists, he conceived the idea of painting the roofs of his restaurants bright orange. Apparently the gimmick worked, and by 1935 there were seventeen roadside Howard Johnson's restaurants in Massachusetts. During the next five years, the number grew to more than one hundred, and the restaurant chain had spread along the Atlantic Coast all the way down to Florida.

Howard Johnson's restaurants not only looked alike; the traveler could also expect the same quality service and food wherever he went. And to help convey the image of a family restaurant, Johnson added another attention-getting gimmick—the stylized picture of Simple Simon and the Pieman of Mother Goose fame. It was only natural that when the first turnpike opened in 1940, it was Howard Johnson who opened the first turnpike restaurant.

The Howard Johnson franchise continued to expand until World War II brought on the rationing of food and gasoline. Travel restrictions kept customers away from Johnson's roadside restaurants, and those that did have customers had difficulty getting food. Most of the Howard Johnson franchises either went broke or closed, and the company faced bankruptcy. But Howard Johnson figured that if his restaurant techniques worked well for the private sector, then they would work well for the military also. So to keep his company alive, he began providing food to military installations, defense plants, and schools. When the war ended, most of the restaurants were reopened, and many more new ones were built.

An inside view of an early Howard Johnson's soda fountain.

POP OUT PACKAGING

Cleverly designed packages dispense things one by one, giving you only as much as you need.

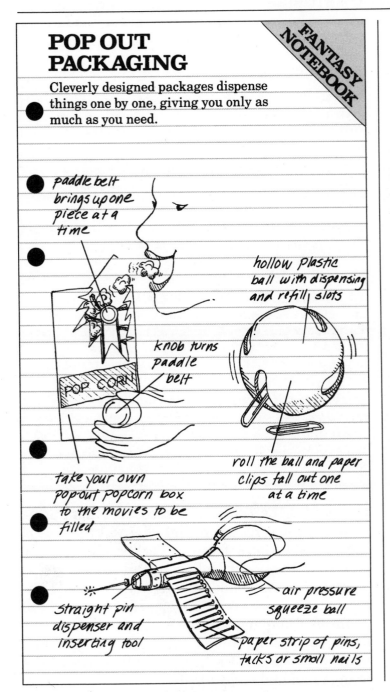

paddle belt brings up one piece at a time

hollow plastic ball with dispensing and refill slots

POP CORN

knob turns paddle belt

take your own pop-out popcorn box to the movies to be filled

roll the ball and paper clips fall out one at a time

straight pin dispenser and inserting tool

air pressure squeeze ball

paper strip of pins, tacks or small nails

This was the standard design for Howard Johnson's restaurants in the 1920s and 30s. The restaurant shown here is from Mineola, New York, in 1933.

Howard Johnson's vision of a motoring public had become reality. By the 1950s, turnpikes with Howard Johnson's restaurants stretched across the country linking nearly every state, and it was only natural that Howard Johnson's should expand once again and go into the lodging business. In 1954 the first Howard Johnson's Motor Lodge opened next to a Howard Johnson's restaurant in Savannah, Georgia. Using the same franchise technique that had built his restaurant business, Johnson began issuing licenses for his motor lodges. The convenience of a one-stop eating and sleeping facility—and the confidence in the Howard Johnson name—obviously suited many traveling Americans, especially families.

In 1972 Howard D. Johnson died, leaving the business to his son, Howard B. Johnson, with the inspiring words "Make it grow." The younger Johnson had grown up learning every facet of the business, taking business trips with his father,

Fantasy Inventions

Howard Johnson was able to anticipate future needs relating to both eating and travel. These ideas may help you think along the same lines as he, to "cater" to dining and travel needs for the future.

SINGLE-EATER TABLE. A restaurant table for the lone eater with a computer TV companion. Eater selects the subject of discussion or the entertainment desired.

SOUVENIR PHOTO MACHINE. Travelers stopping at highway restaurants or rest areas can get a souvenir photo of themselves against the local background with the appropriate description and date—"Taken at Polly's Pancakes in the White Mountains of New Hampshire, October 1985."

BUSINESSMAN'S RESTAURANT TABLE. Has a built-in telephone, tape recorder, computer and calculator, notepads, and other business necessities. The waiter or waitress also serves as a secretary.

RESTAURANT TABLE TV. To watch food being prepared in the kitchen, or to call up descriptions of the dishes on the menu.

DATING RESTAURANTS. Describe to the maître d' the type of person you are looking for, and you will meet a dining companion who is looking for someone like you.

GRAFFITI TABLETOPS. So patrons can leave their marks or messages. When tabletop is completely covered it is removed and becomes restaurant wall decoration.

HIGHWAY RADIO NETWORK. Consistent radio programming at the same place on the dial no matter where you are traveling.

HIGHWAY SERVICE CENTERS. Provide banking, car repair, recreation, health clinic, baby-sitting, movies, and other services for the away-from-home traveler.

PERSONALLY YOURS STORE. A store that specializes in personalizing products. Put your name, initials, message, graphic design on bags, jeans, stationery, clothing, body parts, cars, using tattoos, stickers, rubber stamps, silk screening, heat transfers, carving, printing, engraving.

EATING-BY-THE-HOUR RESTAURANTS. For people who want to sit and talk as well as eat. Charges are per person based on the period of time the table is occupied. There are no additional charges for food.

attending company meetings, and working at a variety of restaurant jobs during school vacations. With an education from Yale University and the Harvard Business School, Howard B. Johnson was well equipped to take over. He opened new chains of Red Coach Grilles and Ground Round Restaurants, but he still paid great attention to the original Howard Johnson's. For a better focus on future growth, Johnson commissioned a research company to analyze the reasons for the company's success. Their report included one conclusion that changed the face of Howard Johnson's forever. The painted orange roof that the elder Johnson had hoped would attract motorists had become one of the best-recognized logos ever developed. The Howard Johnson Company promptly dropped its trademark of Simple Simon and the Pieman, and instead substituted a stylized silhouette of the orange roof and spire.

The Invention of
Life Savers Candy

Every product has a market waiting to be found.

In 1913 Clarence Crane, a chocolate candy manufacturer in Cleveland, Ohio, was having a problem with his product. During the hot summer months his chocolates became soft and often melted into gooey blobs while being shipped to other cities, so candy shops would stop ordering the chocolates until the weather became cool again in the fall.

To get back some of the lost business, Crane decided that during the summer he would offer a hard candy that wouldn't melt during shipment or in the store. Crane tinkered and experimented with a machine originally designed for making medicine pills in the shape of little 0's. The result was a round hard candy with a hole in the center.

Even though Crane put a hole in the candy just to be different, he soon realized that the 0-shaped mints looked much like the life savers used to rescue people from the water. The comparison seemed obvious, so Crane adopted the name and called his hard candy "Life Savers."

Crane then designed the first Life Saver package, using a round paperboard tube to hold a stack of the candies, and printed a label wrapper depicting an old seaman tossing a ship's life saver to a young woman swimmer. He also coined a promotional slogan to help market his product to

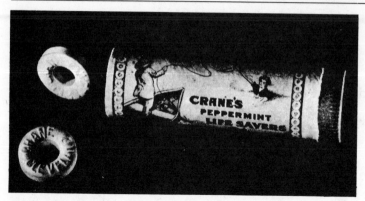

The original 1913 paperboard tube package of Life Savers, which nearly wrecked the product because it didn't keep the mints fresh.

candy shops, "Crane's Peppermint Life Savers... 5¢ ...For that Stormy Breath." But Crane considered Life Savers only a part-time summer business, and he had no intention of taking the innovation any further.

Meanwhile, Edward John Noble, a young New York salesman of streetcar and trolley advertising space (like the ads seen on city buses and in subway cars today) thought differently. He had spotted the Life Saver package in a candy store and on impulse he bought a roll of the candy mints. Noble was so impressed with the taste, as well as the clever Life Saver shape, name, and package, that he

Life Savers' master marketer, Edward John Noble.

took a train to Cleveland to sell Clarence Crane on the idea of advertising the new product in New York's trolley cars.

Noble enthusiastically tried to convince Crane that if he would only "spend some money advertising those mints" he would "make a fortune." But Crane wasn't convinced and he still insisted that his real business was chocolates, not Life Savers!

Edward Noble persisted, so Crane, thinking that he would finally get rid of the salesman, sarcastically suggested that he buy the mint candy idea—along with the converted pill machine—advertise it, and get rich. Noble agreeably asked how much, and Crane, caught off guard, arbitrarily picked the price of $5,000. Noble would have jumped immediately at that offer, but he didn't have anywhere near that much money. He therefore went back to New York and talked the deal over with his longtime friend J. Roy Allen. Together they were able to raise only $3,800, but, being a convincing and determined salesman, Noble got Crane to lower his price to $2,900—leaving $900 for the partners to start the Life Saver Candy Company.

However, what should have been the beginning of success for the two young entrepreneurs quickly became a near-total disaster. As fate would have it, that first roll of Life Savers sampled by Noble tasted good because it was fresh. Only after he purchased the business did Noble discover that the candy went stale after sitting on a store's shelf for only a week or so. In addition, the paperboard tube package absorbed much of the peppermint flavor and gave the candy the taste of the paper wrapper. The partners sadly

One example of the distinctive methods used by Noble to advertise and market his product.

PROMOTIONAL PLANTS

FANTASY NOTEBOOK

Specially bred plants produce leaves or stems with advertising or company logos. A great advertising gimmick that lives on for a long time.

McDonald's Jade Plant

Kodak Palm

Nabisco Geranium

realized that there were thousands of flavorless rolls of Life Savers in candy stores all across America.

Undaunted, Noble immediately devised a tinfoil wrapping to keep the candy flavor fresh, but the store owners who had already been stuck with the original stale candy wanted no more. The best that Noble could do was to exchange the merchants' old stock of Life Savers for his new flavor-tight package.

Noble still strongly believed that, just like himself, anyone who tasted a Life Saver for the first time would immediately be hooked and become a loyal customer. And so to promote his idea, he spent his evenings wrapping up small sample bags of his mints and had them passed out free on street corners.

The brisk business that Noble had envisioned was just not working out, and most of the

An early Life Savers counter display from 1913.

money that kept the candy company going came from the salary of his advertising job, which he had wisely held on to. It was probably fortunate that Noble was more an advertising man than a candy maker. He thought that there was no reason why Life Savers had to be sold only in candy shops, so he began promoting the mints in other types of stores, including barber shops, restaurants, and drugstores. He convinced saloon owners to sell Life Savers alongside the free cloves they supplied to their departing customers, and Life Savers became the first nonsmoking item to be carried by one chain of cigar stores. Noble's marketing plan was simple but clever: he would tell his new customers to "put the mints near the cash register with a big 5¢ price card, then be sure every customer gets a nickel with his change, and see what happens."

Selling merchandise from a display carton near the register (today called counter merchandising) was the turning point for Life Savers. Most people did not come into a store specifically to buy Life Savers, but when at the register with

change in hand they would often be impulsive and buy a roll. The sales of Life Savers began to grow rapidly and Noble was finally making money from his candy business. And as the little round candy with the hole caught on, the mints quickly acquired several other uses—to flavor tea, decorate Christmas trees, and even to hold candles on birthday cakes.

With Noble's success other candy makers discovered that counter displays were also good for selling their "impulse items," and the space around the register began to get crowded with all kinds of merchandise, including several other candies. To avoid having to compete for the best counter space, Noble designed and built a large counter display (called a "merchandiser") that would hold all the other candy makers'

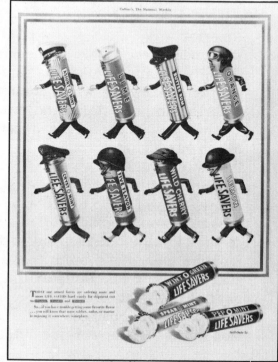

This clever Life Savers advertisement was used during World War I to promote the fact that the Armed Forces were a large consumer of Life Savers.

An inside view of a Life Savers factory and another one of Edward Noble's imaginative promotional gimmicks.

products—and of course display his own Life Savers right up front.

But Edward Noble didn't rely on his counter display to sell his candy mints. After all, he was an advertising man at heart, with a simple philosophy: "Make someone smile or laugh and they are more likely to buy your product." And so the typical Life Saver ad described the candy by using jokes and puns like "enjoy-mint," "hole-some," "content-mint," and "refresh-mint."

Life Saver candies with the patented hole are still very popular today, and the Life Saver counter display, like the original with the mints up front, can still be found by store registers. All that has really changed is the candy flavors. New flavors are always being tested, and those that don't sell well are eventually dropped. But de-

Fantasy Inventions

Edward Noble was able to draw on a catchy name, a fun, impulse-oriented product, and clever packaging and marketing—all good themes for you to consider in your inventions.

LIFE SAVER CHANGE. A cash register drawer that uses 1¢-, 5¢-, 10¢-, and 25¢-size Life Savers for change instead of coins.

NAMES FOR SALE. A business that creates marketable company names and product names and offers them for sale.

GOURMET TASTE SAMPLER. Each candy in the roll is the flavor of a special gourmet food.

PLEASURE PRODUCTS CATALOG. State your areas of interest and the computer shopping catalog offers items of food, clothing, books, trips, and products that are selected just for you.

FANTASY FLAVOR DREAMS. Specific candy flavors and aromas re-create pleasant memories. Pine tree aroma brings back summer camp or a walk in the woods, cotton candy and popcorn flavors provide memories of the circus.

SMELL PICTURES. An instant film that also records the smell of the environment so you can later see *and* smell what you photographed.

TV SAMPLER CHANNEL. Previews shows coming up on all other channels.

LIFE SAVER JEWELRY. Bracelets, rings, barrettes, pins, and other jewelry are made of hard candy wrapped in a decorative gold- or silver-colored foil. Wear the jewelry and then eat it.

spite new and changing tastes, the original Pep-O-Mint remains the most popular.

The Invention of
Milk Bottles

Marketing is often the true key to the success of an invention.

Since long before recorded history, people have enjoyed animal milk as a nutritious food. Even primitive cultures were known to domesticate various types of animals so that they could drink their milk or convert it into other dairy products such as cheese and butter. The first containers used to collect and store milk were the same as those used for any type of liquid—skin bags. The bag was a form of pouch sewn from animal skins that also contained some type of closure and spout.

More advanced civilizations stored and transported milk (and other liquids) in pottery vessels that were easier to clean and had less chance of becoming contaminated than the skin bags. Also, jugs could be made to hold a much larger quantity of liquid than could a skin bag. In more modern times, metal pails were popular containers in those communities that happened to have a tinsmith.

Many people got their milk from their own cow. However, by the nineteenth century the residents of towns and cities had to buy their milk. Every morning (twice a day during the hot summer), the local dairy farmer would put his fresh milk into 5- or 10-gallon cans and load them onto the back of his horse-drawn wagon. As the dairy-

man came down the street, people would emerge from their houses with some sort of container into which he would ladle out the quantity they wished to buy.

Since there was no refrigeration, it was important that the milk be delivered before it could spoil. The other problem was that the dusty roads and the swarm of insects that usually followed the horse could cause contamination. By the time the milk reached the table it often was in bad condition, and this became quite an issue in many communities. Homemakers and newspaper editors demanded that the dairy farmers do something to ensure that their milk stayed fresh and pure until delivery.

By the 1870 s, some local dairies had begun to use glass jars, and in 1878 the first patent was issued specifically for a milk bottle. The inventor had put a glass lid with a rubber gasket atop a glass jar and then held the two tightly closed with a metal thumb screw. But the closure was considered clumsy and unreliable, and the first milk bottle quickly disappeared from use.

That same year, another inventor patented a milk bottle that looked very much like today's long-necked beer bottle. The closure on this container was made of tin, with a paper gasket, and it was held on to the neck with a crimped wire. However, this and other bottling attempts were just local efforts and their success did not spread beyond the areas that they served.

Several companies tried to popularize the glass milk bottle on a much larger scale, but bottles were still blown by hand and glass products were too expensive to be disposable. Nor did people like the idea of the returnable bottle be-

Hervey D. Thatcher, known as the "father of the milk bottle."

cause, once used, there was no guarantee that it could ever be absolutely clean again—there was no automatic washing or sterilization equipment at that time.

Although there were countless attempts to design and produce various types of milk containers, the one person who receives credit as "father of the milk bottle" is Hervey D. Thatcher. Thatcher, a physician and pharmacist, settled in Potsdam, New York, and went into the drug business. Like many people, he had a cow to provide milk for his family.

With his interest in health care, Thatcher quickly became involved in developing new methods for the sanitary production and care of milk. Soon the work was more than Thatcher could handle by himself, and so he took on a partner, Harvey Barnhart. The first invention of the Thatcher/Barnhart collaboration was a rubber tube that carried the milk from the cow directly to the pail, without human hands touching it.

Fantasy Inventions

There is always a market for clever new ways of preparing and packaging existing products, as Hervey Thatcher proved with his milk bottle.

WINE MAKER BOTTLE. Pour grape juice in the specially lined bottle and overnight the juice ferments to become wine.

SINK FAUCET CARBONATION. Press a button to get carbonated tap water. Instantly make soda and other carbonated drinks.

STRING BEAN PACKAGES. A special fast-growing string bean is placed on the package to be wrapped. When the bean is watered it quickly grows vines around the package, forming a secure wrap. For small packages use a "Spider Web Wrap."

LIGHTPROOF MILK CONTAINERS. So fluorescent light and other artificial lights will not destroy the milk vitamins.

MILK MIXER CUP. Liquid jet action at bottom of cup keeps chocolate and other flavorings well mixed.

TWO-WAY SQUEEZE TUBE. Dispenses substances and sucks back in what isn't used.

They called their milking device the "milk protector," and they immediately incorporated it into their dairy operation. One day Thatcher was visited by one of his former students, who had become a patent expert, and when he saw the milk protectors he encouraged Thatcher to seek a patent. A short time later, around 1884, the patent was issued.

Now Thatcher and Barnhart decided to set up a business selling milk protectors to other dairymen, but first they had to produce the product. Thatcher, being the wealthier of the two, put up $5,000, while Barnhart contributed $1,000 of his savings. Unfortunately Barnhart was an inexperienced businessman, and he almost sank the company with his first decision. He had gone to New York City to find a manufacturer who would produce about 200 of the milk protector tubes. The manufacturer claimed that it would be very expensive to make such a small quantity, about 50¢ apiece, but that if he made 10,000 pieces, he could reduce that price to 10¢ apiece.

Barnhart thought it would surely be shrewd to take the lower price, and he was confident that the product would sell like hotcakes. So he returned to the Potsdam farm with a signed contract for 10,000 milk protector tubes plus a lot of milk pails and covers that he also intended to sell to farmers.

At a retail price of $3.00, the milk protectors didn't sell at all, and Barnhart began to lose confidence. He was nervous about losing his money and tried to convince Thatcher that they should lower the price and maybe just try to break even. But Thatcher wanted to hold out, and he offered to give Barnhart back his $1,000 and take over the company if Barnhart would continue to work for him. With great relief Barnhart agreed, and then with renewed enthusiasm Thatcher set out to discover why the product wasn't selling.

He discovered that although the farmers understood the necessity of keeping the milk clean, they were afraid that their customers would not even know about their efforts, let alone appreciate them. And since the milk was still being ladled out to customers by local merchants or street vendors, they felt it really didn't make any difference how many precautions they took. An investment that increased the cost of the product was not considered worthwhile unless the customer knew what he was paying for.

With that explanation fresh in his mind, Hervey Thatcher saw something that inspired him to invent and distribute a milk bottle. In the summer of 1884, as legend has it, Thatcher was taking a walk down a street where the local

The first milk bottle, with glass closure, and an early advertisement for Hervey Thatcher's Milk Protector system, both bearing the slogan "Absolutely Pure Milk."

dairyman was ladling milk into a jug being held by a woman. Suddenly the woman's three-year-old daughter accidentally dropped her dirty and tattered rag doll right into the milkman's pail. The little girl shrieked and the milkman quickly picked the doll from the milk. He could not afford to throw away the contaminated milk, so he went on his way and hoped no one else had seen what happened. But to Thatcher the incident confirmed what the farmers had said—that even though they could guarantee fresh milk from the cow to the pail, they had little control over the way the merchants handled it.

Then Thatcher had an idea. If he could sell the dairy farmer a milk *system* that consisted of his milk protectors plus glass bottles, then people could see how much more sanitary the product was. The farmer could advertise that he used sanitary means to milk the cow, and the customer could see the purity in the glass bottles.

Thatcher was something of a woodcraftsman, so he went to the lathe and turned a wood pattern for a milk bottle and lid. After filing for a patent on his new bottle design, he went to a New York glass company to see about having it made. With a few modifications to aid in production, Thatcher had a quantity of the handmade bottles manufactured to sell with his milking system. His first sales call was to the largest dairy farmer in Ogdensburg, New York, next to his hometown of Potsdam. It was not difficult to convince the dairyman that the Thatcher milk protectors and bottles would greatly benefit the customer and thus the dairyman who advertised his sanitary system. Thatcher also argued that individual bottles of milk would ensure that each customer got just the right amount of cream. He had almost sold his first system when the dairyman asked which other farmers in the area he might be selling to. When Thatcher replied, "Anyone who is interested," the farmer refused to buy, saying that if everyone supplied a superior product then he would have no advantage. Thatcher then went on to the next-largest dairy farmer in town, and the next and the next, and at each stop he got the same response: "If other farmers are going to use it, then I don't want it." But Hervey Thatcher was learning to become a businessman, and he realized that to sell his sanitary milk system he was going to have to try a different

The classic milk bottle shape lives on in the form of a carry-out restaurant located in Massachusetts.

approach. He returned to the first farmer and offered him a new proposal. The farmer would receive the exclusive right to use his patented products (for the seventeen-year life of the patent) if he was willing to pay a $50 licensing fee and buy all of his bottling and milk protector supplies from Thatcher. Thatcher agreed that he would not sell his milking system to any other dairyman in the area of the farmer's distribution. The two men agreed to a deal and Thatcher walked away with an order for $418 worth of merchandise. Thatcher applied the same marketing technique to other towns and was soon pulling in enough orders to hire two road salesmen. The Thatcher milk system found takers in every town, and Hervey Thatcher was convinced that his sanitary milk bottle would soon completely replace the dairyman's tin milk pail and ladle.

To help promote his products, Thatcher had designed his milk bottle to include the molded image of a cow being milked by a dignified man in a suit and fancy top hat, and the embossed inscription "Absolutely Pure Milk." In August 1884, the first batch of bottles was manufactured and shipped to the Ogdensburg dairyman. Thatcher personally delivered a supply of milk protectors and instructed the farmhands in their use. The next day, the dairy filled the bottles with clean, fresh milk and secured a glass cap to each one. Because the bottles were breakable, the dairyman placed them in a bed of hay on the wagon. By the time the driver reached his first customer, he was in for a big surprise. The jostling of the wagon had not caused the bottles to break, but it had caused quite a bit of leakage—the closures were not quite leakproof. The driver returned to the dairy to fill up his half-empty bottles, but the results on his second trip were the same. The farmer was furious, thinking that Thatcher had cheated him, but an adequate temporary seal was quickly developed and Thatcher's milk bottle survived.

By 1890 Thatcher had sold his interest in the company to Harvey Barnhart and his brother Sam. Thatcher went on to produce a number of other inventions, including, in 1896, a "disposable paper milk bottle," an invention years ahead of its time.

The Barnharts continued to develop a better seal for the bottles, creating a dense paper-fiber cap that was pressed into the neck. Called the "common sense bottle," the paper cap made the bottle virtually leakproof, which quieted many of the complaints from customers. The milk bottle business had now taken hold and soon a number of competitors entered the business. The Thatcher Manufacturing Company responded with an aggressive advertising campaign, claiming to produce the "handsomest, cheapest, and best milk bottle ever offered for sale in the market," and managed to stay one step ahead of the competition.

The company was sold again around 1900 to Frances E. Baldwin and his associates, with Harvey Barnhart as their General Manager in Potsdam. Thatcher Manufacturing Company went on to great success, while Hervey Thatcher himself continued his inventing. But his first invention was by far his most successful—so much so that when automatic glass-blowing machines were introduced, the first machine-made bottles were milk bottles.

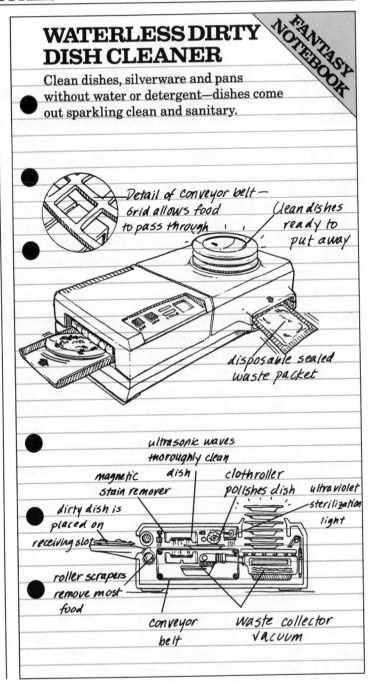

FANTASY NOTEBOOK

WATERLESS DIRTY DISH CLEANER

Clean dishes, silverware and pans without water or detergent—dishes come out sparkling clean and sanitary.

Detail of conveyor belt— Grid allows food to pass through

Clean dishes ready to put away

disposable sealed waste packet

ultrasonic waves thoroughly clean dish

magnetic stain remover

clothroller polishes dish

ultraviolet sterilization light

dirty dish is placed on receiving slot

roller scrapers remove most food

conveyor belt

Waste collector vacuum

The Invention of
Drinking Straws

Look at designs in nature for solutions to invention problems.

In 1888 Marvin Stone was a manufacturer of paper cigarette holders, with a factory in Washington, D.C. After work, he would frequently walk down the block to the local tavern and stop in for his usual drink, a mint julep.

To Marvin, the process of making a good mint julep was a science, and it was especially important to keep the drink chilled. When warmed, a mint julep loses its flavor, so people would drink them through natural grass straws so their hands wouldn't need to touch the glass. These natural straws were cut from the hollow stalks of common wild grass, usually rye. Unfortunately, natural straw was a far from satisfactory solution because it tended to make the drink taste like grass. What's more, the reusable pieces of straw would crack and get dusty when dried—hardly a fitting accompaniment to a fine, well-made mint julep.

Stone saw a connection between the process for making his paper cigarette holders and the possibility of making a paper-wound artificial drinking straw. Excited by the prospect of having an even better tasting mint julep, he started testing his idea by winding long thin strips of paper around a pencil and fastening the loose end with a dab of glue to keep the paper from unwind-

An etching of a Virginia hotel bar from 1861, which includes a man sipping a mint julep through a natural grass straw.

ing. Stone made several of these artificial straws and had the tavern bartender hold them for his personal use. Soon other patrons noticed Stone using his paper tube straws and wanted to try them for their own mint juleps.

Lemonade was also a very popular drink in the late 1800s, and Stone reasoned that people would enjoy drinking lemonade through a straw as much as he enjoyed sucking away at his mint julep. So he designed an 8½-inch paper straw with a diameter just wide enough to prevent a lemon seed from getting lodged in the tube. He used a paraffin-coated manila paper so the straw would not become soggy when put in liquids.

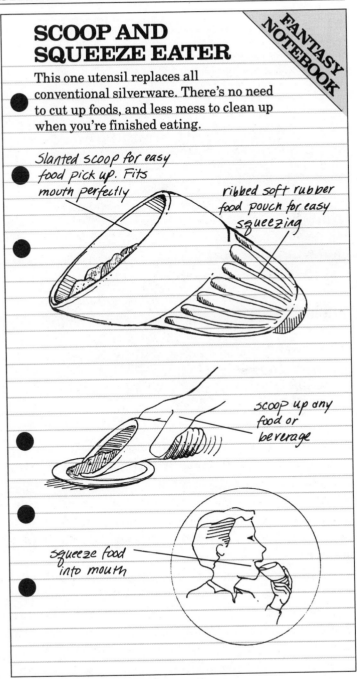

FANTASY NOTEBOOK

SCOOP AND SQUEEZE EATER

This one utensil replaces all conventional silverware. There's no need to cut up foods, and less mess to clean up when you're finished eating.

Slanted scoop for easy food pick up. Fits mouth perfectly

ribbed soft rubber food pouch for easy squeezing

scoop up any food or beverage

squeeze food into mouth

Recognizing the universal appeal of his invention, Stone patented his drinking straw and suggested that it be used for all types of beverages. Stone's straws quickly became so much in demand (and fun to use) that even the railroads began carrying "lemonade straws" for their passengers.

By 1890 most of the employees at the Stone Cigarette Holder Factory were winding artificial straws. Stone's Drinking Straws were selling faster each month, and Stone had to move and enlarge his plant several times. Marvin Stone died in 1898, but the Stone Paper Tube Company

(as it was then called) continued to make straws and improve the product. By 1906 the first machine-made drinking straws were being manufactured with a steam-powered engine that was later redesigned and used to make all kinds of paper-wound tubes, such as those in the center of rolls of paper towels.

Despite the fact that Marvin Stone also invented a pencil sharpener, a fountain pen holder, and sundry other items, it was the invention of the artificial drinking straw that gave him his claim to fame. Nine years after patenting the first artificial straw, Stone obtained another patent on a "double-barrel" straw that presumably let you drink twice as much or twice as fast. But it seems to have passed into oblivion.

Since then several newer types of drinking straws have also come and, mostly, gone. Plastic

straws, which don't kink, and bendable straws have been the winners, but others, such as flavored straws, loop-the-loop straws, and drinking glasses with the straw built in have not remained popular. In many ways, this illustrates that once the most truly useful purpose for an item has been identified, it is almost impossible to improve on it, and variations will go the way of all fads after a brief flash of popularity.

Straws make any drink more enjoyable, with no tell-tale signs of soda moustaches to cause embarrassment on important dates.

Fantasy Inventions

These fantasy ideas focus on imaginative kinds of straws, but they also cover new ways of serving food, along with special kinds of foods.

FOOD BITE SIZER. Chops solid foods into the proper size for small children to eat. Can be used on meats, fruits, vegetables, or any prepared food.

ICE STRAWS. A double-walled drinking straw with ice insulation. The beverage is cooled as it is sucked through the cold straw. Eliminates the need to refrigerate drinks.

PUMP STRAW. Automatically does the sucking.

VITAMIN STRAW. Inside surface of the straw is coated with vitamins. Drinking through the disposable straw provides the minimum daily vitamin requirement.

TEMPERATURE-REGULATED SPOON. So the food that goes into your mouth is always at the perfect temperature.

FLAVOR LINER STRAWS. Inside surface of the disposable straw is coated with a specific taste (chocolate, strawberry, banana) to flavor the drink.

REFRIGERATOR STRAWS. These protrude from the refrigerator door and are connected to beverage containers inside. You can conveniently get a drink without opening the door.

STOMACH BYPASS VALVE. A surgically implanted on/off valve that can bypass the stomach once the food has been tasted and swallowed. Great for dieters and people who like extra desserts.

FEEL-FULL SNACKS. Just a few bites will expand in your stomach so you feel full. For dieters and compulsive snackers.

FLAT SODA REFRESHER. A carbonization pill that livens the bubbles in flat soda or makes regular soda super-bubbly.

ULTRASONIC TOOTHPICK. Removes stuck food from teeth with ultrasonic vibration rather than a sharp poking point.

The Invention of
The Zipper

If necessity is the mother of invention, persistence is the father.

The invention of the zipper is the story of three determined men who eventually overcame a long string of mishaps and bad luck. It all began in the late 1800s with a chubby man named Whitcomb L. Judson. The stylish clothes of that time required bulky undergarments with layer upon layer of outer garments—including shirts, vests, and jackets—all fastened with laces, cords, or rows of buttons. Sometimes it would take almost half an hour to get dressed or undressed. Even the fashionable shoes were tightly fitted boots that were buttoned or laced all the way to the knee.

Well, Whitcomb L. Judson, in his overweight state, had great difficulty getting his boots laced. Judson was already quite a prolific inventor with several patented items to his name when he decided to create a new invention to button his shoes more easily and quickly—he called it a "slide fastener." Through Judson's business associations, he met Colonel Louis Walker (not really a colonel, but a shrewd lawyer and businessman who used the title). Walker was very impressed with Judson's slide fastener and together they formed the Universal Fastener Company.

After two years of research and development, the Universal Slide Fastener for shoes was launched into the marketplace. The "Universal" was a chainlike contraption consisting of sheet-metal hooks (looking like tiny battle-axes) connected with wire rings. These chains of hooks on opposite sides were drawn together and fastened

As good a closure as the zipper is, it is not without its problems. For every one that zips up smoothly, there is one that manages to snare anything in its path—shirttails, loose underwear, bits of thread. Even when all seems safe and secure, remember, it never hurts to check, no matter what your age.

by using a "slider." But before the user could actually fasten his boots, he first had to attach the device to his shoes with ordinary shoelaces.

Of course, to help publicize the new product, both Judson and Walker wore and displayed their own slide-fastened shoes. Business was not bad, and it even began to grow, but unfortunately each pair of fasteners had to be painstakingly made by hand. Both men decided that if the market for slide fasteners was going to develop, they would have to create a machine that could produce the product economically. Judson went about making a model of such a machine and then had it built. Unfortunately, the full-scale version proved to be too complex and too costly to operate. Judson had to hire two full-time engineers just to keep the

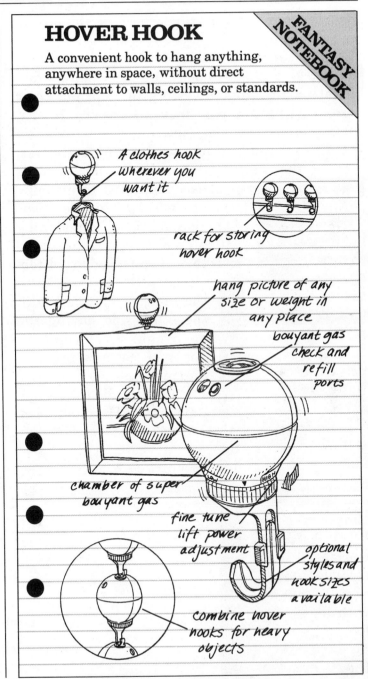

HOVER HOOK

FANTASY NOTEBOOK

A convenient hook to hang anything, anywhere in space, without direct attachment to walls, ceilings, or standards.

A clothes hook wherever you want it

rack for storing hover hook

hang picture of any size or weight in any place

bouyant gas check and refill ports

chamber of super bouyant gas

fine tune lift power adjustment

optional styles and hook sizes available

combine hover hooks for heavy objects

machine going. After only two years, the project was abandoned.

The Universal Fastener Company, however, did not go out of business, and in seeking additional money from investors to continue their research, the company moved from city to city, ending up in Hoboken, New Jersey.

By now, Judson had worked out a new version of the slide fastener that could be more easily adapted to machine production. This new version consisted of fastening elements that were attached to the edges of fabric tape. On one side were the pins, or "hooks," with the other side having the openings, or "eyes." In honor of the new product, Judson named his new company the Hook and Eye Company of Hoboken, New Jersey.

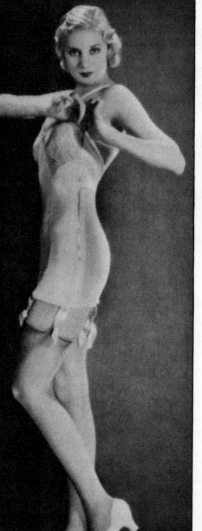

A model demonstrates the new, easy-to-use zippered corsette.

Colonel Walker's enthusiasm for the project was rejuvenated and, once again joining Judson, the two men reentered the marketplace with a new product name and a new slogan: "The C-Curity Fastener: A Pull and It's Done."

However, instead of promoting the fastener only for shoes, the product was now also promoted for women's skirts, men's pants, and other types of clothing. Although Judson's new version of the device could now be made quickly and cheaply by machine, the new name, "C-Curity," proved to be inaccurate. The slide fastener was far from secure, and skirts and trousers would pop open unexpectedly (and embarrassingly) if the device was not used exactly as instructed. It could not be bent, twisted, or washed.

For these reasons, clothing manufacturers distrusted the slide fastener, so Judson and

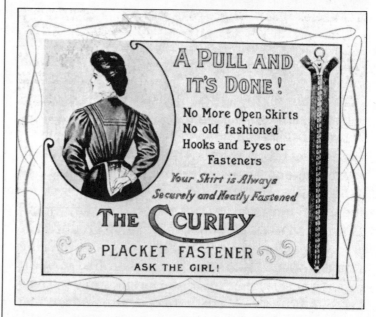

A 1907 advertisement of the C-Curity Fastener Company.

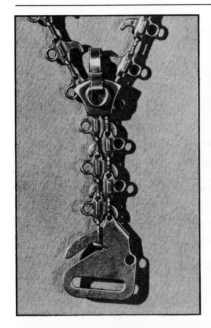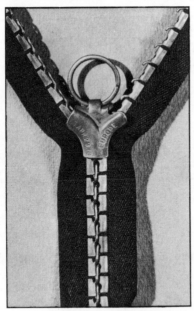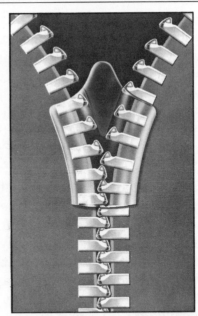

The Judson slide fastener from 1891 (l.), the Plako Fastener from 1906 (c.) and a modern-day zipper (r.).

Walker tried hiring salesmen to sell the C-Curity door-to-door. Although sales were not brisk, the product was novel enough to earn some profit.

In an attempt to improve the slide fastener yet again and then attract the lucrative garment industry, Judson and Walker hired a young engineer, Gideon Sundback, who had already shown great interest in the slide fastener patent while he was employed at Westinghouse Electric in Pittsburgh. First Sundback made several improvements in the manufacturing process, and then he concentrated his efforts on eliminating the shortcomings of the C-Curity fastener, especially its tendency to pop open.

By 1908, after two years of effort, the Hook and Eye Company of Hoboken once again tried to attract the attention of clothing manufacturers. At the time the style of women's clothes included plackets on skirts. To go with the new fad, the newest slide fastener was called Plako. But the fashion didn't last and the Plako name didn't stick, either. The Hook and Eye Company went back to selling their products through door-to-door salesmen.

By 1909 the Hook and Eye Company was on the verge of bankruptcy, and Judson and Walker were operating with only two full-time employees, Sundback and a bookkeeper. All that kept the business alive were sales to people who enjoyed the novelty of the slide fasteners and to actors who needed to make quick costume changes.

However, Judson and Walker still did not lose hope, and they encouraged Sundback to continue his research and experiments for improving the product. It took nearly four years, but Sundback's work paid off. In a radical departure from hooks and eyes, Sundback created the first truly practical, smooth-working, unpoppable slide fastener very similar to today's zipper—and he designed the machinery to produce it.

It all seemed so good that Colonel Walker raised more money from investors to start a whole new operation he called the Hookless Fastener Company. The newest venture went full steam ahead, preparing to launch the best slide fastener ever, but just before the machinery started churning, a flaw was discovered: Sundback's new fastener wore out much too quickly.

Rather than risk yet another rejection in the clothing industry, Walker decided to hold off and have Sundback go at it again. One year later, in 1914, the "Hookless #2" was introduced.

The Hookless #2 worked just fine and had

Fantasy Inventions

Here are a few ideas to inspire thoughts on more new kinds of fasteners.

TICK-ER-TAPE. (The ER stands for Easily Removed.) A ribbon material coated with clinging tick-like tiny feet that hold firmly onto any surface. To remove, just pet the tape and it will let go.

BURR FASTENERS. The alternative plant version of Tick-ER-Tape.

ZIPPER-IN SHOWER CURTAIN. Positively keeps water inside the shower.

ULTRASONIC SEWING MACHINE. Ultrasonic vibration permanently "sews" fabric together by intertwining and fusing fabric fibers.

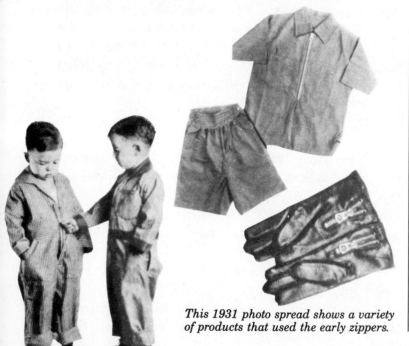

This 1931 photo spread shows a variety of products that used the early zippers.

none of the problems that had plagued the C-Curity and the Plako, but still garment manufacturers were leery. Sales trickled in for three years before the first large order was received—24,000 slide fasteners to be used in sailors' money belts. Over the next several years, other manufacturers found uses for the Hookless #2 slide fastener in diverse products, including Navy flying suits, gloves, and tobacco pouches.

The real turning point did not come until 1923, when the B. F. Goodrich Company introduced a style of rubber boot featuring the Hookless slide fastener. It was one of the executives at Goodrich who coined the name "zipper" by exclaiming that to wear the boots you just "Zip 'er up or zip 'er down." With this catchy name, "zipper," the Hookless #2 slide fastener finally became accepted for use in all sorts of products, including garments.

The Invention of
Teabags

An invention works the way the user perceives it, not necessarily the way the inventor intended it.

In 1904 an Englishman named Richard Blychenden rented a booth in a pavilion of the Louisiana Purchase Exposition, which was being held in St. Louis. He wanted to promote an Indian tea blend his company exported to America. The booth was set up like a Far East teahouse, complete with natives of Ceylon in bright traditional dress serving freshly brewed hot tea. Unfortunately the St. Louis weather turned hot and sticky and Blychenden's teahouse had no customers. On the other hand, the nearby booths serving iced drinks had lines of perspiring people eager for a refreshing cold beverage.

Blychenden was not about to quit, so he decided to give the public what they wanted. Although no one had ever thought of drinking tea any way but hot, Blychenden decided to serve it cold. First he got a chest full of ice and several tall drinking glasses. Then he filled a glass with ice chips and poured in the hot tea. A hastily made sign went up advertising his new cold drink—"iced tea." A trickle of fairgoers turned to a torrent as they all crowded into Blychenden's booth to try the new copper-colored iced drink.

Today tea is the world's most popular drink next to water, and iced tea is America's most popular summertime drink.

Coincidentally, the tea bag was invented in the same year as iced tea. Thomas Sullivan, a New York tea and coffee importer, followed the customary tradition of sending small samples of tea to his customers so they could select the variety they wished to order. But the tins used for packing the samples were becoming increasingly

The tea ritual at the turn of the century meant a pot of hot tea, another of hot water, a creamer, sugar bowl, and perhaps some thin sandwiches and small cakes as accompaniments. What would this proper young woman think of today's teabag, hanging out the side of a saucerless mug?

expensive, and Sullivan tried to think of a cheaper and smaller container he might use—one that would keep the tea fresh without it looking as if he were skimping.

Thomas Sullivan got a bright idea: he would send the tea samples in small hand-sewn Chinese silk bags. The bags were far less expensive than the tins, yet he thought his customers would be impressed. Sullivan sent out the silk sample bags of tea and waited for the orders to come in. He did receive orders for his tea, but his customers also wanted their tea packed and delivered in the little silk bags. It seems that most people thought the bags were meant for a new brewing technique rather than being a substitute for the tins. Sullivan had inadvertently invented the tea bag, and his business boomed.

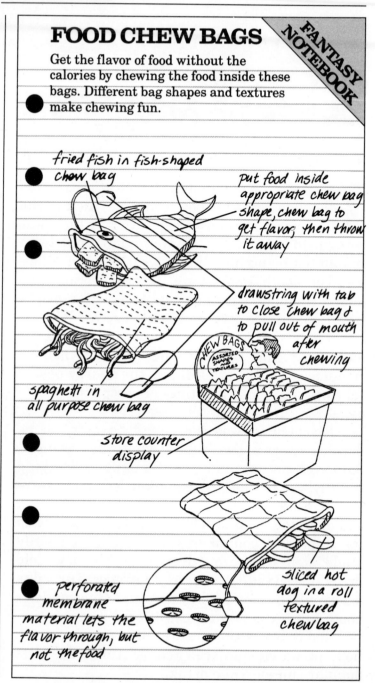

FANTASY NOTEBOOK

FOOD CHEW BAGS

Get the flavor of food without the calories by chewing the food inside these bags. Different bag shapes and textures make chewing fun.

fried fish in fish-shaped chew bag

put food inside appropriate chew bag shape, chew bag to get flavor, then throw it away

drawstring with tab to close chew bag & to pull out of mouth after chewing

spaghetti in all purpose chew bag

CHEW BAGS ASSORTED SHAPES TEXTURES

store counter display

sliced hot dog in a roll textured chew bag

perforated membrane material lets the flavor through, but not the food

The more modern gauze paper tea bag was invented (this time on purpose) by Joseph Krieger. Around 1920 Krieger was trying to devise an easier way for restaurants to brew large quantities of tea. He invented a super-large gauze tea pouch which worked quite well. It was then just a short time before yet another tea importer put the two inventions together and produced a smaller gauze tea bag for brewing individual cups of tea.

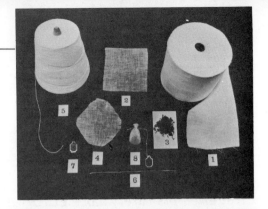

This numbered photograph shows all the stages in making the first tea bags, from raw gauze (1.) to finished bag (8.).

Shown here is a woman sewing gauze tea bags, taken in the mid-1920s.

Fantasy Inventions

The tea bag came about accidentally, but its success shows the potential for new ways of preparing and packaging foods, the theme on which these fantasy ideas focus.

NONSPILLABLE SPONGE CUP. A soft sponge drinking cup with a flexible waterproof outer skin. Sponge soaks up beverage (making it unspillable), then cup is squeezed to get the drink.

FOOD CAN COOKERS. Foods are cooked in the cans they come in. Magnetic accessory handle holds cans of various sizes. Sanitary, no waste, and no pots or pans to clean.

FLAVOR-DIP POSTCARDS. Peel off the protective clear coating and dip the postcard in hot water to get a drink that has the "flavor" of the place or of the message.

FLAVOR-DIP BAGS. For making soups, drinks, dressings, gravies, etc., by just dipping the flavor bag in hot water, milk, or other liquid.

FLAVOR-BREW CUP. A drinking mug for brewing tea or coffee. Ground tea or coffee is placed in hollow wall of cup and brews through tiny holes in inner wall when hot water is added. When beverage is perfectly brewed a twist of the cup closes the brewing holes.

The Invention of
Scotch Tape

First attempts rarely work exactly as planned, but clearly show the remaining work to be done.

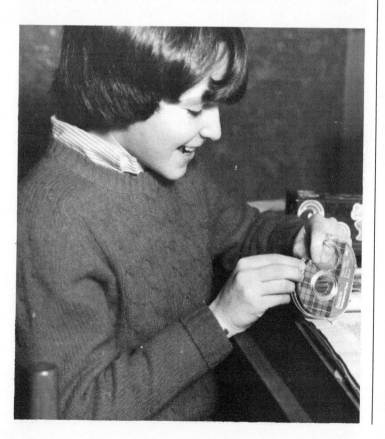

In 1902 five Minnesota businessmen started the Minnesota Mining and Manufacturing Company (3M) with the idea of mining an abrasive mineral called corundum and selling it to grinding-wheel and sandpaper manufacturers. However, during the several years it took to get the manufacturing operation under way, a new and better artificial abrasive material was invented by another company. To make things worse, it was soon discovered that the mineral 3M was mining was not corundum at all, but a low-grade material (anorthosite) not really suited for abrasives. The company almost went broke.

After raising some more money to keep 3M alive, it was decided that the company would try the sandpaper manufacturing business itself. Working out of an old Duluth flour mill on the shore of Lake Superior, 3M went about making various sandpaper products using anorthosite. Though some orders trickled in, the product wasn't very good, and the company once again found itself teetering on the verge of bankruptcy. At this point, a single share of stock in 3M sold for less than 2½¢, but the founders didn't give up.

The turning point came in 1910 when the major investor in 3M, Lucius P. Ordway, insisted that the company move to his hometown of St. Paul, Minnesota, where he then built a new manufacturing plant. The company set out not only to improve the quality of its sandpaper but also to create a new way of selling it. Instead of 3M

STATIC CHARGE GLUE GUN

A gun that fastens and unfastens any kind of material with positive and negative static charges. Eliminates the need for glue, staples, paper clips, nails and tape.

flip-top reverses polarity (+ is for glueing - is for unglueing)

glue strength control for temporary or permanent fastening

activate switch

plug in battery recharger

tip applies static charge to hold any materials together

salesmen calling on company executives, they tried to get into the factory workshops to talk directly to the people who used their sandpaper. In that way, the salesmen could get useful information that would help 3M continue to improve its product.

The results paid off. By 1916 the company had overcome its debt and was making a profit. Over the next few years 3M continued to grow by improving its sandpapers and inventing new ones. Soon some of their biggest customers were the coach builders who made car bodies for the automobile industry. The 3M salesmen would call on craftsmen working in the body shops—and

The 3M Company's first office was on the second floor of this building in Two Harbors, Minnesota.

An automobile worker used the original Scotch masking tape to prepare sections of a car for painting.

it was through that association that Scotch tape was invented.

In 1925, along with raccoon coats and flapper styles, cars with two-tone paint finishes were all the rage. The problem that auto makers faced was how to achieve a clear, sharp edge where one color met the other.

Sharp-edged newspaper and wrapping paper had been tried, to mask one color while spraying another. The idea was fine, but the glue used to hold the paper in place stuck too tightly and frequently had to be scraped off—taking some of the paint with it. They had even tried using surgical tape.

The 3M sandpaper salesmen were repeatedly asked if they knew of any product that would do a better masking job. What the car makers wanted

was a tape that would stick tightly at a touch, yet remove easily without harming the finish.

Richard G. Drew, a 3M laboratory worker, began working on the invention of pressure-sensitive masking paper, and he finally produced a light tan paper tape with a rubber-based adhesive that stuck well and could be removed easily, as the car manufacturers had requested. Drew figured that he needed to put strips of adhesive only on the outer edges of the tape since one edge held the masking paper and the other edge had to stick to the car to provide a sharp, straight line for spray painting. He didn't think there was any

Richard Drew (c.), one of the inventors of Scotch tape, shown here with his co-workers.

Fantasy Inventions

New tapes and sealants are still being created all the time. These imaginative ideas may help you invent another specialized tape.

BODY GLUE. A small dab will hold any object securely to bare skin. Great for attaching watches, jewelry, bathing suits, shoe soles, eyeglasses, etc.

STRETCH TAPE. Can be stretched to fit the exact length needed.

TIME DELAY TAPE. Tape can easily be positioned and repositioned without sticking, until firm pressure is applied.

GRAVITY GLUE. Two chemicals, when mixed, create a gravity field that will attract and hold together any two materials. The amount of glue used determines the strength of the attraction.

ANTI-GRAVITY PASTE. The opposite of Gravity Glue. Mixed chemicals form a paste that when applied makes the object float away from all other objects.

SELECTIVE SURFACE TAPES. A variety of sticky tapes with adhesive surfaces specifically formulated to stick only to certain materials. Harvesting tape sticks to and pulls out crops, cleaning tape picks up dust and dirt, specific stain tapes pull out stains.

---

need for adhesive in the middle, and that would save 3M some money.

When one body shop tried the new "masking tape," it promptly fell off, and the message to the 3M salesmen was loud and clear: "Take this tape back to those Scotch bosses of yours and tell them to put adhesive all over the tape, not just on the edges."

The reference to the reputation of the Scotch for being thrifty was heeded and 3M immediately corrected the product. When the salesmen returned with the improved masking tape, the workers had already nicknamed the product "Scotch Tape," and the name stuck. The company decided to go along with it, and the brand name "Scotch" has since become the trademark for all the company's pressure-sensitive tapes.

The most famous member of the Scotch Tape clan came along shortly after—Scotch transparent tape. Today there are over 400 varieties of Scotch brand pressure-sensitive tapes, as well as a host of other magnetic tapes for audio and video recording—and 3M still advertises itself as the company that listens to what the consumer needs.

The Invention of
Sneakers

Product recognition is the main ingredient of marketing success.

How rubber-soled shoes with canvas uppers became known as "sneaks" or "sneakers" is not exactly known. The reason may be the obvious one—rubber and canvas shoes are very quiet. But the phenomenal popularity of the sneaker has more to do with its comfort and style than with the ability to sneak around quietly.

The story of the rubber-soled sneaker begins with the development of rubber. For many centuries, the natives of Central and South America commonly used the gum that oozed from the bark

This drawing shows how the Mayans made shoes by covering their feet with melted rubber.

of certain trees to cover and protect the bottoms of their feet. Their technique was to apply the gum directly in thin layers, curing each layer with gentle heat from a fire. The result was a coating that covered the bottom of the wearer's foot and protected it from rough land.

A British traveler, in the late 1700s, became fascinated with these strange-looking foot coverings, but he was even more intrigued with the possibility of using the gum to make other products. He collected several samples of the gum and the products the natives made from it and returned to England, where he showed the new substance to his chemist friend Joseph Priestley. Priestley's first discovery was that the gum had the unique ability to cleanly erase pencil marks by briskly rubbing the paper with it—so he enthusiastically named the substance "rubber."

For the next fifty years, several products made of rubber were manufactured—mostly waterproof containers and coverings to protect all kinds of things from the rain. And by 1820 someone finally designed a rubber cover that the wearer could stretch over his leather shoes to protect them in wet or muddy weather. These rubber "overshoes" quickly found their way to America, and the new novelty product became an instant success—but not for long.

In an attempt to make money on the popular imported fad, many New England shoe manufacturers hastily set up factories, making rubber overshoes in various styles that incorporated hand-painted designs and other decorations. But within just a few years the attraction had diminished, as wearers soon discovered that pure rubber became obnoxiously smelly and sticky in hot weather, and brittle enough to crack into small pieces during cold weather. By 1823 no one wanted anything to do with rubber overshoes.

About that time, Charles Goodyear, a young out-of-work hardware salesman, decided to take on the challenge of eliminating rubber's shortcomings. Goodyear's interest became a hobby and then a serious undertaking. Soon he was dedicating all his time and money to making rubber a more stable product. Goodyear believed that the solution involved adding certain chemicals to the pure rubber gum and finding the right way to cure the mixture.

Experiment after experiment failed, and Charles Goodyear went broke. He borrowed

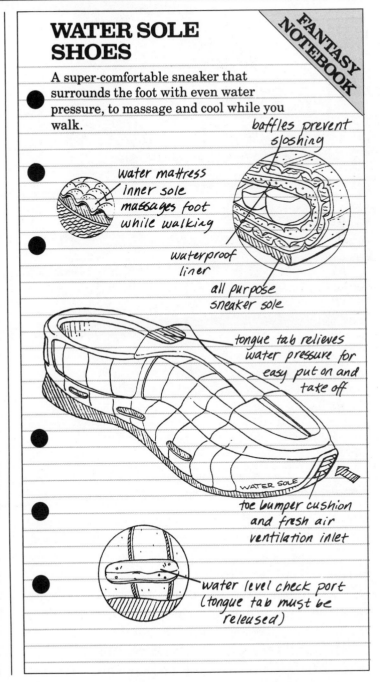

FANTASY NOTEBOOK

WATER SOLE SHOES

A super-comfortable sneaker that surrounds the foot with even water pressure, to massage and cool while you walk.

baffles prevent sloshing

water mattress inner sole massages foot while walking

waterproof liner

all purpose sneaker sole

tongue tab relieves water pressure for easy put on and take off

WATER SOLE

toe bumper cushion and fresh air ventilation inlet

water level check port (tongue tab must be released)

An artist's rendition of Charles Goodyear at work, just as he discovered the process of vulcanization.

patented a process for attaching rubber to the soles of shoes and boots with uppers made of leather, but the combination did nothing to eliminate the original problems with rubber.

By 1838 Charles Goodyear was at his experiments again; this time another rubber enthusiast, Nathaniel Hayward, joined him. They discovered that if they mixed sulfur with the gum rubber and then left it in the sun to bake slowly, the mixture would form a rubbery but not sticky outer skin. Goodyear was sure he was on the track to the solution, but Hayward wasn't so convinced. So Goodyear paid Hayward for his contribution and optimistically went on experimenting alone.

One year later, Charles Goodyear got lucky. He was mixing up a batch of gum rubber, sulfur, and white lead when a glob of the mixture fell off his stirring utensil and onto the hot stovetop. When the mass cooled and Goodyear went to remove it, he discovered that the rubber had

money from friends and businessmen, but he still couldn't find the right formula. Eventually Goodyear was arrested and put into debtor's prison for failing to pay back his creditors.

While the shoe industry still tried to bring back the fad by introducing various new styles of rubber overshoes, the sticky, smelly, and often brittle substance found little acceptance as footwear. In 1834 an inventor named Wait Webster

A print of Charles Goodyear's exhibition of rubber products at the famous Crystal Palace in Sydenham, England, from 1893.

cured perfectly—consistently rubbery throughout and not sticky at all! He then discovered that his new "metallic" rubber (he called it "metallic" because of the lead in the mixture) was more elastic and considerably less brittle. Goodyear named the process for making metallic rubber vulcanization, after the Roman god of fire, Vulcan.

Now that a better rubber had been invented, a better rubber shoe could be made. Goodyear licensed his vulcanization process to several shoe companies and also to manufacturers of all types of rubber products. Some companies made rubber-soled shoes, rubber shoe covers, or even all-rubber shoes, and one shoe manufacturer, Thomas Crane Wales, made a waterproof boot of rubberized cloth with a rubber sole, called "Wales patent Arctic gaitors." But the first real sneaker with laced canvas uppers and vulcanized rubber soles came in 1868 from the Candee Manufacturing Company of New Haven, Connecticut. These canvas-and-rubber "croquet sandals" were made to appeal strictly to the wealthy, and they were sold through the exclusive Peck and Snyder Sporting Goods Catalog.

Fortunately, the Candee Company's marketing scheme didn't work as planned, and people who never thought of playing croquet began wearing the light and comfortable canvas-and-rubber shoes. By 1873 the shoes were commonly called sneaks or sneakers. And by the beginning of the twentieth century, everyday people often wore 60¢ canvas-and-rubber sneakers, while the rich wore more expensive models with silk, satin, and white duck uppers, trimmed in bows for women and elk skin for men.

While the sneaker became increasingly popular as a comfortable, stylish casual shoe, it also was being used as a sporting shoe. Special types of sneakers were being made for all kinds of popular sports and games. In 1909 the basketball

An early advertisement for Spalding tennis shoes, and a picture of those early shoes in action.

Fantasy Inventions

The sneaker has come a long way since the early twentieth century and there is no reason you can't invent another variation on this old favorite.

SLUG GLUE DISPENSER. A healthy live slug is placed inside the glue dispenser carrying case. When glue is needed, a portion of the case bottom is removed and the slug is allowed to walk across the area to be glued.

SHOE SHINE VENDING MACHINE. Provides a quick shoe shine for people on the move. Shine selection options include rainy day waterproofing, military spit shine, different color shade, and a computerized shoe condition report.

NEW SNEAKER SMELL RENEWER. A spray that gets rid of old sneaker smell and replaces it with the smell of a new pair of shoes.

HEADLIGHT SHOES. Shoe toe headlights and red heel taillights provide safety for nighttime joggers and walkers.

sneaker was introduced, and a year later the Spalding Company invented a rubber sneaker sole with molded suction cups for better traction. In 1915 the U.S. Navy ordered nonslip sneakers to be used aboard ships.

In 1917 Henry McKinney, the public relations director for the National India Rubber Company (owned by the U.S. Rubber Company), decided it was time to call the canvas-and-rubber shoe something different from the ever-popular sneaker. After reviewing more than 300 suggestions, he selected the name "Peds" (from the Latin word meaning "foot"). However, McKinney soon discovered that another company used "Peds," and he quickly switched to the now-famous brand name "Keds." The idea worked, and for a while the Keds name was just as familiar as sneakers.

Many other companies tried to create new sneaker fads, and some succeeded. Over the past seventy-odd years, "new, improved" models have appeared with features such as arch cushions, colored uppers, colored rubber soles, side venting outlets, waffle soles, and most recently, curved-sole "running" shoes. Today the sneaker is by far America's most popular and comfortable shoe style, accounting for over one-quarter of all shoes sold—and very few are worn for croquet.

Grace Valentine models a pair of tennis shoes; a Converse model from the early twentieth century.

The Invention of
Roller Skates

An idea becomes an invention only when you can demonstrate that it works.

The roller skate is an invention that clearly was inspired by the popularity of ice skating. When the spring thaw melted the ice on a local pond or river, avid ice skaters could do little but wait for next winter's freeze. For over a century many inventors tried to design a wheeled skate to use on land that worked like a blade skate on ice. But nothing worked quite well enough until an American inventor, J. L. Plimpton, created the four-wheel "trunk" design in 1863.

The first recorded account of roller skates describes a makeshift wheeled shoe device used purely for entertainment. But rather than starting a boom, they caused quite a crash!

In the mid-1700s, a Belgian musical instrument maker named Josef Merlin concocted a pair of roller skates to wear to a London masquerade party. Each skate had only two wheels in a bicycle-type design—one in front and one in back—with no provision for stopping or turning. An account of the festivities describes Merlin being announced to the party-goers and then rolling across the floor while playing his violin. To the shock of the startled guests (and Merlin himself) he was unable to stop, and he smashed into a huge, expensive mirror at the opposite end of the hall. The crash broke the mirror and his violin to pieces, also causing severe injuries to Merlin himself. It was another forty or fifty years before anyone heard of roller skating again.

The next appearance in the checkered life of roller skates was in a Berlin theater around 1818. For a winter ballet scene it was impossible to make ice on stage, and so a pair of homemade roller skates (with several wheels in line) were used for the ice skating scenes. There is no report as to how well the skates worked.

One year later, a Frenchman patented a similar pair of roller skates and tried to stir up interest in outdoor street skating. But because of the in-line wheel design, the skates could move forward only in a straight line. Turning even a slight corner required great strength and skill, and so the wheeled skates were declared too dangerous for just anyone to use.

A few years later, a British inventor patented a skate using small in-line wheels in the front and rear of the skate and a side-by-side pair of slightly larger wheels in the center. By rocking forward or backward and to either side, the skater could effect a turn. This improved skate was attached to the bottom of the skater's shoe and allowed greater maneuverability than had any previous design. The design also provided "hooks" at the front and rear of the skate as an assist in stopping. However, the sport still didn't catch on, and roller skating remained an oddity.

During the 1820s and 1830s, several other versions of roller skates were patented that attempted to duplicate the control and maneuverability of ice skates. There were three-wheeled tricycle designs, skates with large outrigger wheels on either side of the foot, and even a one-way skate with ratchet wheels that prevented the skate from rolling backward (which supposedly allowed the skater to travel uphill with ease).

One Berlin tavern featured pretty waitresses on roller skates, and an opera was created specifically to feature a troupe of roller skaters. Two roller skating rinks opened briefly in London during the late 1850s to provide a "diversion for the wealthy." But roller skating did not become a popular activity until after 1863, when the ingenious and wealthy J. L. Plimpton patented a

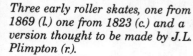

Three early roller skates, one from 1869 (l.) one from 1823 (c.) and a version thought to be made by J.L. Plimpton (r.).

Fantasy Inventions

It is often said that the greatest invention ever was the wheel. Indeed, the wheel has been a key to many designs and inventions for centuries. Here are some new twists on one of the world's oldest products.

KITE SKATING. The skateboard rider is pulled along by holding on to the cord of a flying kite.

HITCHHIKER ROLLER HEELS. Permits the hitchhiker to be pulled behind the host vehicle. Not for highway use.

TRACTOR TREAD ROLLER SHOES. For fast walking by stepping and sliding. Safer and more controllable than wheeled skates.

ROLLER TREES (PLANTS AND SHRUBS). Decorative tree, plant, and shrub planters in all sizes with casters so landscaping (indoors or out) can be rearranged as desired.

HAND AND KNEE SKATES. For skating on all fours. Skating in the crawl position gives better stability and maneuverability.

MARBLE ROLL-AND-SLIP SKATING. The entire rink floor is covered with a layer of hard rubber marbles. The skater can wear any flat shoe. Bare feet not recommended.

WATER WALKERS AND WAVE SKIS. Buoyant foot pontoons allow the wearer to walk on smooth water and ski on waves.

WIND SAIL SKATEBOARD. A single, clear plastic sail attaches to an oversized skateboard.

ROLLER STAIRS. Rubber-padded conveyor-type rollers in place of stairs. The rollers turn freely in only one direction, so a person can slide down the stairs on the spinning rollers and walk up on the locked rollers.

ROLLER SHOPPING BAGS. A shopping bag with pop-out roller wheels for lugging your purchases.

---

skate that had two parallel sets of wheels—two wheels in front under the ball of the foot and two in the rear under the heel. This simple "trunk" design used rubber "action pads" between the wheel axle support and the base plate, which was attached by straps to the wearer's shoe. It was the rocking action of the trunk design that permitted the skater to carve a turn to either side simply by leaning in the direction he wanted to go. Eureka! At last, a roller skate had been designed that allowed the skater to maneuver around a wooden floor with the ease and precision of an ice skater on a smooth frozen pond.

Plimpton's motivation had been to create a roller skate strictly for himself so he could have a substitute for his favorite pastime—ice skating—during the warmer months. But his skate worked so well that he decided to share it with others by going into the roller-skate manufacturing business. To encourage people to buy his skates, Plimpton organized the New York Skating Club and built a $100,000 skating rink in Newport, Rhode Island. During the summer of 1867, the wealthy and the adventurous flocked to Newport's Atlantic House rink to try a spin around the floor on a pair of Plimpton skates. Plimpton's roller skates made skating easier, safer, and more enjoyable than ever before.

Another avid ice skater of the 1860s, E. H. Barney, resented the discomfort he and other skaters suffered from the tight straps used for holding the ice blades to the bottom of the wearer's boots. And so Barney patented a design using clamps to hold the blade to the sole of the skater's shoe. A special key was used to tighten or remove the blades. Several years later, the same Barney design was used to clamp roller skates firmly to shoe soles, and the skate key became a well-recognized symbol of the sport.

In 1881 there was another major design improvement in roller skates. A man named Raymond invented and patented the "Raymond extension skate," which allowed the shoe plate of the roller skate to be adjusted to fit different shoe sizes, adapting to a young skater's growing feet.

During the 1890s the popularity of roller skating boomed in America. Roller skates were finally easy to use and comfortable to wear.

A fashionable couple taking a spin on the rink, from approximately 1910.

This etching shows the gala opening of a roller skating rink in New York City.

Plimpton's patent expired in 1880, and nearly all skates manufactured since have used the Plimpton trunk design, although there have been several different fashionable and functional styles to choose from. Most skates were designed for indoor rink use and had wheels made of wood, rubber, metal, or expensive ivory attached to a wood or metal shoe plate. These indoor skates were called "parlor" or "club" skates, and indeed the roller rinks of that era were like country clubs. Roller skating rinks (or parlors) were built mostly in the wealthier sections of town, some with smooth (and hard!) marble floors. It was quite fashionable to take a date roller skating on Saturday afternoon and to play roller polo on Sunday.

For the next twenty or thirty years the basic Plimpton design remained unchanged except for each manufacturer's particular way of attaching the skates to the wearer's shoe. Some had one, two, or three foot straps with padding for comfort; some had various clamp arrangements that required strong, rigid soles; and one manufacturer even had a step-in, snap-on clamp similar to a present-day downhill ski binding.

With the onset of the Great Depression of the 1930s, the popularity of roller skating quickly declined. As older, once wealthy sections of cities became run-down, the roller rinks began to decay with them. However, as parlor roller skating was abandoned by the upper classes, its popularity grew with the kids on the street.

The clamp-on, all-metal roller skate was as popular as a baseball glove in most homes during the 1940s and 1950s, and in the 1970s the quieter and better-riding urethane skate wheels brought renewed interest and popularity to the sport. Street skating became a practical means of transportation for some and lent a fashionable image to others. The roller rink was now reinterpreted (and redecorated) as a roller disco ballroom. In the late 1970s, the most recent evolutionary stage of the Plimpton-style roller skate was introduced: "Pop Wheels." The skater needed only to flick a lever on his normal-looking, everyday street shoes and out popped a set of roller skate wheels, ready to go!

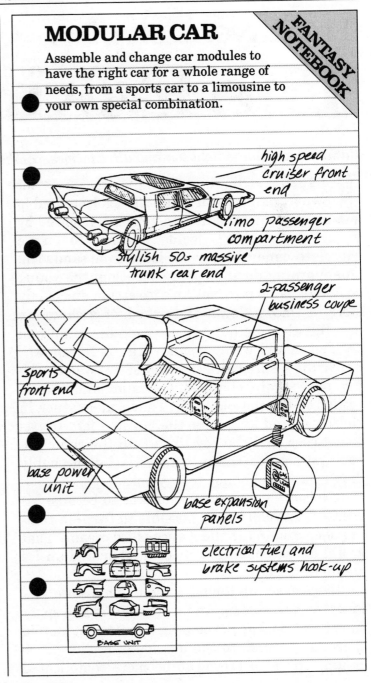

MODULAR CAR

FANTASY NOTEBOOK

Assemble and change car modules to have the right car for a whole range of needs, from a sports car to a limousine to your own special combination.

high speed cruiser front end

limo passenger compartment

stylish 50s massive trunk rear end

2-passenger business coupe

sports front end

base power unit

base expansion panels

electrical fuel and brake systems hook-up

BASE UNIT

The Invention of
The Eskimo Pie

Rather than choose between two alternatives, combine them to make one product with both features.

In 1920 a struggling young ice cream parlor owner named Christian K. Nelson had a bright idea for a new taste treat, inspired by a boy who couldn't decide whether to buy a chocolate candy bar or an ice cream sandwich. One morning during spring vacation, the young customer came into Nelson's ice cream and candy store in Onowa, Iowa, and asked for a chocolate bar. But then he quickly changed his mind and decided on an ice cream sandwich. As Nelson was preparing a slice of ice cream and two wafers, the boy once again changed his mind and finally settled on the chocolate bar. The incident stuck in Nelson's mind long after the boy had left. It was easy to see that the boy liked both the chocolate bar and the ice cream sandwich, but probably didn't have the money to buy both.

Nelson's next speculation was to become his great idea: Would it be possible to freeze a coating of chocolate around a slice of ice cream? That would be like having a chocolate bar and an ice cream all together.

Nelson set up the back room of his store as a laboratory-workshop, and whenever he had spare time he worked on developing a way to get melted chocolate to stick to the outside of a slice of ice cream. The idea proved to be more complicated

Chester Nelson displays the old and new packaging for his Eskimo Pie.

than he had expected. No matter what he did to get the coating to stick, the hot chocolate would melt a thin skim of ice cream and slide off, or the chocolate would cool too fast and become a thick blob instead of a thin coating.

One day while discussing his dilemma with a candy salesman, Nelson learned that chocolate candy manufacturers varied the amount of cocoa butter (a main ingredient in chocolate formulas) to make the chocolate cling better to nuts, taffy, caramel, and other types of candy bar centers. Nelson went back to his store workshop and began a new series of trial-and-error experiments, this time using varying amounts of cocoa butter. Late one night he finally found a proportion that worked. He took a slice of ice cream at below-freezing temperature and dipped it into a pot of his chocolate formula heated to about 85 degrees. Then he put the ice cream into his refrigerated chill box and the chocolate coating solidified instantly, sticking fast to the vanilla ice

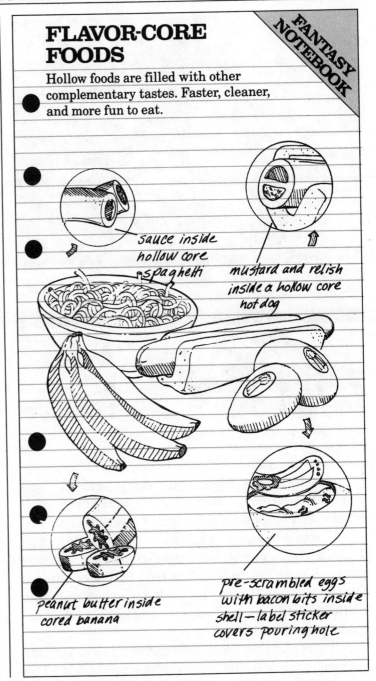

FLAVOR-CORE FOODS

FANTASY NOTEBOOK

Hollow foods are filled with other complementary tastes. Faster, cleaner, and more fun to eat.

sauce inside hollow core spaghetti

mustard and relish inside a hollow core hot dog

peanut butter inside cored banana

pre-scrambled eggs with bacon bits inside shell—label sticker covers pouring hole

A customer helps himself from one of the well-loved Eskimo Pie street dispensing coolers.

Fantasy Inventions

Many of the inventions covered in this book have shown the success of new food combinations and products. Here are some more ideas to start you thinking about your own new food inventions.

CRUNCHY CHEWING GUM. A crunchy chewing gum texture that lasts and lasts.

KETCHUP ROLL. Semi-solid ketchup in a roll that can be sliced. Slice off the amount and thickness you want.

CHROME-PLATED FOODS. A shiny chrome, edible food coating that makes eating fun. Can be used to make chrome cookies, chrome hamburger rolls, chrome spaghetti, chrome chocolate bars, etc.

FOOD WALLET. Super-insulated "wallet" carries portion-control slices of various foods for on-the-go snacks and meals.

FLAVOR CHANGER FOOD WRAP. A flavored edible food wrap that improves or changes the flavor of the food it is wrapped around. Available in all flavors, including special gourmet tastes.

SANDWICH-SHAPED SLICES. Sandwich foods (including meats, cheeses, vegetables, and condiments) are made and sliced to the exact shape of sandwich bread.

NEW TASTE RECIPE COMPUTER. Invents new food combinations and computes the recipe for such dishes as: chocolate-coated fried spinach; crisp-frozen, mint-flavored corn on the cob; butter-popped mushrooms; and cotton cauliflower.

cream. Months of labor had finally paid off. Nelson named his creation the "I-Scream Bar"— maybe after his own reaction at his success.

Customers went wild over I-Scream Bars and Nelson knew he had a successful product. He was granted a patent on the bar, and full of optimism for his new business, he took on a partner who could provide both financial backing and some knowledge about marketing.

Together they decided that the I-Scream Bar needed a new name and a clever package. The name should sound cold like ice cream, but also sound sweet like the candy coating. So, out of hundreds of possibilities, they chose "Eskimo

Pie." Their package also projected the cold, sweet candy image by using a blue foil wrapper with dark blue printing.

The first commercially produced Eskimo Pies were sold in Des Moines, Iowa, but sales and popularity of the new ice cream treat grew so quickly that within one year Eskimo Pie franchises were set up all over America, and by the early 1920s more than 1 million bars were being sold each day!

Christian Nelson became a wealthy man and a celebrity almost overnight. The Eskimo Pie business was so big that it even revived the slumping dairy industry and created an overwhelming demand on the worldwide growers of cocoa beans.

Chris Nelson next developed an insulated jug for selling Eskimo Pies at newsstands, street-vendor carts, trolley stops, and other locations that did not have refrigerated cabinets. A sign on the jug read, "The new Eskimo Pie, bracing as a frosty morning," and each morning the jugs were refilled by Eskimo Pie delivery men.

Today the Eskimo Pie corporation is still going strong with the same innovative attitude that Christian Nelson pioneered. The company maintains extensive laboratory facilities to experiment with new combinations of flavors and coatings. Remembering the youthful customer who couldn't make up his mind, the Eskimo Pie people know very well that sometimes it *is* possible to have the best of both worlds.

Eskimo Pies were so tasty they made people want to sing. This picture is the cover of the music for Dale Wimbrow's tribute to the Eskimo Pie.

The Invention of
The Ballpoint Pen

Advertising entices people to try a product once, quality and value convince them to buy it again.

The first great success for the ballpoint pen came on an October morning in 1945 when a crowd of over 5,000 people jammed the entrance of New York's Gimbels Department Store. The day before, Gimbels had taken out a full-page ad in the *New York Times* promoting the first sale of ballpoints in the United States. The ad described the new pen as a "fantastic . . . miraculous fountain pen . . . guaranteed to write for two years without refilling." On that first day of sales, Gimbels sold out its entire stock of 10,000 pens—at $12.50 each!

Actually, this "new" pen wasn't new at all and didn't work much better than ballpoint pens that had been produced ten years earlier.

The story begins in 1888 when John Loud, an American leather tanner, patented a roller-ball-tip marking pen. Loud's invention featured a reservoir of ink and a roller ball that applied the thick ink to leather hides. John Loud's pen was never produced, nor were any of the other 350 patents for ball-type pens issued over the next thirty years. The major problem was the ink—if the ink was thin the pens leaked, and if it was too thick, they clogged. Depending on the temperature, the pen would sometimes do both.

The next stage of development came almost

fifty years after Loud's patent, with an improved version invented in Hungary in 1935 by Ladislas Biro and his brother, Georg. Ladislas Biro was very talented and confident of his abilities, but he had never had a pursuit that kept his interest and earned him a good living. He had studied medicine, art, and hypnotism, and in 1935 he was editing a small newspaper—where he was frustrated by the amount of time he wasted filling fountain pens and cleaning up ink smudges. Besides that, the sharp tip of his fountain pen often scratched or tore through the newsprint (paper). Determined to develop a better pen, Ladislas and Georg (who was a chemist) set about making models of new designs and formulating better inks to use in them.

One summer day while vacationing at the seashore, the Biro brothers met an interesting elderly gentleman, Augustine Justo, who happened to be the president of Argentina. After the brothers showed him their model of a ballpoint pen, President Justo urged them to set up a factory in Argentina. When World War II broke out in Europe a few years later, the Biros fled to Argentina, stopping in Paris along the way to patent their pen.

Once in Argentina, the Biros found several investors willing to finance their invention, and by 1943 they had set up a manufacturing plant. Unfortunately, the pens were a spectacular failure. The Biro pen, like the designs that had preceded it, depended on gravity for the ink to flow to the roller ball. This meant that the pens worked only when they were held more or less straight up, and even then the ink flow was sometimes too heavy, leaving smudgy globs on

Ballpoint pens used to be sold in vending machines like this one.

the paper. The Biro brothers returned to their laboratory and devised a new design, which relied on "capillary action" rather than gravity to feed the ink. The rough "ball" at the end of the pen acted like a metal sponge, and with this improvement ink could flow more smoothly to the ball, and the pen could be held at a slant rather than straight up. One year later, the Biros were selling their new, improved ballpoint pen throughout Argentina. But it still was not a smashing success, and the men ran out of money.

The greatest interest in the ballpoint pen came from American flyers who had been to Argentina during World War II. Apparently it

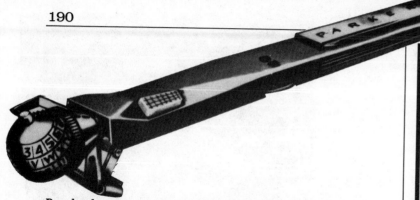

Pen development continues to this day. This sketch shows a Parker model that would respond to the human voice and produce clearly printed copy.

was ideal for pilots because it would work well at high altitudes and, unlike fountain pens, did not have to be refilled frequently. The U.S. Department of State sent specifications to several American pen manufacturers asking them to develop a similar pen. In an attempt to corner the market, the Eberhard Faber Company paid the Biro brothers $500,000 for the rights to manufacture their ballpoint pen in the United States. Eberhard Faber later sold its rights to the Eversharp Company, but neither was quick about putting a ballpoint pen on the market. There were still too many bugs in the Biro design.

Meanwhile, in a surprise move, a fifty-four-year-old Chicago salesman named Milton Reynolds became the first American manufacturer to market a ballpoint pen successfully. While vacationing in Argentina, Reynolds had seen Biro's pen in the stores and thought that the novel product would sell well in America. Because many of the patents had expired, Reynolds thought he could avoid any legal problems, and so he went about copying much of the Biros' design. It was Reynolds who made the deal with Gimbels to be the first retail store in America to

Fantasy Inventions

Pens are used widely every day and there is sure to be a market for useful variations on this essential product.

FINGERTIP TYPERS. Preinked typing balls fit on fingertips for direct typing onto paper or any surface. Finger position determines which letter on each ball is printed.

SKY-WRITING PEN. The pen nozzle emits a white smoke line for drawing three-dimensionally. A propeller on the other end works as an eraser.

CHECK-WRITING PEN. Computer memory records and displays the current balance in your checking account.

TIME DELAY INK. A printing and writing ink that is invisible for a specific period of time. Thirty-day time delay ink is good for answers to quizzes and puzzles in magazines, or "your account is overdue" notices on bills. One- or two-day time delay ink keeps documents secret until after they are delivered.

FADE-OUT PEN. In time writing fades and becomes invisible. Allows paper to be reused.

LOST-PEN ALARM. Sounds a warning whistle when pen is located more than 10 feet from its owner.

FINGERTIP PENCIL POINT. A pencil lead holder that fits on the fingertip for fast, comfortable writing. The adjoining fingertip holder has an eraser.

ANY-COLOR PEN. An adjustable slide control mixes three primary ink colors to produce any writing color wanted.

sell ballpoint pens. He set up a makeshift factory with 300 workers who began stamping out pens from whatever aluminum was not being used for the war. In the months that followed, Reynolds made millions of pens and became fairly wealthy, as did many other manufacturers who decided to cash in on the new interest.

The competition among pen manufacturers during the mid-1940s became quite hectic, with each one claiming new and better features. Reynolds even claimed that his ballpoint could write under water, and he hired Esther Williams, the swimmer and movie star, to help prove it. Another manufacturer claimed that its pen would write through ten carbon copies, while still another demonstrated that *its* pen would write upside down. However, the effect of the slogans and advertising wore off as soon as the owners discovered the many problems that still existed with the ballpoint pens. As the sale of the pens began to drop, so did the price, and the once expensive luxury now would not even sell for as little as 19¢. Once again, it looked as if the ballpoint pen would be a complete failure. For the pen to regain the public's favor and trust, somebody would have to invent one that was smooth writing, quick drying, nonskipping, nonfading, and—most important—didn't leak.

A member of the Papermate research and development team shows how thick and elastic their new Eraser Mate ink is—the new ink can be erased as easily as pencil lead.

Two men, each with his own pen company, finally delivered these results. The first was Patrick J. Frawley, Jr. Frawley met Fran Seech, an unemployed Los Angeles chemist who had lost his job when the ballpoint pen company he was working for had gone out of business. Seech had been working on improvements in ballpoint ink, and on his own he continued his experiments in a tiny cubbyhole home laboratory. Frawley was so impressed with his work that he bought Seech's new ink formula in 1949 and started the Frawley Pen Company. Within one year, Frawley was in the ballpoint pen business with yet another improved model—the first pen with a retractable ballpoint tip *and* the first with no-smear ink.

To overcome many of the old prejudices against the leaky and smeary ballpoint pen of the past, Frawley initiated an imaginative and risky advertising campaign, a promotion he called Project Normandy. Frawley instructed his salesmen to barge into the offices of retail store buyers and scribble all over the executives' shirts with one of the new pens. Then the salesman would offer to replace the shirt with an even more expensive one if the ink did not wash out entirely.

Two of the most successful marketers of ballpoint pens, Patrick J. Frawley (far left), who created the Papermate, and Baron Marcel Bich (left), creator of the inexpensive Ballpoint Bic.

The shirts *did* come clean and the promotion worked. As more and more retailers accepted the pen, which Frawley named the "Papermate," sales began to skyrocket. Within a few years, the Papermate pen was selling in the hundreds of millions.

The other man to bring the ballpoint pen successfully back to life was Marcel Bich, a French manufacturer of penholders and pen cases. Bich was appalled at the poor quality of the ballpoint pens he had seen and he was also shocked at their high cost. But he recognized that the ballpoint was a firmly established innovation and he resolved to design a high-quality pen at a low price that would scoop the market. He went to the Biro brothers and arranged to pay them a royalty on their patent. Then for two years Marcel Bich studied the detailed construction of every ballpoint pen on the market, often working with a microscope. By 1952 Bich was ready to introduce his new wonder: a clear-barreled, smooth-writing, nonleaky, inexpensive ballpoint pen he called the "Ballpoint Bic."

The ballpoint pen had finally become a practical writing instrument. The public accepted it without complaint, and today it is as standard a writing implement as the pencil. In England, they are still called Biros, and many Bic models also say "Biro" on the side of the pen, as a testament to their primary inventors. There are literally hundreds of styles of ballpoint pens to choose from, at prices up to $100. But high prices reflect packaging, not inherent workability. Inside every ballpoint pen is a precision roller-ball mechanism that is pretty much the same as that found in a 29¢ Bic.

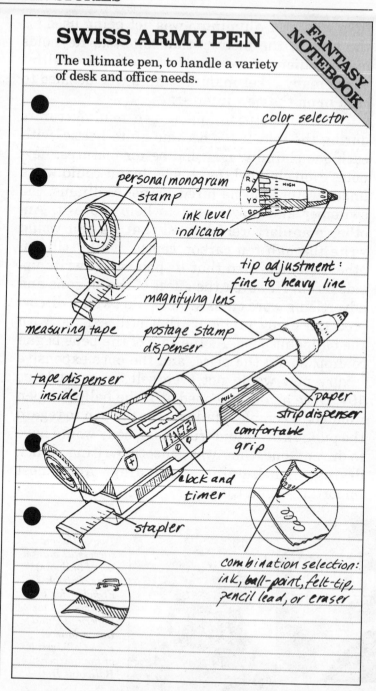

SWISS ARMY PEN

FANTASY NOTEBOOK

The ultimate pen, to handle a variety of desk and office needs.

color selector

personal monogram stamp

ink level indicator

tip adjustment: fine to heavy line

magnifying lens

measuring tape

postage stamp dispenser

tape dispenser inside

paper strip dispenser

comfortable grip

clock and timer

stapler

combination selection: ink, ball-point, felt-tip, pencil lead, or eraser

The Invention of
The Xerox Machine

Big successes often start from small ideas.

Chester Floyd Carlson knew only hard times as a young boy. His father was arthritic and could not work, and Chester's mother died when he was only fourteen. Young Carlson became the sole support of his family, taking on odd jobs, washing windows, sweeping out stores, and working as a printer's helper. Those early, struggling years not only taught him how to survive but also gave him the determination to succeed. In pursuit of that goal, Carlson borrowed enough money to attend the California Institute of Technology, where he received a degree in physics.

With a college degree and a chance to land a high-paying job, Carlson sent out eighty-two applications for work, but he received only two replies, for it was the 1930s and the United States was in the middle of the Great Depression. One of those two replies offered a $35-a-week job as a research engineer at Bell Telephone Laboratories in New York. Carlson took the job, but his great personal drive and immense interest in invention led him to study patent law at night.

He eventually was hired by a law firm, and it was while working on legal matters that Carlson became frustrated with the difficulty of making copies of all the documents he had to review and transmit to others. At that time, the only way to make a copy was either by photography or by a photostat process—both methods quite time-consuming and costly.

Chester Carlson was convinced that a

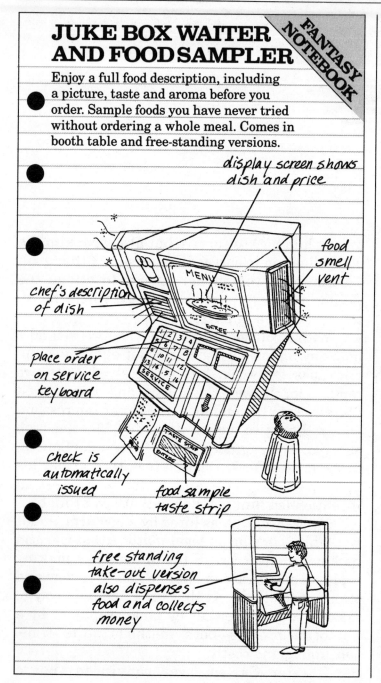

JUKE BOX WAITER AND FOOD SAMPLER

FANTASY NOTEBOOK

Enjoy a full food description, including a picture, taste and aroma before you order. Sample foods you have never tried without ordering a whole meal. Comes in booth table and free-standing versions.

display screen shows dish and price

food smell vent

chef's description of dish

place order on service keyboard

check is automatically issued

food sample taste strip

free standing take-out version also dispenses food and collects money

Chester Carlson with an ancestor of today's Xerox machine called an electrophotographic apparatus. The model was built for Carlson in the early 1940s.

cheaper method of copying documents was possible. So, with money he borrowed from his mother-in-law, he set up a small workshop in the back of a beauty parlor in the Astoria section of Queens, New York. For three years, Carlson spent nearly all of his spare time tinkering and fiddling in his workshop, and for three years the neighbors complained about the strange odors from the chemicals Carlson used in his work.

Carlson was so convinced that his idea would work that before he had even built a working model, he filed a patent application for his theoretical "electrophotography" process. His idea was now protected, but he was quickly running out of money. Carlson tried to interest several large corporations in his new invention. But all that he could show them at this point were his theories and his enthusiasm. Companies like RCA, IBM, Remington, and General Electric all said "No, thank you." Carlson went back to his laboratory and tried to build a model of what he had envisioned.

He was getting closer and closer to his goal of producing quick and inexpensive copies, but his process was still very time-consuming. So in 1937, he solicited help from his engineer friend, Otto Kornei.

On October 22, 1938, Carlson and Kornei succeeded in producing the first dry-process image copy. For the experiment, Carlson inked the date and the word "Astoria" on a glass slide. Then, using his pocket handkerchief, he rubbed a sulphur-coated metal plate to give it a static

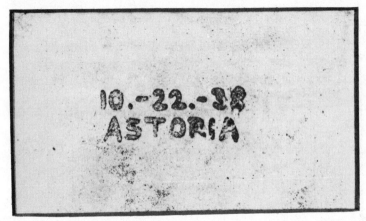

The first Xerox copy ever made.

charge. He attached the inked glass slide to the metal plate and exposed them under a flood lamp. When he dusted the plate with powder the inked inscription appeared. Next the plate with the powdered inscription was pressed against an ordinary paper sheet and the image was transferred. Finally the exact duplicate image on the paper was "fixed," using heat, to prevent it from smudging or fading. His theoretical process had worked and he named it xerography, for the Greek words for "dry writing."

After continuing his experiments and improving the process of transferring the image to plain paper, Carlson and Kornei finally created the first copying machine in 1944. In the ten years it had taken Carlson to get this far, he had made great strides in the copying process, but his copy machine still was not perfected and he still could not find any corporate support. Carlson knew of hundreds of more improvements he could make on his machine if he only had the money. To interest people further in his machine, Carlson wrote about his idea in a magazine called *Radio News,* and he wrote letters to several research organizations.

One privately endowed research company, the Battelle Memorial Institute of Columbus, Ohio, responded to his inquiry and invited him to demonstrate his process. Several people at the Battelle Institute were impressed with Carlson's work and agreed to give him some additional research money—but not much.

Then came Carlson's big break. Almost a year after the article appeared in *Radio News,* a copy of the magazine was read by Dr. John H. Dressauer, the research director for the Haloid Company, a manufacturer of wet-chemical-process photocopy machines. The Haloid

Dr. John H. Dressauer, shown here in 1963, the man who convinced the Haloid Company (later known as Xerox Corporation) to buy the rights to Chester Carlson's copying process.

Fundamental
new way of
office copying

The first continuous copy Xerox machine, the 1955 Copyflo, and an ad for the early sixties Xerox 914, the first fully automatic copier.

Company had not been doing well and they were looking for new products to help beef up sales. Dressauer convinced Haloid to buy Carlson's patent rights, and they promptly shortened the name "xerography" to "xerox."

On October 22, 1948, ten years to the day since the first xerox copy was made by Carlson, the Haloid Company gave their first demonstration of a marketable Xerox machine.

The Haloid Company's first Xerox copiers were not an instant success, and it was not until 1959, after several improvements, that the Xerox copier became widely accepted. It was also that same year that the Haloid Corporation decided to change its name to Xerox Corporation.

Nearly everyone who had been involved with the early development of the Xerox machine became wealthy from it. One New York City taxi driver who had invested $1,000 in the Haloid Corporation later found his Xerox stock to be worth over $1.5 million. The Xerox Corporation has of course gone on to become one of the largest and most successful companies in the United States.

Fantasy Inventions

Copying sheets of paper is convenient and useful, but just try to imagine the possibilities of copying all kinds of things, such as works of art, into all kinds of forms, including a 3-D reproduction.

DE-XEROX MACHINE. Takes any printed matter and removes all printing to turn it back into clean, unprinted paper. The machine also presses out paper folds and wrinkles.

BOOKSHELF FACADES. Inexpensive molded plastic book spines made to look like real books. Spines snap together in any order to fill empty bookshelves, as decorations or to impress friends.

COPY SCULPT MACHINE. Any object placed into the machine can be copied in 3-D form, color, and texture, exactly like the original. The machine operator can select the material for the copy if it is to be different than the original.

FINE ARTS DUPLICATOR. Exactly duplicates any work of art including the original color, texture, and technique.

STEREO NOVEL. The right-hand page gives the story line and dialogue, and the left-hand page describes the characters and setting.

COOL-TOUCH-ENERGY-SAVER LIGHT BULB. Recycles the bulb's heat energy back into electricity to operate the bulb. Energy is conserved and the bulb stays cool.

The Invention of
Kodachrome Color Film

Often the novice, not the expert, succeeds at what "can't be done."

People were taking black-and-white photographs for nearly a hundred years before two professional musicians—finally succeeding where scientists around the world had failed—introduced the first practical, true-to-life color film on April 15, 1935.

The Kodachrome story began seventy years earlier, in 1865, when the famous scientist James Clark Maxwell first produced a color picture. He used three projectors, each projecting a different color of the same image—one red, one green, and one blue. The projectors were pointed at the same screen so that the pictures overlapped, creating a blurry but full-color image on the screen. For the next fifty years, most scientists trying to invent color film used the Maxwell "optical approach." But none improved very much on the colorful but murky images that Maxwell had created. That is until 1916, when Leopold Godowsky and Leopold Mannes became involved.

Godowsky and Mannes had a lot in common besides their first names. Both of their fathers were famous classical concert musicians; they both went to Riverdale High School in New York;

LIGHT BULB PROJECTIONS

Projects a wide variety of images onto walls, floors, ceilings and furniture. Fun for parties, or inexpensive, variable room decoration.

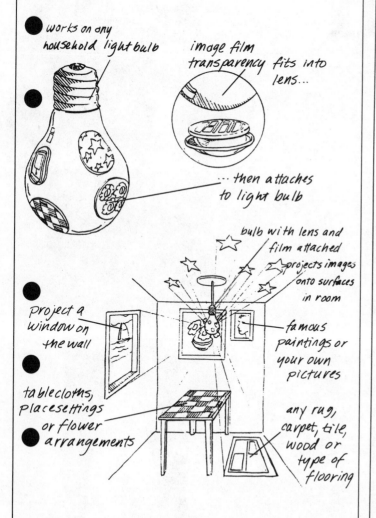

- works on any household light bulb
- image film transparency fits into lens...
- ...then attaches to light bulb
- bulb with lens and film attached projects images onto surfaces in room
- project a window on the wall
- tablecloths, placesettings or flower arrangements
- famous paintings or your own pictures
- any rug, carpet, tile, wood or type of flooring

they both considered music more important than anything else in life; and they both were fascinated by the idea of making color photographic film.

The two Leopolds often worked together in the high-school physics lab, experimenting with film techniques and processes, and in 1916 they duplicated Maxwell's results without even knowing it. Soon the two Leos had improved the Maxwell method so much that they received a patent on their own version of making color photographs by overlapping light. But the results were still blurry and quite crude.

Godowsky and Mannes were perfectionists in their music and they were the same way about their scientific hobby. Despite the progress they had made using the optical method, they weren't satisfied. They both envisioned a color photograph that showed things exactly as the picture-taker saw them through the camera, with every color bright and clear. So in 1921, five years after reinventing Maxwell's optical process, Godowsky and Mannes decided to tackle the problem in a different way. They began using a chemical approach to color photographs—a totally original idea.

By now, Godowsky and Mannes had begun their musical careers, but they continued their chemical experiments when they were not playing concerts or teaching. The two quickly realized the amazing possibilities in using chemicals to create color film. They also realized how much money their experiments were costing, and they couldn't make enough from their music to pay for the testing they knew had to be done. Fortunately, by this time the Godowsky-Mannes team

Leopold Mannes (l.) and Leopold Godowsky (r.) shown in their lab in 1922.

had become well known among photography research buffs, and although people thought they were strange because they had two careers at the same time, some important people thought that the two "oddballs" might be up to something worthwhile.

Just in time to keep their experiments going, the two musician-scientists received a $20,000 grant from an investment company and a lot of valuable help from a Dr. Mees, the director of research at the biggest photographic film company in the world, Eastman Kodak.

Dr. Mees' research department had spent many years unsuccessfully trying to get as far as Godowsky and Mannes had come so quickly. Therefore he was eager to supply the men with all the equipment and chemicals they required.

Even with the progress they were making in their scientific work, the two Leos never put their music aside. In fact, for a while their research slowed down considerably when Mannes won a Pulitzer musical scholarship and then a Guggenheim scholarship to study music composition in Italy. While Mannes was away, he often corresponded with Godowsky about their theories, experiments, and results. When Mannes returned in 1930, he and Godowsky began to make some real progress, but it was still slow and sometimes frustrating.

Their plan was to perfect a way of making natural-looking color pictures by using extremely thin layers of chemicals called "emulsions," separated by even thinner layers of clear gelatin. Each layer of emulsion would turn a particular shade of color, depending on the colors that were being photographed. Figuring out how to make the film was difficult enough, but processing the exposed film was even harder. Various chemicals had to be used to create the colors, and years of testing were necessary just to figure out what qualities were needed and how much time was required in developing to get the colors just right.

Dr. Mees now urged the two to come to Rochester, New York, and use the well-equipped laboratory facilities of his research department at Eastman Kodak. They gratefully accepted the invitation, and despite a very cool reception from the staff of jealous Kodak scientists, Godowsky and Mannes continued their double lives as musician-inventors. The Kodak scientists were unhappy because Godowsky and Mannes were not formally trained scientists and because they spent most nights playing music at the renowned

Eastman School of Music (also in Rochester) rather than working in the labs.

Even while Godowsky and Mannes worked in the laboratory, they sang passages from musical pieces. The other scientists thought this a bit strange and unprofessional, but what they didn't realize was that the men sang the passages (with their precise sense of musical timing) to time the chemical reactions in the completely darkened lab. This critical part of their research was being done before modern electronic timing devices and methods of lighting a photographic darkroom were available. It may have been this very special talent of the two musician-inventors that helped them to succeed where others had failed.

By 1933, the unusual team had invented a film that made the best color pictures yet, and two years later, after nineteen years of painstaking research, they invented an even better color process. This prompted Eastman Kodak to announce a most unusual press conference, in which Godowsky and Mannes showed the world's first Kodachrome color slides and then sat down at their instruments to play a violin and piano sonata for the surprised group.

Leo Mannes and Leo Godowsky worked for three or four more years on perfecting their color film, and they received over forty patents on their chemical processes before returning to full-time music careers. Mannes became the head of a

Fantasy Inventions

Here are a number of ideas to help you see the wide range of possibilities for new kinds of film, cameras, and visual projection.

MIND IMAGE PRINTER. Can produce a printed picture of any mental image in color or black-and-white. Makes remembering dreams much easier. A dream recorder and playback machine for continuous dream viewing is also available.

HOLIDAY FILM. A camera film with pre-exposed decorative holiday borders and cut-out silhouettes. Birthday film, Christmas film, Valentine film, anniversary film, wedding film.

TEAR-OFF FILM. Tear off only the film that has been exposed and send it in for developing. There is no need to wait for the entire roll to be shot.

EYEGLASS IMAGE FILTERS. Special eyeglass inserts can give summertime a cool and breezy look, or wintertime a warm, tropical look. By fooling the senses the wearer feels more comfortable.

HOLOGRAPHIC SLIDE PROJECTOR. Creates three-dimensional scenes that the viewer can walk into.

TWO-VIEW VACATION CAMERA. A lens on either side of the camera allows vacationers to simultaneously take a picture of a holiday scene and a picture of themselves at the scene.

PICTURE PERFECT PANELS. Scenic photo backdrops for home picture takers. Select scenes from all over the world and then photograph yourself as if you were there.

FILM IMPRINTER. Keyboard on the camera permits the picture taker to print the date, time, and picture description directly on the frame being shot.

FLASHLIGHT CAMERA. Upon activation the flashlight will take a photograph of whatever the beam is lighting.

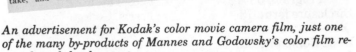

An advertisement for Kodak's color movie camera film, just one of the many by-products of Mannes and Godowsky's color film research and development.

music college and traveled all over the country giving concerts. Godowsky built a luxurious home complete with recording studio and chemical lab and lived a comparatively private but equally busy life. They had always considered themselves musicians first and scientists second, yet neither man ever became as accomplished in music as he had been as a scientist.

Index

Picture Credits

Getting Started
P. 18: Courtesy Dr Pepper Company; p. 20: King Features; p. 22: Courtesy Dr Pepper Company.

The Inventor's Workshop
P. 26: Courtesy Rick Botts, Jukebox Collector Newsletter/ Smithsonian Institution.

Planning
P. 35: Courtesy The Sheffield Tube Corporation.

Breadboard, Model and Prototype
P. 46: Wide World / Courtesy Westinghouse Historical Collection: p. 47: Wide World / Courtesy Heath Company (2) / Wide World / Ideal – CBS Toys.

Naming Your Invention
P. 51: King Features / Signal Corps Photo / Courtesy Ford Motor Company; p. 52 Courtesy Holmes Protection Inc.

Patents
P. 61: Courtesy Eli Bridge Company; p. 64: Courtesy Union Carbide Corporation, Battery Products Division; p. 69: Courtesy Jeff Iula, All-American Soap Box Derby.

Marketing Your Invention
PP. 80–81: The Science Museum / The Smithsonian Institution / The Science Museum / The Science Museum / The Science Museum / The Smithsonian Institution / The Smithsonian Institution / Courtesy of Bell Labs / Courtesy of Ford Motor Company.

Earmuffs
P. 89: Courtesy George Greenwood; p. 90: Courtesy Ronald Greenwood; p. 91: Courtesy George Greenwood / Courtesy Ronald Greenwood; p. 92: Courtesy Ronald Greenwood / Courtesy George Greenwood (2).

Drive-In Movies
P. 94: Courtesy Harry M. Potter, South Jersey Magazine / Wide World; p. 95: Wide World.

The Frisbee
PP. 98–99: Courtesy Dr. Stancil E. D. Johnson; p. 101: Courtesy Wham-O Inc.; p. 102: Courtesy Dr. Stancil E. D. Johnson.

The Band-aid
PP. 104–105: Courtesy Johnson & Johnson.

Chocolate Chip Cookies
P. 106: Courtesy Néstle Foods Corp.; p. 107: Bauman Photography, Inc.; p. 108: Bauman Photography, Inc. / Courtesy Néstle Foods Corp.; p. 109: Bauman Photography, Inc.

The name Toll House is a registered trademark of Nestlé Foods Corp., used by the Toll House Inn under license.

Water Skis
P. 111: Courtesy Jon Samuelson / Water Ski Museum – Hall of Fame; p. 113: Lake City Chamber of Commerce.

Levis
P. 115: Courtesy of Levi Strauss & Co. (2) / Smithsonian Institution; p. 117: Courtesy Levi Strauss & Co.

Basketball
PP. 119–122: Courtesy Basketball Hall of Fame.

The Trampoline
PP. 124–127: Courtesy George Nissen.

Kleenex
PP. 129 & 131: Courtesy Kimberly-Clark Corporation.

Dixie Cups
PP. 133–134: James River Corporation, Dixie/Marathon Products; p. 135: Culver Pictures.

Kellogg's Corn Flakes
P. 137: W. K. Kellogg Foundation / Used by permission of The Kellogg Company. All rights reserved; p. 138: General Foods Corporation Archives / Culver Pictures (Postum is a registered trademark of General Foods Corporation) / General Foods Corporation Archives; p. 139: Culver Pictures (Grape-Nuts is a registered trademark of General Foods Corporation) / General Foods Corporation Archives; p. 141: The Kellogg Company / Culver Pictures (Kelloggs® and Kellogg's Corn Flakes® are registered trademarks of the Kellogg Company. All rights reserved. Pictures used by permission of The Kellogg Company.)

Howard Johnson's Restaurants
PP. 142–145: Courtesy Howard Johnson Company.

Life Savers Candy
PP. 148–151: Courtesy Nabisco Brands Inc.

The Milk Bottle
P. 153: Courtesy Robert A. Wyant, Potsdam Public Museum;

p. 155: Courtesy Robert A. Wyant, Potsdam Public Museum / Ed Clemens, The Milk Route.

Drinking Straws
P. 159: Picture Collection, New York Public Library; pp. 160–161: Culver Pictures.

The Zipper
P. 163: Courtesy Talon Inc.; p. 164: Courtesy Talon Inc. / Picture Collection, New York Public Library; p. 165: Courtesy Talon Inc.; p. 166: Picture Collection, New York Public Library.

Teabags
P. 168: Culver Pictures; p. 169: By permission of Thomas J. Lipton, Inc.

Scotch Tape
P. 170–172: Courtesy 3M.

Sneakers
P. 174: Courtesy Shell Chemical Company; p. 176: Courtesy Goodyear Tire & Rubber Company / Picture Collection, New York Public Library; p. 177: Culver Pictures / Courtesy Spalding; p. 178: Culver Pictures / Courtesy Converse.

Roller Skates
P. 180: Smithsonian Institution; p. 182: Culver Pictures.

Eskimo Pie
PP. 185–187: Courtesy Eskimo Pie Corporation.

The Ballpoint Pen
PP. 190–191: Wide World.

The Xerox Machine
PP. 194–196: Courtesy Xerox Corporation.

Kodachrome Color Film
PP. 199 & 201: Courtesy Eastman Kodak Company.

All uncredited original photographs were taken by the author.

All original drawings in *The Inventor's Handbook* are by Ginger Brown.

All original sketches in *Great Invention Stories* are by Neil Cohen.